W9-CDT-620

REQUIRED
READING
FOR THE ~~DISENFRANCHISED~~
FRESHMAN

REQUIRED
READING
FOR THE
~~DISENFRANCHISED~~
FRESHMAN

KRISTEN R. LEE

CROWN

NEW YORK

Text copyright © 2022 by Kristen R. Lee
Jacket art copyright © 2022 by Mimi Moffie

All rights reserved. Published in the United States by Crown Books for Young Readers, an imprint of Random House Children's Books, a division of Penguin Random House LLC, New York.

Visit us on the Web! GetUnderlined.com

Educators and librarians, for a variety of teaching tools, visit us at RHTeachersLibrarians.com

Library of Congress Cataloging-in-Publication Data
Names: Lee, Kristen R., author.
Title: Required reading for the disenfranchised freshman / Kristen R. Lee.
Description: New York: Crown Books for Young Readers, [2022] |
Audience: Ages 14+. | Audience: Grades 10–12. |
Summary: Upon arriving at the prestigious Wooddale University, seventeen-year-old Savannah Howard comes face-to-face with microaggressions and outright racism— but if she stands up for justice, will she endanger her future?
Identifiers: LCCN 2021036297 (print) | LCCN 2021036298 (ebook) |
ISBN 978-0-593-30915-5 (hardcover) | ISBN 978-0-593-30916-2 (library binding) |
ISBN 978-0-593-30917-9 (ebook)
Subjects: CYAC: Racism—Fiction. | Social classes—Fiction. | Hate crimes—Fiction. |
Universities and colleges—Fiction. | African Americans—Fiction. | LCGFT: Novels.
Classification: LCC PZ7.1.L4174 Re 2022 (print) | LCC PZ7.1.L4174 (ebook) | DDC [Fic]—dc23

The text of this book is set in 12-point Adobe Garamond Pro.
Interior design by Jen Valero

Printed in the United States of America
10 9 8 7 6 5 4 3 2 1
First Edition

To those before me and after me

ONE

The pizza drivers don't deliver here after seven.

Five in the wintertime, when the sun sets earlier. When they do deliver, they don't come beyond the iron gates of my building. We have to walk down to them. They park damn near around the corner, but they still expect a tip.

I have a tip for them: stop being afraid of Black folk.

I search for my low-top Air Force Ones that I've been wearing since ninth grade. Mama taped up the bottom with duct tape to keep the soles from falling apart. She tells me all the time to throw them away, that no matter how poor we are, we don't have to look it, but I can't toss them. These same shoes took me everywhere, and in a few days they'll be coming with me to college. A college I've worked my whole life to get into but, truth be told, I don't want to go to. Not like Mama would give me a say anyway.

"Mama, I'm finna go get a pizza." I stand behind the bedroom door that hangs off the hinges. She takes her sweet time inviting me in. I know better than to enter her room without permission.

"Bring me a pepperoni with extra cheese," she says.

You got extra-cheese money? I want to say, but I don't have time for a lecture. I lean against the wall. "You know they charge more for the extra cheese, Mama?"

"I know that, Savannah. Come get twenty dollars out my pocketbook."

The door hugs my body as I rest against the wall. Mama sits on the edge of her bed, and the cutoff shirt she wears shows the aging in her arms. Soft pink rollers that give her hair a "bump" peek out from underneath her bonnet. Her swollen feet rest in one of them massage buckets boosted from Walmart by my cousin Shaun. Mama's feet ain't no good anymore. Years of standing up on concrete at a warehouse for twelve hours did a number on her body. When she got that good job down at the tax agency, she ran into the house and threw out every pair of steel-toe boots she ever owned. But by then the damage to her feet was already done.

"Don't be out too late. It ain't safe." She gives the same warning each time I step outside. Even if I'm only going toward the back of the apartments to throw out the trash.

"Mama, it's right up the street." I pause. "Besides, you can't keep an eye on me after I'm at college."

It feels funny saying that. Me? College? I'm only seventeen—well, seventeen and a half. One minute I was doing accelerated-learning courses, then dual-enrollment classes, and then the guidance counselor talking about I'm ready for college, if I want to go. I worked like a senior my sophomore and junior years to apply to the best colleges—like Wooddale. Getting into Wooddale meant I made it. That Mama working them long hours wasn't in vain. While my homegirls went to parties, I was prepping for the SAT night and day. It worked because I got a 1500 and accepted to every college I applied to, including the HBU down the street. But Mama said I'm not going to that one because it won't make me successful. Even though people who graduate from HBUs do big things too.

She said I need that fancy Ivy League degree.

And I mean, she right. Life would be so good then. If I got a good enough job with that Wooddale degree, we could even move. Mama wouldn't be worried about crime or nothing. Bet wherever we move then, the pizza people would deliver all the way to the doorstep.

Mama points her half-polished finger at me. "You heard what I said. I don't want you walking them streets this late at night."

I reach into her purse and pull out an Andrew Jackson. I crumple it up and put it in my bra. Mama taught me to never stick money in my pockets. It's the first place robbers look.

"Aight, Mama. Yes, ma'am."

I walk down the stairs and exit my building. Little kids sit out in the patches of brown grass playing hand games with silly chants. I grin. It reminds me of my own childhood.

Summer as a kid was lit.

Staying out all day, riding my bike with the pink tassels coming out the handles. Playing jacks on the porch, if you can call the slab of concrete that. Next day I would wake up and do the same thing over again until school started up in August. Then for at least eight hours I was guaranteed two meals and an air-conditioned place to stay.

My Wooddale degree gone change that, too.

"Savannah, wait up." B'onca, my homegirl since grade school, runs over from the basketball court. "I ain't know you'd be ready so soon. Where we going anyway?"

Meeting B'onca to say my goodbyes is bittersweet. We as good as sisters. Our mamas were best friends growing up— they still are. When you see B'onca, you see me, and vice versa. Pictures of us from pigtails to our first grown-up wraps decorate our refrigerators.

"Figured we'd get pizza."

"Oh snap, pizza? That's fancy." She wipes her chiseled face with the bottom of her shirt. "Your mama must got her food stamps."

"Nah, we got cash money today." I pat the soft spot in my bra. "We getting Marco's. *Real* pizza. Not from the corner store."

"Cool." She looks behind her at her building. Her brows meet. "But I gotta be home . . . soon." Sweat glistens across her chest, and her ombré black-and-brown dreads fly in the wind behind her. She's in the National Honor Society and used to play ball, and not only basketball, neither. Her grades are as on point as her jump shot. B'onca soared in everything she did. Then, in high school, she met Scooter, her boyfriend, and quit all sports. Scooter says his woman ain't gone be "manlier" than him. I told her that's wild, but she in love, and love over- rule anything I have to tell her.

"You good?"

"Yeah. But hold up, one minute." She sprints to the court and picks up her basketball. Scooter must not be around. If he was, she'd be at his house playing wifey. Cooking him chicken, watching Netflix, and folding his drawers. Her nose wide open, like the old folks say.

My foot taps the pavement as her teammates try to con- vince her to stay and play. If you got B'onca on your team, ain't no way you losing. She runs over, dribbling. "Aight, let's go. We good." She catches up to me. "You sure you need pizza?" She pinches the rolls in my stomach, and I slap her hand away.

"Fuck out of here. I'm depressed and food helps."

She twirls her basketball around on her middle finger. "Shoot, depression a white-folk thing. You just sad you leav- ing me, that's all." B'onca kicks at a stray hot-fry bag on the sidewalk. " 'Cause I know you not sad you leaving this ghetto- ass place."

"I'm only seventeen, B. What I know about college? Living on my own?"

"With how much your mama works, you've been practi- cally living on your own since you were what? Fourteen? It ain't gone be that different. Just this time your mama and best friend"—she nudges me with her elbow—"won't be right up the street."

Five months ago when I got the acceptance letter in the mail, Mama musta hollered somethin' fierce. The next-door neighbor, Mrs. Hall, ran over with her walking cane. She waved it in the air, ready to fight off intruders. She did the same shit when the financial-aid package followed.

"A *full* scholarship!" I can still hear the Mariah Carey level of Mama's scream. That's what my lack of a life in high school got me. And even I couldn't fight the tears that day, opening the mail. I'm proud. I have something nobody round here has ever had. Something I haven't seen nobody who look like me do.

Both letters are on the refrigerator, placed behind old Shop & Save grocery coupons and Pillsbury Doughboy magnets. Wooddale's acceptance letter covers the one from Hilbert. Hilbert University, the local historically Black college ten miles away. Mama said it would be real foolish of me to turn down a paid-for university like Wooddale for a school that can't even afford financial aid for every student. Wooddale one of the top schools in the country, while Hilbert don't even make those kinds of lists.

She doesn't understand, though, that my friends from the neighborhood and folks who resemble me attend Hilbert. I scrolled Wooddale's Instagram hashtag the other day and counted on one hand the number of Black folk posting pictures. They don't look like the type of folks I'd hang out with. But I want to make my family proud of me—especially Mama.

Where I'm from, folks can be successful if given half the chance. Hair braiders stand on their feet all day in their kitchen beauty salons, creating styles just as good as anyone with a real beauty shop. Little girls have singing contests on their stoops and sound better than anyone on BET. Women plan extravagant birthday parties for they babies with twenty dollars and a dream. Dreams don't pay overdue water bills, though.

"Two thousand dollars for a one-bedroom apartment." B'onca kicks the plastic real-estate sign and it falls over. "That's more than my mama make in a month."

"These apartments ain't for us," I say.

We pass an empty construction site. Yvonne's Beauty Bar and Mike's Grocery next to it are both chained up for the night. The street full of Black family-owned businesses that have been around way before I was ever thought of. At the corner is a clothing boutique named Elegant, where I got my eighth-grade prom dress. Across from it is the liquor store with the missing *L* in the sign. Folks always going in and out, brown paper bags in their hands.

The bell dings as we walk into Marco's, and the scent of garlic swells in the air. A clerk behind the counter writes down orders and takes phone calls. He got acne deep as craters across his face, but he can't be any older than us. Marco's is family-owned like Yvonne's and Mike's, but they Italian. The namesake bought the store for cheap a few years ago and monopolized the hood pizza game. We stand behind the wooden barrier with the Italian flag folded across it for five minutes and the cashier don't even say hello.

Ten minutes later it's the same silence.

"Aye, boy, you see us standing here," B'onca shouts as she slams her palm on the counter, causing the clerk to jump. She always on ten.

"We want to place an order," I say, reminding him of his job description.

He sighs and slides a folded pizza box out of sight. "What do you want?"

I lean my elbows on the counter. "Hello to you, too." I squint at his name tag. "Jason."

He kisses his teeth in annoyance. I would leave right now, but this the only shop within walking distance. I don't want Tony's frozen pizza from the Shop & Save. I want the real thing, and since they set up shop in our neighborhood, ain't they supposed to serve the people in it?

Ignoring his bad attitude, I place my order. "Could I please have a large pepperoni with extra cheese?" I reach into my shirt and unfold the twenty.

"Sorry," he says with no hesitation. "We're out of pepperoni."

"What about sausage?" I hate sausage, but I hate being hungry even more.

"We're out of that as well." This time a smirk paints his face and I know he's lying, and I know why. The why always make my stomach hurt.

B'onca fakes a hearty laugh before her face changes. "Now how the fuck you out of pepperoni and sausage? This a pizza shop, ain't it?"

I try to give her a look to simmer down, but B'onca ain't trying to hear that.

"I don't have to serve you if you're going to act belligerent." Jason folds his arms across his chest.

"How are we acting belligerent?" I look around the shop. "You made us wait fifteen minutes. You can't be that busy. Ain't nobody here."

His face becomes light pink. "Please leave or I'm going to call my manager."

B'onca ignores his threat and gives him the finger. "My friend wants pizza and it's your job to serve her."

He walks over to the ancient landline phone that hangs on the wall and grabs the receiver. "I *will* call the police. Don't try me."

"Call 'em," B'onca says as she dials 911 on her own cell phone. She flashes the screen to him. "I'm ahead of you."

"Come on, B. It ain't worth it."

There ain't no point in arguing with Jason or none of these other shops that pop up every day. To them, we only rowdy Black kids, and that is all we will ever be.

"This not right, Savannah," she says. "He ain't want to serve us no way."

"It's cool. We can go to the grocery store and get frozen. Better than this shit they serve, anyway." I ball up a half-off-pizza flyer and throw it across the counter.

Jason walks to the door, and before it shuts good, he flips the OPEN sign to CLOSED. Even though it's only six-thirty p.m.

A strange look settles across B'onca's face.

"B?"

She ignores me, looks both ways, and crosses the street to where a sanctuary of rocks is piled.

I walk to the edge of the curb. "Girl, what you doing?"

She grabs one and sprints toward Marco's.

Shit. "B, it's aight, for real."

Through the glass, the clerk's nasty attitude gets replaced with a toothy smile. He stares at us while he yaps on the phone.

"He don't wanna serve us 'cause we Black, but he want to rent space up in our neighborhood. I can't stand these damn folks, acting like they own everything and everyone." Stepping forward, she tosses the rock up and down in her hand and motions for me to move aside. I hesitate, fully aware of what's about to happen. I got accepted into college five months ago. Do they let you defer if you get locked up? Is there a program in jail that lets you out for being a good student? Because if B going down, they gone snatch my ass too, that's for sure. I never heard of no Black person being let out early on good behavior.

B'onca never think shit through. She smart and got more talent in her pinky toe than most folk, but she don't think. She let her feelings eat her up, and later she always regrets the things she's done.

"B, don't. Seriously. It ain't worth the trouble."

"Don't act like he don't deserve it," she says.

He does, but that ain't gone matter when the police got

us facedown on the concrete in handcuffs. The salty taste of sweat pours down my face. Every moment that passes feels like I'm a moment closer to the prison three streets over.

I try to take the rock from her hand. "Let's just get going. Get pizza somewhere else."

For a moment, nothing. Then she drops the rock and I can breathe again.

"They better have the double-pepperoni pizza too," she says as we walk toward the grocery store.

A young couple approaches us, and from the look of fear on their faces, they don't belong here. From the color of their skin to their fluffy dog, they don't belong here. I see them around every now and again. People like them walk their pups up and down the block in the evenings but stay clear of the hood. They live in apartments with coded gate pads and covered parking.

The couple brushes past us and the woman barely touches my shoulder.

"Excuse me. I'm so sorry," she fumbles, and does that fake grin with no teeth, her eyes wide.

I re-create the same smile. "No problem."

She says sorry one last time before they continue their walk.

"She thought you was gone beat her ass about an accident?" B'onca asks, swishing her braids.

"Prolly. You see her shirt?" She's wearing a V-neck Wooddale shirt. I don't know if it's a prophecy or an omen.

"You'll be inside those gated communities in a few years.

11

Looking down your nose at us behind the iron gates," B'onca says.

An omen if I ever heard one. "Those are the type of people who go to Wooddale. Look at them. Now look at me." The woman has gold jewelry that doesn't turn her skin green after wearing it two hours too long. She walks like Earth's rotating just for her. I don't fit in with people like that. Not with my cubic zirconia and slouched shoulders. Even with my Wooddale shirt on, they'd think it was a gift or a find at Goodwill, not that I actually attend the school.

"You need to stop thinking all negative."

"I'm being real. Mama may think I'm some unicorn, but I'm not." The couple is almost a dot in the distance, but I can't look away. They hold hands, giggling as they walk along the trashed curb. They step over Jolly Rancher wrappers and prescription bottles like they're nothing; may as well be flowers. Everything coming up roses in their eyes.

"I'll never be them. And they'll never know what it's like to be me." *Man, this too much.* "I ain't even hungry no more." I switch directions and B'onca follows, the Shop & Save and Marco's behind us. She drapes her arm around my shoulder as we walk.

"Girl, boo," she says. "Go to that fancy school and get your expensive-ass sheet of paper. Come home and help your hood out."

"You coming with me next year, right?"

That was the plan, kind of. We were supposed to attend

Hilbert together, join a sorority together, and dorm together. The location changed, but the plan remains the same.

"Now you know I can't get in that fancy school. You have the book smarts."

I squirm from underneath her arm, the couple now invisible in the distance. "I can help the hood more if I actually stay here."

B'onca turns around, walking backward. "Shit, the way that lady had her purse all open, she was 'bout to help somebody in the hood hit a lick."

"Did you see the dude's watch?" I ask. "I know that's real gold."

"Truth."

Our projects come into sight and we promise to call each other later, one last *so long* before home is in my rearview. B'onca dribbles off and disappears from view. Our apartment is on the second level, and I'm good and out of breath by the time I hit the landing, no matter how many times I've walked them stairs. I step inside and head straight to the kitchen and pour myself a glass of water from the tap. It's warm, but still cools down my heart rate.

"Where the pizza?" Mama asks.

She's at the counter reading through the same Wooddale brochure that I'm sure she can recite verbatim by now.

I halfway lie. "They were closed today."

"Damn, I had my mouth all set for some pizza too."

"I can make us some bologna sandwiches." I set out the

bread. The expiration date says five days ago, but ain't no mold on it.

"That'll do." She smiles down at the brochure. "They got a Black woman as president of the university. Ain't that something?"

"Yes, Mama." We've been through this process a hundred times.

"Uh-huh. Remember that lady I used to do bookkeeping for? With the kids you used to play with sometimes while I worked."

I couldn't forget. During tax season seeing Mama was like spotting the Loch Ness Monster.

"She went to Wooddale. Had the biggest house on the block. Own car, paid for in cash. Now my baby is going there. That's going to be you someday."

"There's plenty of successful people who went to Hilbert, too. Lawyers, doctors, and businessmen right in our community."

People try to play Hilbert. Just because it's in the hood and Black, they give the school a bad rep. I just know I'd be happier there, with people who understand me, but it's like my happiness went out the window soon as that acceptance letter came.

Wooddale's letter stares at me as I open the fridge. I take it down and go over the words for the hundredth time.

Welcome. Congratulations. Proud.

In my hands is a thin piece of paper that represents hours

of missed sleep, unattended parties, long tutoring sessions, and tons of Mama's money spent.

Rummaging through the cabinets, I find the cast-iron pan and place it on the stove. The four slices of meat sizzle when they hit the pan. I lean against the wall and let the sides get almost burnt, the way we been eating them for long as I can remember. This not pizza by a mile. I bet they got pizza where I'm going. The gourmet kind with goat cheese and other random shit like I see on Food Network. Expensive coffee shops on every corner, too. Fresh vegetable stands. Salad bars and hot dinner plates.

Wooddale my gateway to a better life.

I should be excited, but I ain't.

TWO

There's no going back.

We arrive on campus at three p.m. on the dot. Traffic directors stand outside various buildings and keep the cars moving. Our worn-down Honda Civic with the rusted two-tone is an ugly sight compared to the glistening, tinted-window Hummers and Cadillacs that follow us. A girl my age waves us around the traffic circle. She has on a dark blue shirt with white **WELCOME TO WOODDALE** letters.

Mama and I get out of the car and stretch something fierce. That old car been our home for the past two days. A group of students walk up to me and ask for my room number. Five of them, each a different level of perky, grab most of my bags and scurry off into the dorm.

"You even got your own concierge at this place," Mama says. "Hell, I wish I would have gone to college."

I take a glimpse at the other parents. Soccer moms with thin butts and expensive yoga wear stand nearby, chatting with one another. Business dads yap away on their cell phones, making money off someone.

Then there's us.

We can pass for sisters or cousins—anything other than mother and daughter. Mama got on her pink bedazzled T-shirt with the word *Queen* written across the chest and tight light-blue jeggings that I begged her not to wear.

Cox Hall, the dorm I'm staying in, sits tucked on the far edge of campus. Behind a forest of trees that you have to bend your neck to see the top of.

The dorm doesn't look like the newer models the university advertises on its website. Moss climbs the walls of old red brick with splotchy dirt patches. The outside furniture is turned over and covered in leaves and acorns. You can't tell where the dirt ends and the chairs begin.

The inside is no better. The walls and furniture are a funky shade of brown. The leather chairs are torn at the seams and the white stuffing inside spills out. A lone golden-framed picture of a daisy hangs near the entrance. The decorator for this place didn't have any type of imagination. A splash of color goes a long way.

We walk down a short hallway, past all the eager freshmen—and ones who look as if they've made the biggest mistake of their lives. Music flows from some rooms; sobbing rings from others.

Nineteen.

Twenty.

Twenty-one.

Twenty-two.

Twenty-three.

I run my pointer finger over the metal numbers. My home away from home for the next nine months. The door is already ajar, and I can hear voices coming from inside.

"No, Mom. I don't want it that way."

"Well, that's the way it's going to be, you spoiled brat," another voice says.

Mama and I give each other a side-eye. I tap lightly on the door before peeking my head inside. From the looks on their faces and the tones of their voices, I've interrupted a quarrel.

"Elaina?" I ask. When I got my roommate assignment a few months ago we talked via social media. She doesn't mirror her pictures. A tiny little thing. No more than five-four, and no bigger than a size three. She's older than me by a couple years and a sophomore. She said she got a bad dorm-lottery number and was only left with freshman dorm options.

Reason 348,298 I ain't got no business in this place.

Try telling Mama that. And I mean, I don't mind being with people older than I am. Everyone called me an old soul in high school, teasing me 'bout my love of black-and-white movies and Motown songs. Can't dance to save my life, but I'll cut up to Earth, Wind & Fire.

"Vanna? I'm so happy you're here!" Elaina shrieks, dropping her bedsheets on the floor and bouncing to the door. She opens it wide and pulls me into a hug. I stand still, not expecting the sudden display of affection. Or the name change.

"Oh my God. I'm, like, so sorry. I'm a hugger."

"It's cool." I give an awkward laugh and set my rolling backpack on the bare blue mattress. I plop onto it and bounce up and down. Great, I'll be sleeping on concrete for the next nine months. Although my bed feels like bricks, the room is large. Larger than my room at home, for sure, with a view to match. It's like all those times when I was younger: I'd get hype to stay overnight at hotels, even though I knew I'd have to go home the following day.

For the next year this is my home.

But there are no passing cars blasting music outside the window. No people who'll greet me each morning with a fast nod or an "I see you, girl."

"This place is nice, Savannah," Mama says.

"Hi there." A blond woman next to Elaina sticks out her hand. "I'm Mrs. Ellen Caruthers. Elaina has told me so much about you. It's like I know you already." A faux fur hangs over her thin shoulders. I want to remind her that it's summertime and damn near ninety-five degrees. I shake her hand and then get to work unpacking.

My eyes fix on a shrine to Elaina. A gigantic picture of her surrounded by four tiny white candles.

"Excuse my manners," Elaina's mom continues. "Is this your sister? Nice to meet you." Mrs. Caruthers extends her hand to Mama. My cheeks burn. I told her not to wear that damn bedazzled shirt.

Mama's lip snares, a familiar gesture of hers that usually gets followed with a few choice words. But she keeps it classy this time. "No, I'm her mama, Freda Howard." Mama takes her hand, but not for long.

"Well, you don't hardly look old enough to be her mother," Mrs. Caruthers says in disbelief. *A young thirty-four, but don't look a day over nobody's twenty-five,* Mama would say. "Did you have her at twelve?" Mrs. Caruthers throws her head back in laughter.

It ain't even that funny, but this lady laughing like it's the funniest thing she's heard all year. Elaina chuckles too. I make a mental note to check when the deadline to switch room-mates ends.

"Sixteen, actually," Mama says between two deep sighs. The calm before the storm. Mrs. Caruthers only got a few more of those slick jokes before she bring the projects out of Mama.

Mama steps around Mrs. Caruthers and unzips my suit-case. She begins folding my underwear on the bed, all out in the open. Parents always find a way to embarrass you.

"Mama, I got it." I gather all my things and begin to make a pile. Least she can do is let me sort my clothes the way I want to.

She throws her hands up. "You don't got to tell me twice not to fold clothes."

I unpack the family pictures of Mama, Big Mama, and Uncle JR and set them up in a neat row on the wooden dresser behind my bed, which also serves as a headboard.

Mrs. Caruthers places a stack of laundry on Elaina's dresser. "It's nice they are adding more diversity to the campus. When I went here, there weren't many African Americans. N-not that I see color or anything."

"It was the seventies, Mom," Elaina says.

"Black people existed in the seventies," I remind them.

Elaina don't have anything to say to that.

Mama makes a stank face that only I catch. She sucks her teeth and passes me a bag. I decorate the drab white walls with posters of Maya Angelou, Toni Morrison, and Angela Davis. A *Wakanda Forever* decal plastered on my full-length mirror. Diana Ross strikes a diva pose on the door of my closet. Yet it's nothing compared to Elaina's side. Faux fur everywhere. A golden frame with vintage photos of Elizabeth Taylor hangs over her bed. The glow of vanity lights hurts my eyes.

Elaina's phone chirps and she sits up at the notification. "There's a welcome-back fair going on in the courtyard. We should check it out."

"Mama, can I go?"

Elaina picks up her pocketbook and is almost halfway out the door. She don't even think to ask permission.

"You still got all these things to unpack and you know I have to leave in the morning."

"Mama . . ." Mama hates begging, but I test my luck. My eyes lower and I stick my lip out farther than need be. I need to get out of this room. It's suffocating me.

She sighs, folding her arms across her chest. "If you ain't here in an hour, I'm going to the hotel. Then you'll have to put away all these clothes yourself."

A lie. Mama not leaving this room until every sweater is hung up and every sheet is ironed.

"Thank you!" I grab my small pocketbook from the oak desk and leave before Mama can change her mind.

In the hallway, Elain trots beside me, three of her prancing steps for one of mine.

"Your mom always that strict?" As soon as the door opened, Elaina had a cigarette hanging from the side of her mouth. "You'd think we were going to a strip club from how she acted."

"Your mama always that . . ." I search for the right word. "Dense?"

"She is, and trust me, that's not the half of it."

Smoke floats from her mouth and she stomps out the cigarette before we get to the booths. There are twenty tables set up in the courtyard, each decorated to match the club it represents. The baking club has the most people on account of the unmistakable smell of brownies. Up ahead, a long line of frat and sorority tables fills the courtyard with Greek letters, shapes, and all sorts of colors. I'm almost sure I spot Elaina arch her back, sticking out her chest as we walk by.

People stare at us. Well, her, mainly. I spot a table for the Black Student Union. *Now that's what I'm talking about.* A few people stop in front of it, but no one takes the flyers that a redheaded white girl holds in her hands.

"Elaina!" Redhead shouts, and runs from behind the booth. "You finally made it. I thought you'd given up on Wooddale."

"Mom wouldn't hear of it. It's either marriage or college. By next year, hopefully, it'll be marriage," she says.

I feel invisible as they go on about their summer vacations and gossip. Just as I'm about to snag some free brownies and head to Mama, Redhead *finally* acknowledges me. "You're new around here."

Not a question but a statement. From the lack of brown faces, it's extra easy to spot fresh meat.

"Must be the shaking hands that gave me away," I say. "Are you the president of this club?"

If she is, my next question is how'd a white girl get this gig.

Elaina lets out a shrieking laugh. "God, no. Could you imagine? Meggie, this is Savannah, my roommate."

Meggie smirks. "I'm Meggie Weaver. Editor in chief of the *Wooddale Gazette*. I'm just helping a friend pass out flyers."

An older Black lady joins in beside her. She can't be over forty, but she walks like she demands respect at all times.

"And this is the BSU and *Wooddale Gazette* advisor, Professor Daphne Santos," Meggie says. "Savannah's new to Wooddale."

Her eyes light up. "Welcome to Wooddale! You can call me Professor Daphne or Professor Santos."

The first Black guy I've seen since being on campus comes over and stands between Meggie and Professor Santos. "I think"—he coughs between his words—"I got a few new recruits."

"Were you chasing them down?" Professor Santos hands him a bottle of water from the cooler.

He pants; the red undertone of his light brown cheeks shines. "Sometimes you have to be a little aggressive in this business."

"Are you okay?" Professor Santos asks. "Do you need to go to the health center?"

"Nah . . . I'm good. . . . I got asthma, that's all." He wheezes some more before standing up straight. He towers over me by at least a few inches and wipes the sweat off his bushy brow, bringing attention to his dark brown eyes.

"We might have gotten you a recruit ourselves. Benji, this is Savannah," Meggie says, introducing us. "Savannah, Benji."

He reaches into his pocket and pulls out an asthma pump. He takes three hits before sliding it back in his pants. "Nice to meet you. I've never seen you on campus, and since it's only one hundred Black people here at most, I definitely wouldn't have missed you."

"A *hundred*?" I ask. "Where are they hiding out at?"

"You'll see them around sooner or later," he says.

His eyes lock on mine. I look away, pretending to be interested in the science table next to us. "Benji . . . what's that short for?" I ask.

"My government name is Benjamin Harrington the Third."

"You sound like you're from a royal family," I joke.

"He is," Meggie steps in. "His great-great-*great*-grandfather was one of the founding students here. He's got clout."

"Nah, I'm a regular guy . . . and I'm a sophomore, so if you ever need anyone to show you around or anything, I'm your tour guide."

"I'm down for that," I say. "You're a member of the BSU, I'm assuming?"

"The president, actually—this is my baby." He glides his hand across the table. "Created it last year."

"You mean to tell me there wasn't a Black Student Union before last year?"

"There has been one on and off over the years," he says. "Not many of us join the BSU because they think it puts a target on their backs. That no one takes it seriously. Which is understandable. Sometimes there wasn't even an advisor to take on the group. That's why I'm grateful for Professor Daphne."

A target on folks' backs? Kind of BSU is this? Or better question is: What kind of school is this?

"It's my pleasure." Professor Santos pats Benji on the shoulder.

"Do I need to do anything to join?" I ask.

"Breathe oxygen," Elaina answers. "They let anyone in, I bet." She laughs.

"If you're committed to the progress of Black students

on Wooddale's campus, that's all you need," Professor Santos hits back.

I like her already.

"Do you have an idea about what you want to major in?" Professor Santos asks.

"I'm actually thinking about journalism."

Truth is I'm not sure what I'm majoring in. I focused too much on getting into college and not enough on what to do when I got here. Journalism seems dope, though. Like a way to give a voice to the voiceless. Make a difference in some-body's world.

Professor Santos goes to the *Gazette* table beside us. She hands me a folder with INFORMATION plastered on the front. "Well, the *Gazette* is always looking for diverse staff. We only let sophomores join the paper. If you declare this year and keep your grades up, I can guarantee you'll have a spot on the team next year. It's a good way to beef up your résumé."

"Look at you, Vanna!" Elaina hip-bumps me, I guess a way for her to prove she's being genuine. "Affirmative action all over the place."

White people, I swear. "That'd be dope."

Maybe this is one of those opportunities Mama was talk-ing 'bout.

I look through the information folder. Famous journalists who graduated from Wooddale fill the front page. *Dream Big* is written in bright letters, but none of these journalists look like me.

Who are these dreams meant for?

"We should get back to our table," Benji says. "Welcome to Wooddale, Savannah."

He looks over his shoulder at me, Professor Daphne by his side. Not too many boys have looked at me *that way* before, but I know the look. In high school I didn't have time to date, and college won't be any different. I'm only here for one thing: a degree.

"Just who I wanted to see." A hand smacks Elaina's butt loud enough for the entire courtyard to hear, and she spins around, beaming.

"Lucas!" She flings her arms around some dude's neck. He's covered in Greek letters, gold and purple. She presses her lips into his face, and I look away. Ain't nobody trying to see all that. Meggie meets my eyes, grimacing, equally as uncomfortable.

"Meggie." Lucas smiles quickly.

"Lucas," she says flatly. She's not a fan of Lucas, apparently. She murmurs a goodbye as she walks over to her table.

"Who's your new friend?"

"Babe, this is my new roomie, Vanna!" Elaina's squeal doesn't go away as she introduces us. She goes on and on about how they met, Lucas's family's name on the university recreational center, and where they were vacationing over Labor Day weekend. I want to be anywhere else at this point. Elaina wraps her arms around him tighter, like if she lets go, he'll fly away. "Vanna is from Tennessee too! Isn't that a funny coincidence?"

27

"What part are you from?" I ask.

"Knoxville," he replies. "We left when I was a kid but still go back at least once a year."

Never been. I know which cities in Tennessee to stick to. Hell, Memphis can be racist if you go to the right place at the wrong time.

"Memphis is my stomping ground. Go, Tigers." I throw up a fist even though I don't watch basketball.

"I can't fuck with you, then." He imitates an "urban" voice. "We're city rivals."

"He's just joking," Elaina says. "I'm sure you two are going to get along fine."

"Of course. If you need anything, freshman, I'm your guy," he says. "It's my senior year and I know this school like the back of my hand."

I don't think I'll be needing anything from him, but I take note.

"I'll catch you later, Vanna. Tell my mom she can leave," Elaina says.

—

Mama and I sit on the edge of the mattress. Elaina's mom was already gone by the time I showed up, thank God. I ain't feel right talking to nobody's mama like that.

"Mrs. Caruthers headed to dinner," Mama says. "She asked us to join them, at Pierre—some French place across town."

I don't know nothing about French food, besides French toast and French fries.

"I thanked her but said no. Don't have extra money for that, and I'm damn sure not letting Mrs. Caruthers pay for us." She sits still for a beat. "And I don't like her ass anyway."

I snort and Mama bust out laughing.

"You up here fronting for these white folks," I say.

She gives me a knowing look. "You could learn a thing or two about that. Don't be up here being *too* Black."

"What's *too* Black?"

"You know what I mean, girl."

Black culture . . . loved by folks of every color unless that culture come from actual Black folk. Then we called hood. Ghetto. Trashy. I have these cute bamboo earrings that I never wear because Mama says only hood rats wear them. I turn on the television one day and guess what I see? A group of white girls . . . in bamboo earrings. *They* ain't never been called no hood rat neither.

"I can't be myself, you mean."

"Listen," Mama says. "You heard that girl, and especially her mama. These folks already got their mind made up about who you is."

"If they already got they mind made up, then why I'm tryna prove them wrong?"

I check my drawers. Everything neatly folded. Mama came through for me, per usual.

Mama shrugs. "That's the way the world work. No one here your friend. Use them like they gonna use you."

"Mama, you not speaking in no type of sense."

"Girl, don't be talking to me like I'm one of your li'l friends. You think these rich white kids know true friendship? They don't, but they have daddies and mamas who own businesses, who can get you a decent job one day. It's chess, not checkers."

I can tell she's serious. "I'll tap-dance for a job. You happy?"

"Chess." She kisses me in the middle of my forehead. I never seen Mama this happy before. Not even when she won three hundred dollars off a scratch-off lottery ticket that one time. She acted like three hundred dollars was three thousand. When you barely make three hundred a week, it might as well be.

"Do you know how proud I am of you, Savannah?" Mama holds my face in her hands. Her brown eyes that are damn near black fuse with mine.

"You tell me every day."

"That's 'cause I don't want you to forget. I never wanted you to end up like me. You not gonna end up on the street or working a dead-end job to make ends meet. All my dreams for you are coming true. It makes working those long hours worth it. The money spent on those extra tutors was worth it. I know you won't let me down."

"I'm scared. . . ." I study the floor.

"What you scared of?" she asks.

"School, I 'pose . . . I'm afraid of being out of place . . .

a minority." Even the private school I gone to since sixth grade was full of Black folk. Although they wore Jordans and name-brand bubble coats, I still blended in.

Mama grabs my chin and forces me to look up. "You got in fair and square like those other kids. You worked hard for that scholarship. You earned this! You're worthy of this opportunity, and dammit, you deserve it. You hear me?"

Tears flow down my face. I been holding it in so long, I can cry enough to fill the Mississippi River.

"Wipe them tears. Ain't nothing to be crying about," she says. "You have nothing to worry about. You're going to be a wonderful student and make the entire family proud. Repeat after me: I've worked hard. I deserve to be here."

"I've worked hard." The words squeeze my throat. "I deserve to be here."

"Now don't ever forget that. Every morning you wake up, I want you to repeat those words," she tells me.

"Yes, Mama." She pats me on the thigh. The sound of cheerful students outside my window haunts me.

Pressure. Pressure. Pressure.

Wooddale is my only opportunity at greatness. I have to hold on to it.

I don't have money to fall back on like Elaina. I don't have a rich daddy to save me or an elite last name to get me out of trouble.

I can't make one mistake.

THREE

Week two and the pressure has set in.

The pressure Mama was talking about—to not be *too* Black. And I *gotta* make it here. So I should conform. . . .

Right?

I can't afford bundles of pure Peruvian hair, but I can afford this hot comb. Ten dollars to have straight hair that don't block folks' view or invite foreign hands to touch it. *Normal* hair. I grab another strand and slather the heat protectant throughout. The electrical savior touches my hair. The sizzling and crackling sounds it makes causes my stomach to sink. The curls that make me different are no more. *Good hair* is synonymous with *lifeless hair.* I pick up a strand and let it fall to my shoulder. *It will revert,* I pray silently to myself.

With straight hair, I can play the role of Vanna. That's what Elaina's still calling me, and even though I don't want to answer to it, maybe she's onto something.

Vanna turns her nose up at fried pork chops and red Kool-Aid. She prefers the lightness of sushi and LaCroix. She walks the streets of well-lit suburbs, not trash-filled projects.

"I deserve to be here," I say into the mirror. *I almost believe it.*

Because Savannah doesn't have a place here, I walk out the door as Vanna.

The dining hall resembles a princess's ballroom more than a university cafeteria. The ceiling painted with tiny baby angels that dance around the room. Crystal chandeliers hang two apiece above our heads. The large gold-encrusted windows pour in matching golden sunlight that reflects off the laminated flooring.

After the sixth round of looking for edible food, I tap out and walk in defeat to the fruit-and-salad bar. Damn. Where the chicken? The spaghetti? Hell, at this point I'll take some kale, 'cause I know they aren't making no mustard greens in that kitchen. The kitchen staff turn simple dishes into complicated tragedies. They put roasted vegetables in mac and cheese.

Where they do that at?

I pick at the red grapes on my plate and search for somewhere to sit. A place to blend in. Just *be.* Cliques not a thing of the past. The café segregated. Black folks sit with Black folk and whites with whites. A few tables in the back defy this unspoken rule and integrate. I spot a familiar face framed in blond highlights come my way.

"Hey, Elaina, mind if I sit with you?" I ask. I don't know what's worse: sitting with Elaina or by myself like I've been doing because I haven't made any friends yet.

"Of course," she says. "I'm sitting outside on the patio. I hate being stuffed inside on a pretty day like this."

We follow other people who have the same idea. Elaina grabs a table right in the middle of the courtyard. We can see everyone who comes in and out of the cafeteria.

Elaina's eyes move from her plate and lock in on my dome. She didn't come home last night and didn't witness my metamorphosis. "I'm switching up my look." I run my fingers through my hair.

"I like it. Now people can tell you're a college student." She says it more like veiled shade than a compliment.

I ignore it. *Elaina can get me places.*

In retrospect, Elaina been shady this whole time. I chose to ignore it. Ignoring it was easier than acknowledging it. And she was the *only* person I was going to know when I got here. Figured it ain't make sense to piss off the one person I'd know.

Over the summer, when Elaina and I were talking through email, I told her I was on a full scholarship. She asked me was it affirmative action but made sure to mention she supported it.

I wanted to tell her the facts. I'd been solving puzzles since five. Connecting the pieces of the big pictures before I learned to wipe my nose good. "You gone thank me one day," Mama had said. I'm not singing Mama's praises yet.

I can roll out my accolades for Elaina to admire. The honor-roll ribbons I've been getting since grade school. The math tournament trophies Mama keeps in a display case. I can show her pictures of me shaking hands with the principal after I won spelling bees. But it'll be wasting my time. She'll still only see me as an affirmative-action case from Memphis.

I deserve to be here. Mama's words play on repeat in my head.

Lucas rolls up on us. Him and his clique are dressed in different-color pastel shorts that stop above their knees, with bow ties to match. They look the same but with different shades of blondish hair. One dude in the middle stands out—the token Black guy, no doubt. His kinky hair shaved down into a clean cut. His bow tie ain't solid like the rest. There are red polka dots sprinkled on it, I guess his way of bringing flavor into the unseasoned group.

Elaina's eyes gleam with excitement. "Hi, baby," she squeaks.

He pulls her into a hug and then sets his eyes on me. "Vanna, right?"

He's seen me at least five times since school started and still doesn't remember my name.

"That's me." Or at least some watered-down version of me.

I roll another grape around in my mouth. Lucas is your normal white boy from those corny movies about white high school life. He's nothing special, but I'm sure everyone in the world has told him how amazing he is and that's why his head is so big. He bends down to kiss Elaina on the forehead and slides a small white package into her hand before him and his crew leave in a single line.

"You're welcome to some, by the way," Elaina says in a hushed tone. "It keeps me thin and alert."

"I don't do drugs," I say. "Mama would kill me. Then she might just kill you for giving them to me."

"Your mama isn't here anymore," she says.

That doesn't mean my entire upbringing went out the window.

"Anyway." I change the conversation. Getting hooked on drugs isn't my college plan. Networking and getting a job is. "You still haven't told me much about Lucas other than how much you love him."

"I love him." Elaina swoons. "He's the big man on campus, and he chose little ole me."

"What makes him so special?" I ask. He looks basic as hell to me.

"He's a Cunningham." She waits for me to catch on, but I don't. She huffs and rolls her eyes. "He's the president of Gamma Kappa Psi, one of the biggest and oldest fraternities on campus. They practically run this place." She flips her hair. "I mean, come on, Vanna. Everyone knows who Lucas is."

I guess.

"His family is loaded with oil money," she goes on. "And when I marry him, I will be too." She puckers her lips, daydreaming.

Apple don't fall too far from the tree. Her mother proud, I bet.

"Elaina, you're already rich," I remind her, like she reminds me. We been here almost two weeks and she's gone shopping almost every day, coming to the dorm with new purses and expensive makeup she don't use. I went shopping with her one day just to pick up some little things, and the store clerk's blue eyes followed me every time I wasn't near Elaina. She didn't notice and told me I let my imagination run too wild.

"Lucas's family has *money*. We're going skiing in the Alps for winter break." She moves her arms and imitates like she's already on the slopes. "I've only been skiing in Aspen, and to be honest, it isn't that exciting. I get tired of the same slopes, and Mother always acts like it's our first time there."

I suck my teeth at the privilege. Then Meggie comes running to our table, notepad in hand and eyes bugging out of their sockets.

"You guys got to see this!" She so loud, people's heads veer our way. She motions for us to follow.

"First month of school and it's already drama." We leave our trays and follow the crowd out into the courtyard like a fight 'bout to start. Fights in elementary school happened every other day until I went to private school. There, fights were rare. It happened from time to time when one boy got mad at another one for accidentally bumping him or some dumb shit. But fights in college? No way that's what this shit's about. The way everyone running, you'd think Mayweather himself 'bout to square up outside.

I walk toward the business building, Elaina close behind, heels clacking.

There's no fight.

No circle of people tossing bills, betting who'll win.

But something equally painful stands at the center of the growing crowd—a defaced statue. The *only* statue on campus with a broad nose.

Clive Wilmington was the first Black man to be elected president of Wooddale. His tenure didn't last long, but in 1996 he was immortalized with his own statue.

Someone has added a cheap Afro wig to Clive and painted his lips red and exaggerated. A group of students laugh, re-arranging the wig.

"It's not funny." I approach them. They back away as I stand on my tippy-toes (damn near have to jump), snatch the hair off Clive's head, and throw it on the ground.

"That's the most fucked-up thing I've ever seen," I say to Elaina. Her face lacks any expression, shock or otherwise.

"Blackface before Halloween. At least they aren't predict-able." Benji walks up beside me, his eyes meeting the ground. You can't look at things like this too long or they make your heart upset.

Lucas's stank cologne introduces him before his mouth. "What's everyone up in arms about? Even my professor walked out of class." His face glows with delight, not batting an eye at the statue. "Whoever did his makeup did a horrible job. It's funny, actually. Look at his smile."

"That's not makeup," I say. "That's blackface, and whoever did it knew how to perfect it. Makes me sick to my stomach." It's makeup to them. It's pain to us.

"The statue's already of a Black person," Elaina says. "Can Black people do blackface?"

This isn't the time to give a history lesson, and I don't have it in me to. Elaina is ignorant and harmless, for the most part.

I remember what Mama said.

She'll get me to better places.

"Don't make no damn sense," a sharp voice says beside me. Sunlight illuminates her dark skin. She looks me up and down. "Sorry you had to see this, freshman."

She has a body to die for. That I'd give up pizza for. She stands out in the sea of sweatpants and baggy shirts crowded around the statue, in her high pumps and tailored suit. Folks may think it's overkill, but I understand.

You have to be twice as good.

"What gave it away?" I ask. "That I'm a freshman?"

"The shock on your face," she says before extending a hand. "I'm Tasha; this is my second year. You'll get used to the bullshit."

I don't think I'll ever get used to this. We stand as what seems like the only Black people, watching a nasty part of our history be treated like a show at the circus.

"I'm Savannah." I give her hand a flimsy shake.

Savannah to everyone that matters. True friends, that is. Vanna's a persona, not the real me.

"They've gotten bolder this year," Tasha says, shaking her head in disdain. "I can't even form words for how I feel."

I know. That sinking feeling in my stomach that I got when I went to the farmers market on the white side of town and had to deal with invasive stares. The feeling I got each time someone I thought I liked told me how I wasn't like *other* Black people they'd met. The feeling of betrayal.

"Tasha, I don't remember anything like this happening last year." Benji gives her a familiar side hug that screams friends but not *friends*.

"Last year we were too busy trying to survive here—maybe we didn't see it," she replies. "And I bet whoever did this is already on that WooddaleConfessions page. Bragging about it behind a fake profile."

From my summer research, I know that #WooddaleConfessions is a social-media page full of Wooddale's secrets. Sometimes people in the comments decode the anonymous posts and expose whoever is being talked about. If you try to find a post the next day, it's liable to be deleted. It seems extremely high school.

"They'd be real bold to do that," I say.

"Bold as hell."

"I might be sick," I say.

"You three are thinking too deep into it," Lucas jumps in. As if anyone is even talking to him. "The person who did this probably thought it was funny." He chuckles, nudging his friends. "Nothing serious."

I bite down and my inner cheek throbs. This ain't no laughing matter.

"You can't be serious right now." Meggie rolls her eyes. "This is, like, almost racist."

Almost. I swallow a sigh.

"Oh, he serious, from what it looks like," Tasha mumbles in my ear.

She right. He so calm, so entertained, I have half a mind to think he or one of his friends did this. But I glue my lips shut and give Tasha a knowing look. She purses her lips, nodding, like she read my mind.

At least someone here gets me, a small relief.

"Shouldn't I have a say?" Lucas scoffs at Meggie. "Racist? That's ridiculous. I'm not racist. Two of my best friends are Black. Benji and I basically grew up together. Tell them."

Wait, what? I look between the two and see different worlds. Can't imagine them shooting hoops in their gated community or going swimming together during summer vacation. They don't look like people who would be friends, but here at Wooddale you never know. Class almost always trumps race, and with a name like Benjamin Harrington III, ain't no telling how Benji was raised.

"That was a long time ago, man." Benji clears the air like he can tell what's going on in my mind. "Don't use me as your Black-friend card."

"I'm just saying we shouldn't go on a witch hunt for a joke."

Tasha stares at the statue and cuts her eyes over at the frat boys. "Whoever did this is getting expelled. No ifs, ands, or buts about it. I want to go to law school, so I actually read the code of conduct, cover to cover. Vandalism is minor, but a hate crime is expulsion."

"Expulsion a perfect fit for this crime," I say.

"Surely is," she says.

"Whoa, whoa. You two need to chill out. If I knew who did it, I wouldn't think they deserved their life to be ruined over a joke," Lucas says. "It's not a big deal."

"*Do* you know who did this, Lucas?" I ask, the words fumbling from my lips before I can stop them. He studies me up and down. His green eyes rolling across my face make me feel like I'm being cross-examined on an episode of *Law & Order*.

His jaw clenches. "Maybe I do. Maybe I don't. If I did . . . I *wouldn't* make it into an issue." He squeezes his way out of the crowd, and I can't be more relieved. Elaina struts behind him with a shady-ass wave my way.

A sea of paleness and shades of red and blond hair gather around the statue, whispering, taking photos. Some eyes filled with confusion, others with mirth. Before long, there's nowhere to turn without meeting awkward stares of pity or a lack thereof.

Meggie looks curious, her glitter-sticker-covered reporter's notebook in her hand. "I'm going to get the crowd's opinion. Maybe someone knows something about who did it." She says her excuse-mes to about fifteen people before her head disappears out of sight.

"Sis, this ain't right," Tasha says.

"And apparently it's just gone stay here," I add. "Ain't nobody even coming to fix it."

All the white folks just staring; ain't nobody doing shit.

"Seriously, though. Ain't nobody coming to take this mess down?" Tasha asks.

"Knowing them, this might be our new mascot," Benji says.

"Shit, you ain't lying."

If that's what they think of a statue, what do they think of me?

A caricature.

Only meant to be pointed at and laughed at, no matter what I accomplish.

"They are clueless," Benji says. "The worst kind of fool is the ones who don't know they are."

Everyone grows uncomfortable, or maybe they just don't know what to say anymore, so they start to leave. Nothing to say. Or do. Clive sits there grinning until maintenance comes and shoos everyone away before they start cleaning. We settle on the business-building steps, watching as everyone else goes on about their day.

Meggie spots us and heads over, scribbling on her notepad. "It's not usually like this. Well, not this overt, anyway."

"I'd rather they let us know how they feel in front of us." Tasha swats at the mosquitoes that bite at our ankles.

Meggie flips her notebook open. "Benji, I'd love for the

BSU to team up with the *Gazette*. Collaborate on a story about this. Maybe you can host a Talk Back forum? I heard some rumors that Lucas's fraternity may have actually been involved."

"What y'all think? Do you want to be on the panel with me?"

Tasha waves her hands. "Nah, keep me out of all of that. The only thing I have energy for this year is getting an internship on Capitol Hill. My grandma will kill me if I don't get her money's worth out of this high-ass school."

"What about you, Savannah?" he asks.

"I don't know. What would I even say?"

"Speak from the heart," he says. "It won't be too bad, swear. We will cap it at five questions, max. If you don't want to answer one, just pass the mic to me."

"I guess there's no harm in answering a few questions."

"So, you'll do it?" His eyes perk up.

"I mean, let me think about it for a day or so. But, y-yeah, maybe I will."

"Thanks, guys." Meggie returns to the crime scene.

"That's a big job," Tasha says. "Even if it's just a panel, you gotta make it count."

I shuffle on my feet. *I never had to speak up for someone before.*

Mama's words twist in my memory.

I've worked hard. I deserve to be here.

I tap my foot and an eerie silence hangs over us.

I know what I should do even if I don't want to.

44

Clive earned that job, and he may be dead, but we still living. His legacy shouldn't be diminished into this. He was more than that.

If I deserve to be here, his statue sure as hell does, without being ridiculed.

FOUR

There's a welcome-back event in the student union: karaoke. The wackest recreational activity ever, aside from bowling. Which at least gives you a score to feel like you accomplished something at the end. The flyer says pizza will be served, and that's the only reason I'm making an appearance.

I pick up two slices. This pizza is like the kind I can get from Marco's or the frozen-food aisle of Shop & Save. I take a bite, and the texture is reminiscent of cardboard slathered in tomato sauce. I'm not feening for seconds anymore.

I eye the dark room for a place to sit and settle on a table in the far corner. Close enough to view the foolishness but far enough not to be in the way or called up onstage.

"Look who it is," Tasha says. Benji follows behind her. "Mind if we join you?"

"Go 'head." I pull out a chair a little, inviting them into my space. "I didn't think you two would be here." Mostly freshmen come to these things—it's a way to immerse ourselves in the campus—but the only thing I can think about is how most of the people here laughed at Clive's statue yesterday. Blending in at Wooddale mean just smiling at the way they act, the wild shit they say. Elaina not the exception round here. She the rule.

"I needed a break from studying and Benji just wanted free pizza."

"Can't beat free food. That's the only reason to come to these things." Benji stacks two slices of pizza together and eats them like a sandwich.

"I don't see how y'all eat this mess." Tasha picks up her slice of pizza like it's contaminated. "Thin, flat, and lifeless. Like the people around here."

"Here she goes on her 'Chicago grandma-style pizza is the best' rant." Benji turns to me. "Ignore her and enjoy."

"Whatever, you know I'm right." Tasha trades out her pizza for garlic knots. "Man, my little brother would love this. We used to do karaoke battles all the time. When I get rich like Benji that's what I'm going to have, a media room. Where we can sing as loud as we want."

"Get up there and show 'em what you got," I say.

Tasha almost chokes on her bread. "I never said we were good at it."

I take another bite of my pizza and laugh at the show. Everyone claps as an off-brand Chloe x Halle duet leaves the stage.

The table vibrates at the same time. A notification from the university president pops up on our phone screens.

The administration has been made aware of what happened yesterday regarding our late president, Clive Wilmington. We have opened an investigation into the matter and during this time implore you all to remember the values of our university, which include treating one another with respect and kindness. Black lives matter, not only on our campus but throughout our great city. Wooddale University will continue the work of tackling racism head-on and of building communities that are supportive and inclusive for all.

"That was a whole bunch of nothing," Tasha says.

"I'm surprised it took them a whole day to send that out," I say.

"They had to get their story together," Benji replies.

Clive was cleaned up within the hour. Then it was back to our regularly scheduled program. There were whispers, but no one spoke his name out loud. Now it's like everyone has forgotten. Everyone except for us.

"Benji, you talk to your shady friend?" Tasha asks.

"There's no point in talking to Lucas. He always thinks he's right." Benji waves to the new people onstage. The bass of some eighties song starts. "And he's *not* my friend."

"Y'all see that confessions post? Someone said they saw Lucas's frat brothers sneaking around the statue that day," Tasha says. "I know they not that interested in Clive's history to be reading the plaque, either."

I barely saw that post. It got deleted as soon as it popped up. People verified it and everything. Nobody said names, but I wouldn't be surprised if Lucas was in the mix. A real snake in the grass.

"I don't blame you for cutting him off," I say. "He's smug as hell. Sneaky, too. Like you always gotta watch your back and front around him."

"He wasn't always this way." Benji shakes his head. "I actually remember when he wouldn't speak unless spoken to. The shyest person in Boy Scouts. His dad broke him out of that, though."

A quiet Lucas. I can't imagine him not talking. He's big and bad now to make up for lost time.

The gathering dies down, and the staff begins to strip and clean the tables, leaving the last students left to chat quietly to themselves on the sofas.

"Administration still hasn't gotten back to me about the forum," Benji says as we walk outside the building. "The BSU is having a silent sit-in tomorrow."

"Now, *that* I'll come to," Tasha says. "The administration approves all other activities in the snap of a finger, but when it comes to things important to us, they take their sweet time to make sure it doesn't make them look bad."

We find an empty spot on the stairs and sit on the warm concrete.

"I'll try to make it too," I say. I've seen protests, of course, on television, but I've never been to one before. Silent or otherwise. Never really had a reason to raise my voice before. In high school, other people were my advocates, especially Mama. Didn't have to worry about people trying to take advantage of me. Justice a given, not something that had to be taken.

My phone buzzes against my hip.

Mama: You okay up there?
Haven't heard from you in a while.

Me: I'm fine Ma. Might be going to a sit in with some of my new friends.

Mama: A sit in? Why you focusing on things that don't matter? Remember your grades!

Mama didn't see Clive. Couldn't bring myself to take a picture, let alone send it. This might not matter to Mama, but it matters to me.

"Benji and I should be used to this," Tasha says, "this being our second year and all, but you can never really prepare for life at Wooddale. Don't let these people get in your head, Savannah. Trust me, they will try."

I soak in her advice. Remembering Elaina's, Meggie's, and Lucas's comments. To them Clive is just a statue. Nothing weird at all, and now they got me questioning myself. Maybe I am too sensitive.

"It's hard," I say. "I know what Wooddale represents. But at what cost?"

"You'll get your footing," Benji says. "The years will go fast, and by the end you'll have a Wooddale degree."

"*Mm-hmm,* two things can be true. We plan sit-ins *and* get a great education," Tasha adds.

That Wooddale degree is supposed to change everything. Maybe even me. But I'm not sure it's worth it.

FIVE

My outdated alarm clock wakes me up the next morning. I drag myself out of bed and wrap my thin sheet around me.

I settle on a basic-ass plain-Jane outfit that hides the dimples in my thigh flesh. A navy Wooddale sweatshirt, jeans, and plain white Keds. Preppy, but it ain't me. A feeling of sadness settles over me. I can't be me anymore. Pushing the feeling away, I pull out my bamboos and clamp one to my left ear. Then the dainty fake pearl on my right. Seconds change to minutes as I study my face. Elaina's snoring shakes me out of it.

I replace the bamboo with the dainty pearl.

The courtyard floods with freshmen like me who thought taking an early-morning class would be a breeze. Reality hit us like a freight truck. There's fifteen minutes left before class starts. My stomach gurgles for some type of breakfast but I don't want to be late. Students walk zombielike, not saying a word to one another.

"Hey, Savannah!" Tasha comes over, coffee in hand.

"Hey, girl, love the shoes."

"Thank you." She does a quick spin in her red-bottom heels. Her outfit looks as if she has a court hearing and she's the high-powered attorney, not the worn-down perp. Preparing for her future life on the Hill, no doubt. "As you can see, the dress code around here is sportswear and pastel."

"Birkenstocks and Puma."

She chuckles. "What class are you on the way to?"

"African American Literature with Jacobson," I say. "I dropped my American English class for it."

American English is code for White English. Hemingway, Fitzgerald, and Dickinson. People I've never had any interest in reading.

Toni Morrison, Gloria Naylor, and Ntozake Shange more my speed.

I squint at the map on my phone. "I'm having a hard time finding the building, though."

"Lucky for you I'm heading there too. Let's go—we don't want to be late." She walks with grace and assurance. Her ability to grab college by the throat radiates off her. I drag my feet along and lower my eyes, not wanting to draw attention to myself. Blending in is what I came here to do.

Tasha leads us to room 314 of the Barwell building.

She sets her purse on the table right in the front of the classroom. I sit in the plastic chair beside her and pull out my old-fashioned notebook. I can't help but notice everyone else has a laptop, Tasha included.

"I can't wait to get a new laptop." I attempt to save face. I don't want to be labeled the poor girl on my first day. Truth is, my laptop is raggedy. It turns off randomly and I have to jiggle the charger just right for it to work.

"Don't worry. If you miss something, you can have my notes," Tasha says as her MacBook boots up. A poorly tanned man with a salt-and-pepper beard that could use a trim enters the room. His lips are in a permanent snarl position.

"Hello, class." Professor Jacobson's boisterous voice rings out. "Nice to see all your smiling faces."

More like sleepy faces.

Professor Jacobson begins to check off names on the roll sheet.

"Savannah Howard," he says without looking up.

I raise one hand in the air. "That's me. I just registered."

"Get with me after class and I can catch you up."

Lucas walks in just as Professor Jacobson begins the class.

"What is he doing here?" I whisper to Tasha.

"He thinks it's an easy A," she says, not looking up from her color-coded planner.

Lucas takes forever to sit down. Him and three other guys, all wearing the same colors, talk loud as hell, and it's like Professor Jacobson wants to say something but he doesn't. He just glares.

"Sorry, student-body-president business." Lucas takes a seat in the back of the class.

Student-body president? I can't imagine Lucas being the

voice for me on campus. Being the voice for anybody, matter fact. Then I remember the people who laughed. More of them than there are of me. He probably was voted in unanimously.

Professor Jacobson reads passages from a book about the Harlem Renaissance, going over hidden symbolism. I try to keep up with the lecture while taking notes by hand. Eventually I give up and drift away.

"You all can wake up." Professor Jacobson claps his large hands to gather our attention. "I want to raise one more point and then you may leave. Can anyone tell me who Lorraine Hansberry was? And the importance of her work that spanned her short lifetime."

Dead silence.

Lucas's voice cuts through the tension. "Isn't she the lady on the syrup bottle?"

Tasha looks over her shoulder. "That isn't even funny."

"People laughed," he says. "Learn to take a joke."

"Learn to not be casually racist."

"Here we go," Lucas says. "It only took you"—he pretends to check his Apple Watch—"five seconds to bring up the race card."

"It's not a card; it's the truth."

I sit mum as Tasha goes head-to-head with Lucas. My mouth wants to jump in, but it won't open. Mama's words run through my mind each time I try.

I've worked hard. I deserve to be here.

Professor Jacobson snaps his fingers. "Let's move on. Lucas, keep your wisecracks to yourself from now on."

I move my gaze around the room. The place is small enough for me to notice that Tasha and I are the only ones who put the African American in this literature class. I make up my mind right then that I will not be the Black spokesperson. I will not explain to them the meaning of James Baldwin's work. I will not stand on a soapbox about the imagery weaved into Zora Neale Hurston's stories. I for damn sure ain't about to tell them about *A Raisin in the Sun*.

Every time their stares leap to the front of the room, to no doubt wait for us to answer the questions asked, I will look away. Pretend that I don't see how they don't really want to learn about folks like me.

SIX

I sit outside on a white wooden bench across from the university community garden. There aren't any crops in, but lily flowers left over from the summer still sit in full bloom. The only flowers that grow in my neighborhood are weeds.

My books lie beside me, all opened to problems I can't bring myself to complete. This Clive story has been on my mind ever since it happened, almost four weeks ago. I scroll Lucas's social-media pages. Scrolling so far down to when he didn't look so bad.

To when his smile seemed genuine. It's funny how people change as they grow. He has a few pictures still up with Benji. Them leaning on their bicycles in a cul-de-sac. Benji looks different too, like maybe he was supposed to end up like Lucas but took a different path.

My phone vibrates. It's Ma.

Savannah I got bad news

The text lights up the screen of my phone. She usually calls once a day just to say "hello" a.k.a. get into my business. The news can't be that bad since she texting me instead of calling.

> **Me:** Good afternoon to you too

I know the sass in my response is risky, but I've been pushing the boundaries with Mama since I've been in this place. I'm grown, right?

> **Mama:** Don't think I won't get on a plane
> and come light you up. I can't send money
> this week. We're short. The light bill was sky high.

Okay, it *is* bad news. Just bad news Mama didn't want to tell me over the phone. She knows I'd panic and cry. I cry when I panic.

My phone vibrates in my hand. Mama, the queen of double and triple texting if she doesn't get a reply in what she deems a timely manner.

> **Mama:** Troubles don't last forever.
> When you get your degree from Wooddale,
> you'll be sending me money.

That doesn't make me feel any better about now. The lavender body oil I'm wearing is not making me feel relaxed like the lady at the herb store said it would. It feels like my body has started to tighten, and no matter how much I close my eyes and "let go," the tension remains.

Only thing that's keeping me from really panicking is my little living stipend the school gave me along with my full-ride scholarship. I use *living* loosely. They give me like three hundred dollars a month. After buying food, toiletries, and other necessities, I can barely afford an outside burger. Mama usually sends extra to get me over the hump. The little I have left will last me, though. If Mama taught me one thing, it's how to survive.

"You found my favorite place to do homework." Benji sneaks up on me with a stack of papers in hand. "No one usually comes out this far."

"It's the quietest place on campus. I was trying to get some assignments done, but I don't think that's happening." I scoot my books over and make a place for him to sit. "Join me?"

He opens his physics book. Flies through the problems. "Shouldn't you be off doing freshman activities? Rushing? Day drinking?"

"The only activity I have is preparing for this literature exam," I say. "Any news on the forum?"

"It'll be this Tuesday if everything goes right. It's been hard planning events and getting people involved. Especially since only a handful of folks signed up. You're still down to be on the panel, though, right?" he asks.

"I've been thinking that maybe I should sit this one out," I say. "I mean, what can I really say about the situation? I'm new here. No one cares what I have to say."

Benji closes his book and stuffs it into his backpack. "You bring a new perspective as a freshman. I mean, you'd only been on campus two weeks and the Clive thing happened."

"I guess I'm more nervous than anything," I say. "I've never had to speak up in front of an entire student body before."

"No need to be nervous." He scoots closer; his fingers linger near mine. "I'll be beside you, and Tasha will be in the audience. We won't let anything happen."

I pull my hand away. *Eye on the prize, Savannah.*

He notices the gesture and folds his hands in his lap. "Truth? I'm a little nervous too. Sometimes it's hard for me to speak up about these things," he says. "Especially when there's a possibility Lucas is involved. There's only so much I can say before things get complicated."

"He's an asshole, though. That should make it easy to speak up," I say.

"That's easier said than done. Imagine if you grew up with someone and they turned out like Lucas. How'd you react to it?"

I can't think of a decent answer.

SEVEN

Today is the Talk Back forum, and Clive is the topic. His painted face is still circulating on social media. Wooddale ain't going out like that. They need to do damage control, and this is it. An hour-long forum that's only half full. Tasha, Benji, and I sit in the front row, waiting for the beginning of what can be either something good or something extremely bad.

"I wonder where Elaina and Meggie are," I ask Tasha.

"I saw your roomie in the library earlier, but she wasn't studying, just fixing herself in the mirror."

"That sounds like her." Sometimes I wake up early just to get ready first. Elaina has to try on eight different outfits and combine fifty different smells before she's out the door. "I figured Meggie would be here, though. She was the one that set this up."

I look over my shoulder for her. Instead I'm greeted by Darla, a girl in my chemistry class.

"Hey, girl! I sent a Halloween party invitation to your school email. You can bring your friend, too. It's going to be lit!" She's a white pageant queen from Kentucky who ain't realized she can stop smiling at any time. I cringe at her use of the word *lit* and hold my breath at the over-the-top *girl*.

I push down my feelings and smile up at her. "Thanks. We'll try and make it."

"Cool it, you guys. We're about to start," one of the students who's moderating says with her lips pressed against the microphone. Professor Daphne stands next to her, poised. Our eyes meet and she almost allows hers to roll. She gives me a low-key thumbs-up.

"There is a divide on this campus. A divide that wasn't here last year or the year before that."

I shoot her the stank eye. *It was there. You just didn't want to notice it. I doubt racism dropped on campus last month like a special delivery from UPS.*

There have been incidents here and there. I've never seen anything; Meggie told me about them. Subtle things that are gone with the snap of a finger. Nooses hung on trees brushed off as Halloween decorations. A swastika carved on a desk, and the next day the desk was gone. Nothing negative lurks on Wooddale campus for long.

Professor Daphne takes over the mic. "You can discuss with one another, but you are not allowed to talk over each other. There will be no use of slurs, trash talk, or anything of the like, or you will be escorted out and sent to the dean of students. Do I make myself clear?"

Low yes-ma'ams echo through the room.

"Good. Let's get started."

I look around the Jasper Auditorium. About fifty people are here out of the thousands of students who attend Wooddale. Me, Tasha, Benji, and a handful of others who aren't already in the BSU are the only Black faces. I roll my eyes to the back of my head each time they pass the mic around to people who try hard to convince us they mean no harm before saying harmful statements. They make sure to sugarcoat their veiled racist "observations."

"They segregate themselves." One girl wraps her thin fingers around her thinner red hair.

Tasha and I look at one another and then at Benji. We give one another the *look*. The *she done fucked up* look.

"Who are *they* and what does that have to do with Clive?" I say loudly.

I want to get through this thing without my blood pressure going through the roof, but I got to know. A few people sit up in their seats and try to find my voice in the crowd.

Professor Daphne gestures for me to stand up. I hesitate and dig my fingers into my palm. All those eyes looking at me. *Don't trip, Savannah. Say what you got to say and sit your ass down.* I regulate my breathing and stand up tall. I try to seem confident when inside I'm screaming at the top of my lungs.

"Well, um, Black people," the redhead stammers. "You're the second-most represented group on campus, but you still segregate yourselves."

"Girl, no she didn't," Tasha whispers out of the side of her mouth to me.

I close my eyes and shake my head. Professor Daphne said to keep it civil. If I curse her out, the brand of *angry Black girl* will linger over my head. Plus, I don't need a trip to the dean. "How exactly do you figure that we segregate ourselves?" I say through a clenched jaw.

"Well, um, well, um."

"Girl, spit it out." Tasha's leg bounces up and down. I don't know if it's from nervousness about what Redhead going to say, or if she's trying to calm herself from going over there and busting her upside the head with her pocketbook.

"Hey, hey. I said civil. This is a discussion between these two young ladies. If you want to say something, you will wait until it's time to speak," Professor Daphne says.

Tasha makes a *psssh* sound and murmurs something underneath her breath.

"In the café, you guys always sit together," the redhead says, "even though there are a bunch of free seats at the other tables."

Members of the audience agree in low whispers. If I start talking, I won't make any sense, and this is an important moment. I can't blow it. Right now, I'm the head speaker of the minuscule Black coalition of Wooddale University.

I find my voice.

"Do you ever come over to these Black tables that you speak of?" I start. "Have you ever noticed that the number of white tables outweighs the number of Black ones? Or thought that maybe, just maybe, we want something for ourselves?"

"Preach it, sis." Tasha waves her hand like she caught the Holy Spirit.

"Well, no. But—"

I ignore Professor Daphne's warning and don't let her finish.

"There is a reason we have our own tables. It's because y'all"—I point out into the cosigning crowd—"never invited us to yours. In forced rebellion, we made our own. That's not self-segregation. That's self-preservation."

"Wellllllllllll." Tasha copies the old church deacons.

"Whatever. I still think it's wrong." The girl lacks understanding. Understanding me would be admitting that her views are wrong. Something they never do.

"Sit down, Jessica, and listen—you just might learn something," Benji yells out. Jessica huffs and flops in her seat. He sends me a toothy smile and looks away before I get the chance to return the gesture.

Benji reminds me of home. The way he's quick to protect me from these people. I don't need him to wear a cape for me, but it's nice to know he got my back.

One after the other, different shades of white folk stand up and offer their opinions on why they think racism exists. None of them takes the responsibility for their ancestors and their own part in upholding the advantages that have been set up for them. None of them takes any responsibility for Clive.

"Slavery was so long ago. . . ."

"I don't see color but . . ."

"It was only a joke."

"My best friend is Black. . . ." As if that gives them freedom to say whatever they want about things they know nothing about. As if that gives them a reason to put blackface on Clive.

"I would like to thank you all for voicing your opinions on the matter," Professor Daphne says. "It seems we have more work to do on campus, and I and the members of the BSU are dedicated to making that happen." She waves Benji and me to the stage. We sit behind a long buffet-style table. One mic sits in the middle.

I can feel the sweat beads form on my forehead.

If I can take Jessica alone, I can do this.

Benji leads. "This year the Black Student Union will be more active. We will try our best to be a resource for everyone on campus so things like this don't happen anymore."

He passes the mic to me. The #WooddaleConfessions post about Lucas's fraternity being at the statue flashes in my head.

"There has been talk that a popular fraternity on campus may have had something to do with defacing the statue," I say. "If that's true, then it is up to us as a community to make sure that they aren't honored at Wooddale."

"Whoa, can she say that?" A guy in Lucas's frat jumps up, his crew three deep behind him. "Everyone knows who she's talking about."

Professor Daphne takes over. "Savannah, do you have proof of this accusation?"

I squeeze the base of the mic tighter. "Well, not really, but . . ."

"She's only been here for what, not even two months? What does she know about Wooddale and our community anyway?" Jessica hollers out.

"Nothing," another guy chimes in. "She's only a freshman."

Eyes throw darts at me. Whispers float around the room. People snap photos without even turning the flash off. I drop the mic and run off the stage. Benji calls after me, but I don't stop.

"Savannah, wait up!" Tasha yells from behind me. "Girl, if I trip in these heels—"

"I fucked up," I say as we make it to a safe space, leaning against the redbrick clock tower. The sun has gone down.

"You just have to be more careful about what you say. Lucas has mouthpieces everywhere. A person talking anonymously on the internet is way different than you saying it in real life."

"You don't think he'll try anything, do you?"

"He shouldn't unless he's guilty of something," she says. "You didn't name names."

I still can't help but think that I've messed up my last chance at blending in.

The clock tower gives out a sputtering chime that signals the changing of the hour.

"You hungry?" Tasha asks. "My stomach is about to eat itself."

"I want something greasy and comforting."

"Anything but the café, though. I'm paying two thousand dollars for a meal plan to eat yogurt every day. College a scam," Tasha says, like she is making her case in court.

Our stomachs growl in sync. We cut through the secluded alleyway behind the school to get to the street faster.

"Wait up," a male voice calls out of the darkness. His shoes click against the pavement and make me uneasy.

"Girl, who is that?" Tasha looks over her shoulder but keeps up her pace.

"I don't know," I reply. "Let's walk faster. I left my Mace at the dorm."

"Aye, you guys. Wait, it's Benji," he says again. This time, Tasha and I stop and try to find the voice that rang out.

He catches up with us and crouches down. "I know . . . you guys . . . heard me . . . calling you."

"We don't make it a habit to stop in dark alleys," I say.

"Boy, you need some milk or something?" Tasha asks. "Don't come over here dying. We don't know CPR."

"Nah . . . I'm good. . . . My asthma been acting up lately."

"What you want, then? We only have forty minutes before everything closes around here." Tasha blunt, and that's what I like most about her.

"I wanted to check on Savannah," he says. "Why'd you run out like that?"

"I made a fool of myself," I say.

"No, they are fools if they think it isn't possible for Lucas or his frat brothers to do something like that," he says.

"You two used to be tight, right?" Tasha chimes in. "You got to know something about him and his people. That statue didn't deface itself."

He bites his bottom lip. "Just because we used to be friends doesn't mean I keep up with him now."

"You sure about that?" Tasha asks.

I look between the two. Tasha putting her lawyer skills to use and Benji is losing.

He raises an eyebrow. "You don't trust me now, Tash?"

"It isn't about trust. This about loyalty," Tasha replies.

There's an awkward silence as we wait for him to say more, but the more never comes. I can tell he wants to say something: his lip twitches but nothing comes out. Lucas got a grip on him, and I need to know why or how.

Benji breaks the ice and pulls a colorful flyer from his coat pocket. "Listen, I'm having a Halloween party this weekend." He hands the crumpled paper to me. "We're all on edge right now and need a pick-me-up."

Tasha leans in and reads over the paper. This will be my first party of the semester if we go.

"We'll try to make it," Tasha says.

Right now she's still in petty mode, but from the way her eyes gleam, I know she wants to go.

Benji tips his Chicago Bulls ball cap as he walks away. "I hope to see you there, Savannah."

I tuck a frizzy strand behind my ear and study my feet as he walks backward, eyes on me.

Tasha waits till he's out of sight before she bursts out laughing. "Girl, that high-yella boy has a thing for you. I have never seen him this gushy."

My cheeks burn. "Nah, he doesn't. Besides, I'm not here for boys. Especially boys that used to be *that* close to Lucas."

Benji comes with too much baggage by the name of Lucas Cunningham. I already have too many other things to worry about. Don't got time to be looking over my shoulder all the time in the name of infatuation.

She rolls her eyes. "He *definitely* does, and I know I gave him a hard time, but I believe him about not being tied to Lucas anymore."

I brush her off. "It doesn't even matter. He was being friendly, that's all."

"Girl, I know you saw how he was looking at you during the forum. Like you're baked mac and cheese and it's Thanksgiving."

"I bet he got a girlfriend, or in a situationship," I say, shouldering my bag. "He too fine to be out here single."

"Nah, Benji ain't the player type. Plus, he got asthma," she says like a light bulb went off in her head. "You can't have asthma and be a player. He gonna run out of breath tryna come up with lies."

I crack up laughing. "You're a mess."

"It's the truth, shoot. Personally, he ain't my type. Too closed up, but there's no denying he's fine."

"We going to this party or what?"

"Hell yeah, we going." She folds the flyer up. "And don't say you have to study or whatever. College is all about balance."

I've never been to a real Halloween party. Or any party that didn't involve cupcakes, balloons, and pastel colors. I usually spent high school nights when I wasn't studying watching old movies on AMC. Halloween parties I heard about were always about who could be the sexiest. That's more Tasha's lane than mine.

But maybe if I talk to Benji at the party, he'll lighten up and tell me more about Lucas. Hell, maybe everyone there can tell me more about Lucas and his reputation around here.

The people who aren't afraid, that is.

EIGHT

"Has Lucas said anything to you since the forum?" Tasha says into her phone, dancing around my room for her social-media followers. A Spotify playlist of the year's best music blasts in the background. She looks fire in her black spandex catsuit and ponytail that took six packs of braiding hair, plus a ton of carefully placed bobby pins, to create. That suit looks like it's squeezing the life out of her while giving clear view of every perfect curve on her body.

I close my rented laptop, setting it on the bed. "Nope, nothing. I mean, I get a few looks here and there, but no one has said anything to me."

"I'd hate to see you caught up in some drama over Lucas. He ain't worth it in my opinion."

"You think I'd get caught up over this?" I ask. "It's not like I said anything that isn't true. His fraternity *is* rumored to be involved."

"Just be careful. Lucas's power around here is deep," she says. "Even if it is true, that won't stop him or his minions from coming after you. Including the administration."

"Professor Daphne seems cool. Like she'd take up for me if anything popped off."

"Even Professor D might cower to Lucas," Tasha says cynically.

I chew at the tips of my chipped nails. Sometimes I wonder why Benji even wanted me to sit next to him at the forum. He probably scared of Lucas too. Of what he's capable of. Growing up together, I'm sure Benji knows more about Lucas's clout than I do.

"I'm not scared of Lucas or some uppity people in tailored suits."

A front to save face. In reality I want to call Mama, tell her to pick me up like I used to do, but I can't now because technically I'm an adult. I have to fight my battles on my own.

"Well, at least you'll have one night of fun before they toss you out on your ass," Tasha snickers.

"Shut up." I shove her shoulder, careful to keep my face out of her selfies. "Don't say that."

"These white folks are wild. Just be careful. Kicking you out is the most benevolent thing they could do."

The leftover cookies from lunch threaten to come up as I push the same clothes around in my closet. I can't think about that right now.

Tasha throws her phone on the bed as I slip on the least awful outfit I have.

"That's cute. Now, hurry up, girl. I don't know how long this ponytail going to hold up." She stomps over to the mirror in her leather thigh-high boots and stands behind me. "These bobby pins are already slipping." She puts her elaborate hairdo back into place, making it even better than before.

"We can't all look fly on the first try." I press my hands against my stomach and cover the lower bulge, studying myself in the mirror. The white dress plunges low, which would be sexy for anyone else, but I don't have any boobs worth a damn. The matching sheer maxi skirt has a slit that goes all the way up and showcases the dimples in my thigh. I toss some jewels on from my dresser, best pick of what they had at the beauty supply store. The chunky, eccentric gold jewelry adds flair to my outfit and transports me to ancient Egypt.

"Do you like this one?" I ask, flattening out my Cleo-inspired dress.

Tasha grabs my hand and spins me around for a better look. "I *love* it."

"Queen Cleo it is." I add the dramatic Aspen and try not to flatten my curly twist out. I stopped myself from putting the heat to my curls. Since it's Benji's party, it'll be full of other Black folk. I'll walk in and be welcomed by other women with kinky hair instead of ones amazed at how my hair grew out of my scalp. At this party I won't be a spectacle, an "other," like I am at Wooddale. The tension in my chest lets up a twinge.

"Benji is going to need his asthma pump when he sees you." Tasha applies another layer of mascara.

"Yeah, right. All the dudes' eyes are going to pop out when they see you. I wish I could pull off a catsuit."

"You're beautiful, darling," Tasha mocks in an old-style Southern accent. "Just beautiful."

"Why, thank you, sugar," I say, returning her banter. "You looking mighty fine there yourself."

"Now can we go? You taking colored-people time to a whole 'nother level." Tasha grabs me by the shoulders, pushing me away from the mirror and out the door.

———

We follow the crowd to find the party: drunk hipsters who pregamed so hard that they stop to vomit in the trees along the way, and sorority sisters who are dressed as the Spice Girls, singing off-key.

These folks *can't* be the ones going to Benji's. *Ugh.*

As lame as the crowd looks, my jaw drops when Benji's party comes into view. A hologram ghost greets us at the front door of the colonial-style house. Cobwebs cover the entryway.

"How you even get up in here?" Tasha says, reading my mind.

"This live," I say. We feel our way through. The entire way, Tasha screams at every holographic spider that crawls down the walls. Past the long line of cobwebs, we slip down a corridor, finally inside. Music blasts, pumping so loud I can't hear myself think. A male server dressed as Count Dracula offers us "blood" in orange-and-black cups. Tasha takes two.

"*Heyyy,* friends, over here." Benji stands at the entryway, greeting partygoers. "How you guys doing?" He sways on his feet but corrects it with quickness.

He already tipsy. At least he not sloppy with it. He strategically puts one foot ahead of the other to avoid falling over, walking us through the crowd. Mama always told me to stay away from men who'd been drinking. Men in general, honestly. Benji appears harmless, though. Like the type to pick flowers while drunk, not punch walls.

"We're good," I yell over the music.

"I see you guys got the first drink," he says. "Bloody Marys. It's a cliché drink, but you gotta have it at a Halloween party."

"I don't drink." I shake the contents in the cup Tasha handed me. I've only drank once before. Behind the bleachers at a sock-hop dance with half the seventh-grade class. We went around passing the 5 percent–alcohol wine cooler that Troy Johnson stole from his mama. We were so cool, drinking that one small bottle, taking baby sips so everyone could get faded. We got caught by the chaperone, Coach Broderick, and were suspended for four days.

I still remember the whupping Mama gave me when I got home, and the second whupping I got from Big Mama. Those kind of whuppings stay with you.

"She just never been to a party with me before." Tasha takes the Bloody Mary to the head and licks the leftover contents off her full lips. She drinks mine for me.

"You can party without being turnt," Benji says. "That's

what's up. I need to learn from you." He has on white shutter shades and Bathing Ape shoes, looking like Kanye West in the early 2000s.

Benji looks like an entire snack, and even I can't deny I'm famished.

One by one, white boys in white masks and purple-and-yellow capes stroll in.

Lucas's frat.

My entire stomach turns. Why Benji invite them? He said they *used* to be friends. Past tense.

"Why they here?" I ask Benji.

"I don't know," Benji says. "I didn't invite them, but they got one time to try something."

"Lucas's favorite pastime is trying people," Tasha says.

I fold my arms. "Figured it would be more different. This crowd is basically Wooddale 2.0."

He laughs. "You're still going to have fun, trust me. Here, let me get your jacket." Benji reaches for my coat and I jerk away, knocking over the drink in his hand.

"I—I'm so sorry. I—I didn't mean to. *Damn,* I'm so clumsy." I grab some napkins from Count Dracula's platter and dab at the wet spot in the middle of his shirt.

His fingers wrap around my fidgety hand to stop my dabbing. "Vodka is like water. Good thing I didn't have a Bloody Mary, huh?" he says, and my knees get all weird and shit. *You're here for school, Savannah, damn.* "It'll come out, no sweat. Give me a sec. I'll be right back. Help yourselves to the house." Benji disappears behind a giant Frankenstein and a pair of nurse twins.

"Girl, you need to loosen up." Tasha grabs my hand and we shimmy through the room full of sweaty people. We settle at the fully stocked bar.

"They got everything." Tasha shoves my cup of liquid at me. "Henny and Coke, *aye.* Just one."

I don't drink. I sniff it and grimace.

She rolls her eyes so far back I think they might get stuck. "Just one drink, it won't kill you."

"Fine. *One.*" The strong concoction stings my throat and then settles at the bottom of my stomach. I frown and pinch my nose to down the rest.

"The Henny should hit you quick." Tasha takes another shot, and another, scrunching her face up after each one. She's on glass three and already mixing another potion.

She puts another in my hand. "I said *one.*" My chest burns and everything is a little hazy.

"Just hold it. You don't end up wanting it, I'll drink it."

I lift it to my face. The smell makes my eyes burn. "How do you do that just over and over? I'm about to die from sipping that first one."

"Practice, young grasshopper. Stick with me and you'll be a pro in no time."

I ignore her prophecy and take another sip. It burns less. It almost tastes . . . good.

She grins wide. "Better, ain't it?"

It almost is. Until the lights start to feel like they beating at my chest. "I need some fresh air."

"You want me to come with you?" Tasha asks.

"No, I'll be only a second." I follow a line of kids with the same idea. The fresh air makes it easier for me to concentrate on my breathing and less on throwing up.

"You keep trying to ruin things for me." Elaina's voice drifts from the side of the house. I squint to get a better look. She's talking to someone with long red hair. *Meggie.*

I inch closer, crouching lower to the ground to stay out of the light that climbs the building.

"How many times are you going to let Lucas use you? He's dragging you down into the gutter. The statue. Really?"

They talking about Clive. Dammit, I left my phone at the dorm. The wrong time to want to "enjoy the moment." This could have been it. My way to out him for real. To get everyone to see what kind of person Lucas Cunningham is.

"It's not like he did it alone, but you've always had it in for him," Elaina says. "You're worse than Vanna."

"At least Savannah stands for something," Meggie says. "I should have stood up for her at the forum. I'm not scared, not anymore."

Elaina steps forward, her body almost pressed against Meggie's. "Don't think Lucas doesn't have anything on you. Last year you weren't all high and mighty, remember that."

I press my back harder into the brick wall, taking one last breath before I walk back into the party. I follow the music, walking almost zombielike back to the bar. My head spins with questions, questions that only Meggie or Elaina can answer.

"You all right, girl?" Tasha grabs my hand and leads me deeper into the crowd.

"I'm okay. Just needed to get out of here for a minute." I'm not sure if I should tell Tasha. If I should tell anyone. The main question is: When was Meggie going to tell me?

"Hey, freshman." Lucas drags in with three of his frat brothers. Meggie walks behind them, trying unsuccessfully to get around. My entire body stiffens like a board. I instinctively take a step back. Lucas's presence makes my scalp itch.

The melanin-enriched guy in Lucas's crew stands quietly, taking small sips from his Bloody Mary. He floats in his sunken place. I never see him by himself on campus. Even on the one day of the week that the college humors us Black folk and has soul-food day in the café.

Tasha and I both ignore Lucas and greet Meggie, who's dressed like a fox. She slides past the three bodies and gives both of us a hug. I don't wrap my arms around her. The bass of the music rattles our bodies but keeps Lucas from being in our business. He stands on the side, dancing like he has two left feet as we move toward the edge of the dance floor.

I don't drink nor do I dance. Why am I here again?

Oh . . . information from Benji. Now Meggie.

"These three made their way to you before I could," Meggie

says. "Long time no see, Savannah. Have you been hiding out because of the forum?"

"I'm not hiding out. You know how college is," I say. "I've just been swamped."

She looks over her shoulder. "Freshman year was when I had the least amount of work. You need help in any of your classes? I tutor in chemistry."

I ignore her question and point my head toward Lucas. "Why does ole boy act like that? He hasn't stopped looking over here since he walked in."

"He's trying to break you," she says, like it's an everyday thing. "People normally bow at his feet, and when they don't, he tries his best to make sure they do. It's a sick game to him."

"Well, we aren't playing," Tasha says.

"Last year, Elaina and I met in Rotary Club and were like this." Meggie crosses her fingers. "Even though I was an upper-classman and she was an underclassman, we still clicked. She wasn't into drugs or snobby as hell like she is now. Lucas did that. I've known him since freshman year, how he operates and treats women. He sniffed her out, got her away from me, hooked her on drugs, and she hasn't been the same since."

"Damn, that's messed up," Tasha says.

"Super messed up." Meggie's lip starts to tremble. "The last straw was spring break. He knew Elaina and I had already planned a nonrefundable trip, I used most of my savings for it. But he wanted her with him in Turks. I couldn't afford it and he offered to pay. I didn't accept, of course. He would have never let me live it down. I'd always be in his debt."

"Did Elaina end up going?"

She nods. "That's why we aren't as close now. I don't trust him, and sometimes I don't trust her. If she has to choose, she'll always pick him."

Lucas joins our circle and clears his throat.

Ugh.

"It's rude not to include others," he says, nudging an elbow at Meggie. She flinches as if to say *don't touch me,* but she keeps her mouth closed.

"What do you want, Luka?" Tasha asks.

He rubs the side of his mouth with his thumb. "It's Lucas."

She shrugs. "Same thing."

"Why are you so mean to me?" He lays his arm over Tasha's shoulders. "Do I have something in my teeth?"

She moves from underneath Lucas's arm, her nose scrunched up like she's gonna be sick. "I'm not mean. You just do too much too soon. Can you learn my name good before you start being extra?"

He tips his head. "Does that mean you won't dance with me?"

"You're so smart," I say. My chest is warm, that liquor loosening my tongue. "I think that's exactly what she means." Every time I look at him, my face changes, like I smell something stank.

"Ouch." Lucas shakes his hand like it's on fire.

82

"Don't you have Elaina to annoy . . . I mean, talk to?" I squint, searching the crowd. "Where she at?"

"We're not joined at the hip," he says.

"She'd be thrilled to hear you say that, I'm sure," Meggie says.

"Mm-hmm." Tasha purses her lips. "Well, I'm no home-wrecker, so see ya."

"I know what'll make you more receptive. You girls want to party?" Lucas reaches into his pocket and dangles a small ziplock bag in our face. "Pure grade. It'll get you higher than you ever been."

"I like to stay here on the ground, thank you," I say, taking another sip of my drink. I've seen enough people's lives ruined from drugs. When you watch addicts stealing from their own grandmothers to get their next hit, it fucks you up. I made a promise to myself: no matter how hard my life gets, I'll never harm myself that way.

People around laugh at his attempt, but he shoots them a look that shuts them up within seconds. "Oh, you don't like this?" He scrunches his nose. "Guarantee it's better than that cheap shit your people used to."

Wait, what? I ain't know if he means poor people or Black people. Probably both. Equally fucked up.

"We gone catch y'all later." I have to get away from him before the Memphis in me come out. Tasha opens her mouth to speak, waving a finger in the air, but I pull her away before she can go off. We move toward the middle of the dance floor and I take another sip. *Mmm, sweet like vanilla.* I rock clumsily from side to side and concentrate on the dance steps. God ain't pass out rhythm when she created me.

"Why white boys hate the word *no?*" Tasha asks as she moves her waist in slow circles to the reggae song that plays.

" 'Cause they ain't never been told it before." I hold my cup in the air and give my liver a break from the foreign intruder.

Future keeps the party jumping. The strobing orange and black lights make it hard to get a good look at everyone. White kids who can't dance but try their hardest gyrate on the metallic dance floor, singing along. I cringe at flat asses popping awkwardly.

A group of guys taller than the entire crowd—a.k.a. the basketball team, a.k.a. half the Black population on campus—makes a bunch of commotion across the room.

"Check this shit out," Tasha says, pointing. The guys form a circle around a white girl. She does a striptease routine. Her elbows rest on her thighs, and she whips her brunette hair around in a circle. It spins around fast like a tornado. They eat that shit up, slapping hands, smacking her ass.

"Look at them acting like they ain't never seen pale skin before." Tasha grimaces. "All these sisters in here."

The lack of color is noticeable now that I pay attention to it. I don't care that much, but I care enough. "Um . . . the only sisters in here are us."

"Where all the Black girls at?" Tasha shouts to Benji as he comes back wearing a fresh white tee.

"They probably went to the school fifty miles out to party." He pops a Tic Tac and refills his cup with vodka and a squeeze of lime. I'm still on my second cup.

I sip on it more to catch up to them. "What school?"

"Booker T. Washington University. It's a historically Black college . . . if you couldn't tell by the name. They cool people over there. I pop my head in at some of their parties every now and again. They be wilding sometimes, though."

Benji stands with us as we drink and people-watch. We point at the jacked-up costumes and laugh at the not-so-popping dance moves.

Benji's cool. Friendly as hell. Just that—friendly. Only that. And that's cool. Friend zone is A-OK with me. I chew my lip.

"Do you want to dance?" Benji asks.

"Don't mind me." Tasha throws up her hands. "I'll be gone. Y'all go 'head."

I roll my eyes at her ridiculousness. *Friends dance. It's nothing.* "Um . . . I'm not much of a dancer."

"Me either." He imitates a drunk man, looking like Unc at a family barbecue. "But I can two-step with the best of them." He snaps his fingers and hits a Michael Jackson spin.

The corners of my mouth curl into a smirk at his corny act.

"Well, can I at least get your number?" He returns to a normal standing position. He wants to get to know me. That's what friends do. Friends. Tasha stands behind him, making stupid faces, pretending to French-kiss her hands. I choke down a laugh and repeat my number.

"You're not going to put it in your phone?" I ask.

"Nah, I won't forget it." He winks.

"Let's go," I say. "But don't expect no special dance moves."

On the dance floor I'm safe from the trance of his kind eyes and wide smile.

An old track from Kanye West and Jay-Z plays on the loudspeaker. We dance around each other the way the cool aunts and uncles do at cookouts. I grind against him a little, not enough to channel my inner Beyoncé but enough for him to feel what I'm working with. Just because I don't want him don't mean I can't flirt a little.

Tasha winks at us from across the dance floor, then moon-walks her ass up to me.

"Better quit. That booty gone hook him, girl," Tasha whispers into my ear as I wave her off.

"Let's make a video," Benji says.

Tasha jumps in. We dance together for his social-media followers, singing along to the throwback Kanye, drinks raised in our hands.

Lucas finds Elaina. They come over hand in hand and begin to dance, mouthing the words right along with us. We move away, but Lucas pushes closer. Elaina ain't even speak. She's in her own world, hair slick with sweat, dressed like a zombie or some shit, her eyes rolling all over the place as she does some white-girl version of twerking.

Lucas's lips move, singing along.

I bump to the beat, trying to ignore all of them.

His voice grows louder, like he's talking directly to me. "Got my niggas in Paris and they going gorilla."

I stop, rigid all over.

Did he just say . . . ?

It's like on television when the music stops playing and everyone stands still. Except I'm the only one still and the song keeps playing. Folks keep right on dancing.

"Chill with all that, Lucas," Benji says. "We trying to have a good time."

"What did I do?" His words slur together. Elaina grabs on to him for support as she stumbles over her feet.

Feeling the liquor, words flow from my lips with ease. "You know damn well what you just said." I stare between Lucas and Elaina. She keeps dancing, like she can care less.

"You never had a problem with me saying it before." Lucas ignores me and smirks like he got a one-up on Benji.

Benji winces. "That was when we were kids and I didn't know any better. It's called maturity."

"It's just a song," Elaina says between glides, her eyes lower than they should be. "It's not like he walks around throwing the N-word in your face."

She takes out a white baggie full of powder, dips in her

index finger, and rubs it across her gums. Not the first time tonight, I'm assuming.

"Plus, you guys said it too," Lucas adds. "Isn't that a double standard?"

I slide my fingers across my skin. "Call it our privilege— *Black* privilege."

"Elaina, check your man." Tasha stands next to me and rolls her latex sleeves up as much as they can go. "He been tripping all night."

"Why can't I say *nigga* if it's in a song?" Lucas asks, and my blood pressure shoots through the roof.

He did *not* just form his mouth to say it again.

The thing about the word *nigga:* We reclaim it. Make it something between skin folk. Then they dirty it up again. Roll it around in their mouth and spit it out with venom. Even when they don't try to, that is what it feels like. Poison flowing in my veins.

It's *ours.*

They have everything else. But *that—that* they can't have.

"You can't say the shit, period," Tasha says.

"It's a free country, last time I checked," Lucas says, and continues to mouth along to the words but doesn't speak them out loud.

"You can freely get your ass kicked too," Benji says.

Lucas gets in his face. "It was a joke, man. Just like the statue. When did you get so damn sensitive?"

Waaait a minute. The hell he say?

"So that was your little fucked-up work of art?" Tasha asks.

"Yes," he says with venom. "Is that what you want to hear? Does it make you feel better?"

We are the only ones who hear his confession over the sounds of Cardi B. No recording. No witnesses. Us against him. He a racist, getting away with foul shit.

I hate him.

I stare and his red face grows redder, like he can feel my hate.

"What? Got something to say, Affirmative Action?"

Him and Elaina with that shit. She snorts.

If it's a war he wants, I can suit up. My future career, upsetting Mama, none of that will stop me. He's so entitled he don't even know what fear is. I promise myself that he'll fear me.

"I do, actually." I approach him. "I got plenty to say, but not here. You want people to know your name? When I'm done, everyone is going to know your face and what you did."

"Go ahead. No one is going to believe some freshman. No one is going to even listen to what you have to say."

"You gone hear what I gotta say real soon. See who talking then."

NINE

I double-check the last text Meggie sent me and slip my phone in my pocket, darting across the street, off Wooddale's campus and toward the rows of cookie-cutter homes clustered around the school. If I want to expose Lucas, it will be good to hear the truth from the horse's mouth. I have to walk nine blocks and some change to get to Meggie's neighborhood and get her to tell the story. The *whole* story.

Giant houses, mostly where professors live, intermix with frat houses. Cars parked up and down the street. You couldn't find a free space if you wanted to. As blocks and blocks pass, the houses get smaller, narrower, and less statuesque.

Before I know it, I don't recognize anything around me. No street signs, no college folks, no cars buzzing past. I'm transported back to the hood in the matter of a thirty-minute stroll. To streets riddled with empty liquor bottles, cigarette butts, and other nasty trash. Junkies pace the sidewalks; these ones have decayed teeth instead of marked-up arms. Stray dogs fight over abandoned chicken bones as toddlers clothed only in soiled diapers run about. Mamas hang out on their porches with a baby in one hand and a lit cigarette in the other. Daddies stand by, drinking their bloating beers, preparing for the next day of their low-income jobs.

White ghettos are a little different, but in a way they are the same.

Sunny Waters Trailer Park is scribbled on a flimsy cardboard sign at the entrance of the down-and-out property. Sunny Waters the uncolored version of my old hood. Each home stands five feet away from the others. Instead of small units so compact that you can't breathe without the people next door hearing you, Sunny Waters has trailer homes the size of eighteen-wheel tractor containers.

"Savannah, I'm over here," Meggie shouts.

The shutters don't hang off her windows like at the one next door. Her trailer looks brand-new. I'd call anyone a lie if they'd told me Meggie was poor. That she lives in a trailer-park community that hasn't been functional in years. That her neighbors are folks named Ray and Billy Bob. Not folks named William III and Ellen Caruthers. She ain't look like a poor person. I suppose I don't either.

"You live so far out," I say.

Mama taught me never to turn my nose up at people's situation, but I'm almost in shock at this one.

Meggie dressed down in sweats, and now I feel overdressed in my button-down shirt. If I knew Sunny Waters was a trailer park and not a subdivision, I would have worn my Memphis clothes.

"They cut the white trash off from everything else. People think poverty doesn't exist in this town," Meggie says.

Black folk must have been cut off from the white trash as well. There are a few who live in mansions around the school, but I ain't seen nobody who wears hoop earrings instead of dainty pearls.

"Come on in. My mom isn't home, and my dad is asleep, so try not to make too much noise, please." She leads me inside.

I check my surroundings once more and follow her inside.

"Sorry about the mess. . . . We don't get much company." The screen door slams closed behind us, startling me. So much, I almost miss the small dog that runs up and begins humping my leg.

"Cupcake." She claps and the poodle scurries away. A stuffed animal in the corner becomes its next victim. "Sorry about her." Meggie gestures at a tattered brown couch with holes in the cushions. "Have a seat. You want some Pedialyte? My hangover was killing me earlier."

"Nah, I'm good." My one and a half drinks didn't affect me much. Tasha still knocked out, though. Or at least I think she is. She ain't been answering my texts.

Meggie lowers herself into the reclining chair. She puts her tiny feet up on the coffee table. "What was so urgent? Something you're having trouble with?"

I stroke Cupcake's curly fur. "It's about Clive's statue." I hesitate, and she tilts her head at me. "Sorry . . . not gonna lie. You not being rich is blowing my mind."

Meggie rocks in the recliner. "People don't know I'm poor unless I let them know. Usually I meet the people I tutor at the library."

"How come? Why you let me into your business?"

"I knew you wouldn't judge my living conditions. You're not stuck up. You're real," Meggie says.

I rub the back of my neck. "How you figure that?"

She moves to the kitchen and pours herself a glass of milk. "We are two peas in the same pod. Elaina told me about the neighborhood you're from."

She stops to sip her milk.

Ugh, Elaina. I join Meggie in the kitchen. The linoleum counter topped with old newspapers and Pizza Hut coupons. "What she tell you?"

"That you don't come from some rich family. She said your good grades got you in here, which is hard for 'people like you.'" She makes air quotes with her fingers. "That's a direct quote, by the way. But I read between the lines. You can't take half of what Elaina says literally. I inferred you pulled yourself up by your bootstraps."

"I ain't even got boots," I say, eyeing a coupon flyer on her counter. Bet the pizza drivers still deliver here.

"Most people don't."

"You got every pair."

"Why do you think that?" For a second, she looks shocked.

Offended, even. The lines in her face disappear, and she takes another sip of her milk. "Look around, Savannah. We aren't lounging in the Taj Mahal."

White privilege don't begin and end in suburbia. Store clerks follow me around even though they only make ten dollars an hour. White privilege don't have a set economic background. I ignore her question. That ain't her world, and it ain't my job to make her see. *I shouldn't even be here right now.* "Vanna" will definitely regret this in twenty years, when I'm not invited to reunions or alumni meetings. When my attendance here ain't nothing but a faint memory of how I got bullied out or, worse, kicked out. Meggie's laptop dings on the kitchen counter, and she pulls it open. "You ready to tell me why you're here?"

My heart pumps faster than it should. "I heard you talking to Elaina at the party. I know Lucas is the one that defaced Clive's statue, and now I want to know what else you know."

"I knew you'd find out eventually. Didn't think it'd be this way, but secrets never stay that way for long." Meggie hugs her knees to her chest. "Elaina told me Lucas did it. But not until three days after it happened. I was so disgusted I didn't even want to run it in the paper anymore."

I sit down on a stool near the counter and pick at the lifting linoleum. "Did Elaina know? She didn't try to stop him?"

"I don't think she did. Even so, when Lucas puts his mind to something, there's nothing stopping him."

"Then why'd you put us in the mix? You could have just

gone to the dean and there wouldn't have been a need for a forum."

"I had . . . have faith that the Black Student Union could get people talking." She rakes her fingers through her hair with a deep sigh. "That somehow Lucas would finally have to face accountability for his actions."

Black people being forced to the front line again. Being used to do other folks' dirty work. History has shown that never ends well for us.

"That's real grimy, Meggie," I say.

She snaps her laptop closed. "Lucas knows things about me. From sophomore year. If I exposed him, he would have exposed me."

"What does he have on you?" I ask.

She picks up her pace, eyes darting around the room. "I can't tell you."

I start to leave. I have no time to be playing with Meggie. "Well, maybe the dean of students wants to hear about it."

"No, wait!" She grabs my wrist and sighs. "I used to take Lucas's online exams for him."

I loosen her grip. "Go on."

"I know this isn't shocking, but Lucas isn't that smart," she says. "He paid me a lot for those exams, and as you can tell, I need the money. Now he's blackmailing me. Keeping me in my place. Making sure I never speak bad about him. It's exhausting."

"Does Benji know about this?"

"Kinda," she says. "He knows that I took exams for Lucas, but he doesn't know anything about the Clive statue. At least I don't think he does."

"Lucas snitched on himself at the Halloween party. Told me, Benji, and Tasha that he did it like it was the most casual thing in the world."

Meggie settles on a spot on the floor, tapping her pencil. Cupcake crawls into her lap. I sit in the reclining chair and fold my legs up.

"I wasn't brave enough to come forward. I know I should have, especially after the statue. If I rat on Lucas, then I'm a casualty too. I don't want to be in a trailer park for the rest of my life."

"What else do you know about Lucas?" I ask.

"I mean, pretty much all of it. Elaina is an open book when she's zooted. Lucas has loose lips himself." She leans in closer, as if we aren't the only two people here. "I know for a fact that Lucas didn't get into Wooddale on his own merit."

My eyebrow rises. "He cheated?"

She nods. "I'm not in on the specifics, but if you're around Lucas enough, he'll brag about it. How Daddy's checkbook saved him from going to a plan-B school."

Lucas's mother should have taken a Plan B. Folks like me have to do everything right, give up everything to go to schools like this. While people like Lucas can cut a check and walk right in. It ain't fair.

"I had to miss sleep to get into this school. My mama worked sixteen-hour days to pay for my tutors, application fees, and school fees. If Lucas got into this school based off a check, don't you think that's something people should know?"

"Don't get me wrong, I get it. But, Savannah, this could have colossal backlash."

"Anyone who takes places from people who actually earn them deserve any backlash they get," I say.

"Not them, *you*," she says. "The statue is one thing, but unraveling an admissions scheme . . . that takes guts. If Lucas did get into Wooddale unfairly, his family . . . the Cunninghams wouldn't want *anyone* to know that." Her eyes get real big, and a chill sweeps up my arm. "His uncle is a senator, or was one or something. His last name is on the damn recreational center. These are powerful people you're trying to go up against."

"I ain't tryin' to go up against no one. I'm just telling the truth."

B'onca's home right now balancing cooking for her family, washing their clothes, studying for school, and practicing for her SAT. No one from my neighborhood in Memphis can write a check for Wooddale or buy a building in their name. The only thing going for B'onca is how smart she is. I grit my teeth. Pisses me off that she can earn something fair and square and it go to someone else just because they wallet fatter. "If I don't tell the truth, who will?"

"A few years ago, a professor tried to accuse the administration of racial profiling. She was fired. Moved out of town right after that."

"I know I'm putting a lot on the line if I expose Lucas. I understand if you don't want anything to do with it."

"Listen, this pisses me off as well. I had to fight to get into Wooddale myself, and it's a daily fight."

"Are you on a scholarship too?" I ask.

She nods. "Not a full one, though. Wooddale only covers my tuition. Everything else is out of pocket. That's why I live at home. It's much cheaper."

I bet no one thinks she's an affirmative-action case. I bet no one asks her how she got into Wooddale. Asks her questions about where she from. Assumes she from these busted trailer parks.

"I'll do my absolute best to back you up on this, Savannah. If exposure is the route you want to take, maybe I can even find someone who can interview you. Someone with pull. The *Gazette* won't cut it," she says. "I'll ask Professor Santos. She has her own radio show, you know."

"I want to talk about it anonymously. Keep the heat off me. But, regardless, I need proof. People who will step up if need be."

I can't have a repeat of the forum. That'd ruin every piece of credibility I have.

She taps her lip. "Hmm, proof . . . I do have a connection

to a guy in Admission Records. . . . He owes me a favor. Let me see what else I can find out."

Her lips spread into a devious smile. "In the meantime"—she pulls out her phone—"you ever hear of WooddaleConfessions?"

"I looked at it over the summer. It seems dead now."

"It is," she says. "But you can revive it. It can keep you anonymous while also spreading the word about Lucas. The perfect short-term solution until I can find more evidence."

I never thought about using social media as a tool, but it makes sense. People get exposed for ignorant shit. Might as well use it for something worthy.

"Keep your posts simple," she says. "Straight to the point, yet provocative."

"Say less." I offer her dap, but she just stares at it, so I put it away. "And, Meggie, let's keep this between us."

"Oh, for sure," she says. "Lucas won't know what hit him."

TEN

Lucas Cunningham is a racist.
#WooddaleConfessions

I press send and yeet my phone to the other side of Tasha's room. It buzzes beside her dresser.

"Why the fuck did I do that?" I pace the floor. This the riskiest thing I've ever sent out. My stomach tightens and I damn near want to vomit, but I know nothing will come up. I haven't been able to eat. Worry fills me every day that there will be consequences, even behind a fake profile picture.

"It's done now." Tasha cradles my phone, checking for cracks. "The comments are coming in."

I cup my face in my hands. "I mean, of all the things I have to worry about. Math, for one. I'm struggling to get a C, and instead of studying I'm doing this. All because I want people to care."

There's almost a hole in Tasha's fur rug by now.

"Stop all that fidgeting. Now you're making me nervous." Tasha grabs a bucket of hair supplies and tosses a pillow on the floor. "Sit. Maybe getting your hair done will calm you down."

I sigh and sit down on the pillow, giving her full access to my tightly coiled hair. "You better not be heavy-handed."

She grabs the rattail comb and parts my hair into four sections before she begins to twist it. We sit in silence for three *Moesha* episodes. My phone beeps every other second. Notifications, I'm sure, of people talking to the fake profile picture.

I'm scared of what they have to say.

"Can you check for me?" I ask.

Tasha puts my twisted hair up into two ponytails before wiping her hands and checking her phone. "These comments."

She reads some of them off.

Not surprising.

Anyone surprised?

His hair screams it.

He comes from a long line of them.

"You think he's going to know this me?" I mean, yeah, I used a fake profile, but knowing Lucas, he probably has someone tracking the IP address as we speak. That's how controlling he is.

"How could he? Lucas has more enemies than I have shoes," Tasha says. "If you worried, though, you can lay low here with me for a while. I mean, it's only one floor up from your room, but people know not to come to my door with mess."

I spin around so fast I almost break my neck. "You serious?"

"It'd be nice to have some company around here," Tasha replies. She gathers the clothes and hair products that decorate her extra bed. "It's all yours. Shout-out to my roommate for never showing up."

A weight of relief falls off my chest. Elaina's indifference has made it difficult for me to sleep next to her at night. She didn't apologize for her role in Partygate. She doesn't care. It's only a word to her. Matter fact, all I've heard from her are excuses that Lucas is such a great guy.

A great guy wouldn't do what he did. A great guy wouldn't feed her cocaine like it's fifty-cent Jolly Ranchers. Lucas keeps her supplied and in the palm of his hand. I left one drug-filled community to go to the next. Cocaine ain't that different from crack. Only difference is the price tag and the folk that use it.

"Listen to this one," Tasha says. " 'This about what happened at Benji Harrington's party? This isn't the first time Lucas has been racist on campus,' " Tasha recites. " 'Last year an offensive Wi-Fi name was linked to his frat house, but everyone pretended they didn't see it.' "

"You think it's true?"

"I heard about that last year," Tasha says. "It disappeared as soon as it was found. Anything related to Lucas is always swept under the rug."

We pass Cheetos back and forth as we watch the likes and comments climb.

"All these allegations. It seems everyone has a Lucas story, but no one wants to talk about it," I say.

One man can't have that much power. Lucas seems untouchable, like he wrapped in barbed wire.

"If your posts keep going mini viral, he won't be for long," Tasha says. "You want me to go with you to get your stuff?"

I slip on my slides and start for the door. "Nah, I think I got it. Besides, I don't want you to be around Elaina's foolishness unnecessarily."

"All right, call me if you need me," she says. "Elaina can't fight, so if she gets too bigheaded, you can take her out yourself."

The floor between Tasha's room and Elaina's is like a safety net. Soon as I get to Elaina's door, I feel the harness snap.

I take a deep breath and push the door open. Elaina doesn't believe in locks. Another trait of privilege. I don't say hello before I start throwing clothes into my empty backpack. I tell Elaina, "I'm moving in with Tasha."

"What? You don't have to move, Vanna." Elaina sits crisscross on her bed, watching me pack. A line of coke sits on the textbook in front of her.

"Sa-vann-ah," I correct her. Vanna will never be seen again. I know people shorten names to show familiarity. That's what I wanted to be in the beginning. Familiar. So I never had to explain the other side. But if being at Wooddale has shown me anything, it's that Mama right.

I *do* deserve to be here, and I'm going to be here—as me.

All me.

Hair and voice to the sky.

"And, yes. I do have to move. I don't want to see Lucas every time he comes to see you."

"There's a lot you don't know about Lucas." Elaina takes a hit, her voice nasal like she holding her breath. "I mean, it isn't all black-and-white, you know?"

"No, I don't know, and to be honest I don't give a damn. He called me and my friends a racial slur and then wouldn't apologize for it. *And* he admitted to defacing that statue. Not to mention how he has you all doped—" I stop myself; she so *far* up his ass it doesn't matter what I say. "All that explains a whole lot about his character."

"He said he didn't mean it like that, and I believe him," she says. "I know my boyfriend better than anyone."

Elaina is every too-in-love-to-see-what's-right-in-front-of-her-face woman—or, in her case, too high. The clock tower rings and Elaina scurries to put away her stash. Today is random-inspection day, but it ain't too random because everyone knows.

"He's an asshole." *And you're a cokehead.* But one hard

104

truth is probably as much as she can handle in a day, so I keep my mouth shut.

"Lucas is the nicest, most gentle guy I've ever dated."

The deadpan look doesn't leave my face. "That's sad."

"You're being unreasonable, Savannah."

Oh, now I'm Savannah. "No, I'm being realistic. I'm not stopping until Lucas gets the punishment he deserves for *everything* he's done. I don't care if I have to shout what he did from the rooftops of the White House. People are going to know his name, and not in a good way."

Lucas thinks he is invincible. You can see it in the way he talks and the way he treats people. Everyone is disposable to him. It's his way or no way. It pays to be on his team, literally. Everyone in his circle gets benefits for selling their souls to the devil.

Elaina stands and faces me. "Savannah, if you take this further than need be, you'll possibly be ruining way more lives than just Lucas's."

Privileged people always think they the victim when they world shakes up a little bit. Shit, Elaina couldn't be me and accomplish what I have on her best day. She the victim . . . Bullshit.

"Oh, you mean yours? You won't get the trips, the last name, or his fortunes?"

She doesn't say anything. "It was *just* a statue and a word. Don't go causing problems. In the end, you might be the one squashed in the rubble."

I raise an eyebrow. Elaina looks everywhere but in my eyes.

"That a threat?"

"Just drop it," she says.

The knock from the RA startles Elaina. She almost tips over the Tide container as she slides her drugs inside.

"Girl, get your life. I'm outta here." I toss her one last look, pity more than anything else, and open the door for the RA on the way out.

ELEVEN

Have y'all heard that Lucas bought his way into school? "Allegedly"? #WooddaleConfessions

Last year, he cheated the whole time in my advanced chemistry class, no lie.

Yooooo! I knew it. No way that dude can even do long division.

Remember that time he misspelled his own fraternity name?

A racist and an idiot. Pick a struggle.

Chill. Lucas passes all his classes. Besides, I doubt he'd have to buy his way in. He's a legacy.

Okay? You guys are taking an
anonymous account way too seriously.

Dude you're an anonymous account
and you're right here with us.

I'm just saying. Cut him some slack.

No.

TWELVE

The *Gazette* offices are in the oldest building on campus and it shows. Spiderwebs hang in each corner, and I'm sure there are plenty of ghosts haunting this place.

I tap two times on the covered window. Benji peeks from behind the curtain before opening the door. "I'm almost ready for lunch. Thanks again for coming down here. The BSU hasn't gotten their own office yet."

He ushers me inside. There are three desks pushed against the wall and one larger desk in front scattered with papers. Must be Meggie's. "You don't get scared working down here alone?"

He returns to his desk. "Not really. The real boogeymen are outside." He types away at the document on the screen. "Just have to finish this piece."

I pull up a chair next to him. "What are you writing about?"

"Professor Daphne stuck me with the BSU announcement column this week," he says. "School fairs, blood drives, and other things no one cares about."

"About the blood drive—do I have to actually watch them take the blood out?"

I volunteered to help Benji with that. It's the least I can do after slacking on club duties all semester.

"Nah, you can just pass out the cookies after," he laughs. "Social work isn't always glamorous, as you can tell."

"Social work always been in your cards?"

"Not at all," he says. "I was groomed to take over the family business, but I went off course, and, well, here we are. I'm officially the black sheep of the family unless I end up winning a Nobel Peace Prize or something."

"They just want you to be set in the future, that's all," I say. "You can't really blame them for that."

"It's not always about the money."

I wave him off. "Only people with money say that. If you want to continue to throw parties like the Halloween one, you should listen to them."

"I can downgrade if that means being happy. My parents are rich in money but not life. They don't smile much and are always putting off going on vacation, or anything else enjoyable, for tomorrow. So what's the point?"

"I guess I can't relate. I grew up poor, and money could have solved at least eighty percent of my problems."

He rubs the back of his neck. "I guess I do sound like a typical rich boy. Sorry."

"Don't apologize for who you are," I say.

"How are things going for you?" he asks. "Freshman year

was a killer for me in terms of classwork. I partied way too much."

I fiddle with loose notebook paper. "Classes are okay. I'm waiting on my midterm grades, but I know I flunked them. I didn't expect my freshman year to start off like this. I'm supposed to be making fun memories. Not fighting racism before it's even winter break."

Sometimes I wish I had the confidence of Lucas. He doesn't deserve to be here, but he walks and talks as if he's the baddest man on the planet. I don't have that even though I proved ten times over that I'm meant to be here.

"I feel you. Wooddale is not the typical college experience. White kids get to join sororities and frats. We have to fight tooth and nail to have a damn Black Student Union."

"Sometimes I want to up and leave," I say. "You know, go someplace where I'm not an other."

"It's better to fight within the system than to leave," he says. "If you leave, then you're giving them what they want."

I rest my head on the desk. "That's fine with me. I have nothing to prove to them."

"You need a pick-me-up. Turn that frown upside down. Let me show you something cool." He hops up from the computer and gestures for me to come.

I follow Benji down a dark corridor and then down an even darker staircase. A flickering light above us flashes one last time before it dies. Probably a sign from God to not go down to creepy basements with boys you barely know. I grip the railing, trying to ignore that all signs point to this being a scary movie. Benji stops at the bottom of the staircase, and his voice echoes off the walls. "They keep the archives down here." He flips a switch on the wall and a buzzing blue light fills the basement hallway.

Next to the entrance sits a row of beige filing cabinets with rusted drawer pulls. At the end of the row is a red cabinet. The only red cabinet.

"Uh, what is all this? And why is that one red?"

"It's the 'just in case' archive cabinet." He senses my confusion. "Anytime someone has a story they're researching or digs up any evidence that may need revisiting, it's kept here. Evidence, conversation logs, reporters' notepads from the biggest stories the *Wooddale Gazette* has ever covered . . ." He pats the top of the cabinet, loosing a cloud of dust. "It all goes here. Just in case. When people graduate, they leave stuff here too. Meggie and them haven't finished scanning everything to the system."

"Ah, okay." I pull, and the top drawer creaks open. "How old are these stories?"

"I found an article in here once from the fifties," he says. "I have much respect for people who used to report with a typewriter."

"They the true MVPs," I reply.

We pull out articles from time periods that seem like so long ago, but the topics are still the same.

WOODDALE STUDENTS
DEMAND CAMPUS INTEGRATION

He holds up a picture of a woman in a dashiki with a big ole 'fro. "Guess that integration protest worked."

I squint at the date. "Mm-hmm, only took them until 1971."

All these years and still nothing has changed. Wooddale integrated in name only. Black students are merely tolerated. Used to meet quotas. I thought things would . . . could be different.

"Why hasn't anyone done anything?"

"Done what?"

"Brought *real* change to the campus," I say.

"*Change* is a loaded word," he replies. "To some folks change meant letting Black people on campus in the first place."

Damn. The sad thing is he's right. We're here and we should be happy, no matter what happens to us.

Benji moves closer and turns his head slightly. "Are you going to the scholarship dinner tomorrow?"

"I don't really have a choice," I say. "They need me to be the face of diversity."

He rubs his hand on his pant leg. "I'm going to be there since my parents are donors. Maybe we can go together? I mean, not as a date or anything. I can pick you up from your dorm and we can ride over together."

"That sounds like a date to me," I say.

"N-no," he stammers. "I mean, if you want it to be. I don't want to pressure you or anything."

Benji is all wrong for me. He listens to NPR and keeps up with the stock market "for fun." He never had to struggle. Mistake fireworks for gunshots. Never had two separate wardrobes.

"We can go as friends." I can almost hear the wind being knocked out of him. There's a part of me that wants to say *sike* and take a risk, but being at this college already is my biggest risk right now. I can't take on any more.

Besides, Kool-Aid and caviar ain't never going to mix.

Benji retreats, flicking through more pages. "It's because of Lucas, isn't it?"

I run my fingers over the dusty files, chewing my lip. Lucas's snide remarks swirl in my head, and Clive's face comes to mind. Not his statue face, but his real face. I looked him up after the incident, learned about his untimely death, the controversy around him being hired president here. The policies he enacted, the ones he tried but failed to get passed, and the ones that he was able to. He fought within the system and ended up with a bunch of college students disrespecting his memory.

"I know you're not like Lucas." I place my hand on his. "I'm just not ready to date right now. You understand, don't you?"

He nods. "I get it. When you're ready, I'll be here."

Benji squeezes my hand and I can't help but squeeze back.

We continue to sift through paper. Laugh at the fashion of days gone by and how some things never really change. I start to loosen up.

Feel better, even, until . . .

I pull open a folder on my lap and unstick the pages. A small folder sits between them, the initials LCJ scrawled on it.

I scan the first sheet of paper, covered in scribbly erratic handwriting all over the page. Henry Rutherford III. He was a freshman last year when he joined the Gammas. According to this article he paid someone to write every term paper he had. The professor who caught him unexpectedly resigned. *Weird.*

My heart pumps faster as I go through the papers, skimming words and connecting dots. My stomach wriggles and I pull my sweater tighter over my shoulders.

I turn the page.

More articles.

Next Gamma Kappa Psi member in the pile is Simon Ford. He was arrested last year for a DUI, but it was swept under the rug as soon as he made bail. Pages stick together like they haven't been touched in forever. The words wanting to be freed and read by the masses. This is damning. Sex parties, drugs, hazing, and vandalism. All committed by the Gammas. All starting two years ago, when Lucas Cunningham Jr. became president.

My tongue sticks to the roof of my mouth and the paper shakes in my trembling hand.

The articles don't end there, but I hesitate to turn the page. To know more.

I turn it, and a handwritten note falls in my lap. I unfold it, bringing it closer to my face.

To whom it may concern,

As a freshman I entered Wooddale under the impression that all were welcome here. However, since moving into Baron Hall, I've never felt more unwelcome. At the hands of Lucas Cunningham, I've suffered more verbal abuse and microaggressions than ever before. The most recent incident of anti—Black language being shouted to me as I crossed campus is what has caused me to write this letter and call for the expulsion of Lucas Cunningham and the suspension of his fraternity until this matter is settled.

Signed,
Natasha Carmichael

THIRTEEN

The café line out the door today. I wait in line as folks swipe in and out. Other students stand by, whispering to one another. Probably about me, since each time I look up they look away. I don't know any of them, but they know me. Or whatever Lucas or Elaina has told them about me. I take my phone out, pretending I don't hear the snickers, and text Tasha.

> **Me:** Want to get lunch?

My phone chimes.

> **Tasha:** Where?

> **Me:** I'll send you the address.
> It's 20 minutes away.

Chime.

"You going incognito now?" I ask as Tasha sits down with her cup of yogurt. She has on a gray hoodie that swallows her and thick, dark sunglasses. Her hair is in a messy bun. I've grown so used to seeing Tasha dressed up that she looks weird dressed down.

"Even I have my off days. This is a weird place to pick for lunch, but I don't hate it." She takes off her sunglasses, setting them on the small flower-decorated table. I found this place while walking back to the dorms. It's a yogurt spot for kids but I don't care. They got the best toppings, and we don't have to worry about running into anyone from campus. It's a spot to chill and be free. I notice that Tasha's eyes are starting to look sunken because she hasn't slept for days. All her free time and sleep time is spent studying for the LSAT, doing regular classwork, or prepping for internship interviews. I don't want to bring it up since I'm about to lay another burden on her.

"Tasha, I have to ask you something."

"Yes, marshmallows and chocolate chips will give you a bunch of cavities."

"I'm serious, Tash."

"Sorry, go ahead."

I unfold the letter in my hand and smooth it out on the table. "You didn't tell me about last year with Lucas. Why?"

Tasha drops her spoon; chocolate cream splatters out against the table. "How'd you get that?"

"I found it along with some other stuff in the newsroom," I say. "All this time and you didn't say a word about Lucas harassing you last year. *He* hasn't even said anything."

"He doesn't know I wrote the letter," she says. "Well, I don't think he does anyway. I took that to the dean, and he didn't do jack shit about it. I figured I'd dodged a bullet, since I saw how much Lucas truly controls this campus. I changed dorms, since he damn near lived next to me, and tried to forget all about him."

"He still never brought up last year."

"You know people like that always forget the bullshit they do. While you bear the scars forever."

"Damn, you at least could have told me," I say. "It could have made a world of difference."

"It would have made things messy," she says. "Lucas never found out, and I'm glad he didn't. I got a fancy recommendation letter from the senator's office—that wouldn't have been possible if Lucas made my life a living hell."

My face lights up. "That's the biggest hurdle to getting an internship."

She brushes her shoulder off. "You know how I do."

"I'm glad one of us has good news. It's like Lucas is an

unwinnable battle." I roll the strawberry yogurt in my mouth. "Unless . . ."

"Unless what?"

"Tasha, I know you don't want to do this, and I wouldn't even ask if it wasn't important, but I need your help. If we tell your story publicly, it'd be easier to take Lucas down, *permanently*."

Tasha shakes her head. "No."

"But, Tasha—"

She stops my plea. "I'm *real* close to reaching my goals, Savannah. I can't let nobody take that away from me."

"Tasha, if you speak up, we can take him down. We can get Lucas suspended."

"Getting him suspended won't stop him. There will always be another Lucas ready to take his place."

"I know that, but don't you want justice?" I look at her with pleading eyes.

"I'm not like you, Savannah," she says.

"What's that supposed to mean?"

"All this activism stuff." She pushes the letter toward me. "That's more your lane than mine, and I respect it, but I can't be a part of it, not in the way you want me to be."

"Tasha—"

"I'm sorry, girl, I can't, and I hope you can understand why." Tasha flips her sunglasses on. Leaves her yogurt to melt on the table.

I understand Tasha but at the same time I don't. Her name

would be out there. A sacrifice that she isn't willing to make. I didn't want to be an activist, not at first, only Savannah. A college student who goes to parties and ignores homework assignments until the last minute.

If I have to be an activist to make this right, then I will. The need to fix things here is strong. Someone has to do it, or it's going to keep being the same song and dance. I can't be looking over my shoulder for the next three years, wondering what else is going to happen.

I can't tell Tasha's story for her. Only she can do that.

I can only tell mine.

Even if it doesn't come with a happy ending.

FOURTEEN

They must have gotten a new chef for Soul Food Friday. The chicken wasn't dry today and the dressing was dressing and not stuffing. #WooddaleConfessions

Okay!! Wooddale stepping up their game.

Ban green stuff in the mac and cheese!

Seasoned to perfection too. Wooddale said they might not give us a safe environment but here go some seasoned salt.

It's all a distraction!!

. . . . . . What is chicken distracting us from?

That Lucas thing. You see how no one talking about it anymore?

Damn. Black folks can't do anything for themselves. We can't even enjoy dinner in peace.

I'm just saying. #STAYWOKE

FIFTEEN

"Are you nervous?" Benji places his hand on my shoulder, giving a reassuring squeeze. Tonight is all about me, allegedly. In reality it's about impressing a bunch of folks who wouldn't look my way any other time. Even among all the scholarship kids, I'm one of the only *regular* Black faces. I mean the ones who ain't grow up with a silver spoon in their mouth.

"No way," I say, and my heart skips a beat at the lie. Everyone here write checks that can cover four years of my tuition, plus some. Benji used to this. Galas, balls, and charities are regular occurrences in his life.

"Lying ass . . . Don't worry, most of them don't bite." He opens the door and soft jazz plays. Black-tie servers hold silver platters with flutes and sample-sized foods. Hairdos fried, dyed, and laid to the side. Tuxes crisp and dapper. People float about holding drinks in their hands. They air-kiss only for a few seconds and then go on to greet the next person. Shiny pieces of fabric get stuck in places they don't belong. I pull at my bunched-up sequined dress and check my breath. Fresh, thanks to my emergency stash of Tic Tacs. I lick my tongue over my teeth and tuck in stray braids. Check my phone one last time before putting it away.

"You've been pressing the home button on your phone for the last ten minutes," Benji says, waving toward some people our age. "You become a celebrity overnight?"

"Nah, I wouldn't be talking to commoners if I did," I say, stifling a laugh.

He nudges me with his shoulder. "Ha-ha, real funny. For real, what's got your attention?"

"Do you follow the WooddaleConfessions hashtag?"

"Nah, it isn't my style," he says. "I'm surprised you follow it."

"It's good for some things."

I still haven't talked to Benji about how me and Meggie plan to out Lucas. Haven't found a time that feels quite right. It's been awkward, full of little silences where I feel like he knows I ain't telling him something.

But ain't no time like the present.

"Come here." I pull his arm and guide us to a quiet area. "I need to tell you something. You have to promise not to say anything."

"You in trouble or something?" he asks.

"Not in trouble per se," I say. "It's a long story."

I explain everything about #WooddaleConfessions, Clive, Meggie, Lucas, and my next steps if I ever get someone to back me up.

"That's been you the whole time?" Shock written all over

his face. "Normally that hashtag is full of silly shit like who's cheating on who, and then things changed."

"I thought you didn't follow it," I mock.

"That isn't the point. Savannah, dead this. Now."

Okay, *that* isn't the response I expected. I wait for his tone to change. For his eyes not to feel like a thousand stingrays.

"Dead it? I thought you'd want Lucas to get what he deserves. He's a racist, a cheat, and he doesn't deserve to be here."

"I do. You know I do, but this isn't the way, trust me. If you keep exposing Lucas, he will go after you."

Why justice and trouble for people like me go hand in hand so much?

"What do you want me to do, then? Walk away? Pretend this ain't happening?"

His gaze meets mine. "I've been in this school, this town, longer than you have. I know how this is going to end. Dead it!"

This isn't the Benji I know. He never raises his voice at me, and he definitely wouldn't stop me from raising mine. "Benji, I'm not giving this up," I say. "I don't even know why you'd expect me to. I mean, we ain't exactly the same, and I know y'all used to be friends, but you a brotha, too."

He starts to speak, but a chirpy voice floats by, interrupting him. "Benjamin, darling." A woman glides across the room. "Is this Savannah?" She asks out of curiosity or disbelief, I can't tell.

"Dead it," he says one more time, low in my ear. But

somehow it sounds more like a threat than a warning. I move two steps away from him.

"Mom, this is Savannah. Savannah, this is my mother, Billie Harrington."

I extend my hand and she takes it with no hesitation.

"Nice to meet you, dear," she says, smiling.

"Likewise." I do a double take at the bougieness in my voice.

"Benjamin says you received the full Jamison scholarship," she says. "You have to be mighty smart to pull that off."

Allegedly. I'm not that smart, especially not here. Work piling up right now. I'll get around to it this weekend. This Lucas thing taking up too much of my time.

"Hello, everyone."

Speak of the devil.

"Lucas." Mrs. Harrington's voice is full of excitement. She pulls him into a hug that lasts a second too long. "It's been forever. You never come by the house anymore."

"Benjamin has forgotten all about me." Lucas flashes a smile. "I think it's because of how much time he spends with Savannah here." He bows in front of me. "Nice to see you again."

I try my hardest to get rid of the disgusted look on my face. "Hi."

"We have to change that," Mrs. Harrington says. "Isn't that right, Benjamin?"

"Let's not," Benji says low enough for only me to hear.

Lucas drapes his arm across Benji's shoulders. Like they're back in Little League. "Don't worry. We're going to come together again real soon."

"May I borrow your date for one moment?" Mrs. Harrington asks me, and before I can respond, her arm is scooped inside Benji's. "Mingle, dear—this is for you, after all," she says over her shoulder as they disappear behind wide glass-paned French doors.

"You can leave now, Lucas." I sway to the jazz music that plays overhead. "I don't need people to think we're together."

"They would never think that," he chuckles, and then starts working the room. He brings a smile to everyone's face except for mine. It's like I have a permanent scowl each time our eyes meet. He's revered here. Everyone wants to touch the hem of his garment, like he's a god. No one here knows just how much a devil he can be.

I stop the server and he describes the dishes on the tray. I ain't never heard of mushroom-and-goat-cheese bruschetta. I take one to be polite and curl my nose at the aroma, standing against the wall, nibbling at the tiny toast.

I wish Tasha could have come with us. These are her people. She's used to rubbing shoulders with high-powered folks like this, all buttoned up as Natasha Carmichael, future Capitol Hill lawyer. A few folks from local news outlets, politics, and high-society web columns cluster in groups, laughing, talking. Some Black folks too. Uppity, but Black nevertheless.

Do they still know that? Or does their vision become cloudy after they reach a certain tax bracket?

"Now, why you over here holding up the wall?" a short older Black woman asks. Light reflects from her diamond elephant brooch, shining in my face. I've seen her floating around. Taking up space with her laughter. I want to ask her how she does it. How she copes with being the minority. "You should be having fun."

"I'm waiting for my 'date.'" I make air quotes. "He left."

"That means you need to find another date in the meantime." She nudges me.

I laugh and wrap the bruschetta in a napkin. She must notice my sly move because she winks.

"I can sneak you some real food from the kitchen a little later," she says.

I sigh, thankful. "I will forever be in your debt. I'm starving."

"I don't know why they insist on feeding us bird food," she says.

"Does it ever make you feel weird?" I ask. "You know, being one of the only Black people at these things?"

She flags over the waitress. "Not particularly. After doing it so long, you don't notice it, and besides, I'm not here for them. I'm here to help you students.

"Bring us some of the real food," she whispers to the waitress. "My new friend and I are famished."

"You don't have to do that," I say. "I think I'm leaving soon."

"You going to let that sharp dress go to waste?"

I smirk. "The dress came from the thrift store and cost me fifteen dollars."

"Don't matter. You're wearing it well. I only wish I'd had those hips at your age."

I smooth down the fabric over my hips. "Those folks inside here can smell I don't belong." I sit at an empty table. "I don't belong anywhere. Not at home. Not here at this bougie school."

"Someone got the blues." She sits beside me. "Are you friends with Benjamin? I saw you walk in with him."

"Yes, but I'm not a legacy like him. I'm one of the scholarship kids."

"That don't matter none. It's not how you start out in life; it's how you end it."

This lady thinks she know about me. I look her up and down. Dainty pearls hang from her neck, and her hair is swept up into a bun. Sparkling jewels dot her earlobes and fingers. What she know about my life? Where I'm from?

"Where did *you* start and end, Ms. . . . ?" I ask.

"Flowers," she says. "Izola Flowers. I started out as a sharecropper's daughter and retired as a self-made multimillion-dollar businesswoman." Her expression doesn't hold boasting or inflated pride. She says her truth as fact and not as a bragging right.

"Multimillion-dollar." I rest my chin on my hands. "Why you sitting here talking to me, then? I can't even picture that amount of money."

She frowns. "That'd be very shallow of me."

The tightness in my chest eases a bit. "You're down-to-earth," I say.

"I'm no better than anybody else," she says. "Money is to pay bills and that's it. Money or lack of money doesn't define a person's character."

She ain't lying. Look at Lucas.

She nudges me with her shoulder. "And you, darling, have outstanding character." She winks. "I can tell. That's why I'm talking to you. Anyone looking at you funny isn't worth the time of day. Not your time *or mine.*"

That's nice. The knot in my chest is almost gone. Almost.

"You feel a little better now?" She wraps her arms around my shoulders and shakes me lightly.

I nod. The server comes by with small finger sandwiches. They look more edible than anything else I've seen here. I take two and eat them within seconds.

"Now go mingle," she says. "You might meet more antiques with good advice." She winks at me again and leaves my corner of the room to talk with a few other folks, all wearing matching elephant brooches. I catch snippets of conversations around the room. Politics and personal gossip are the two main topics. The server makes his rounds again. This time, liquor sits on the tray. I look around, pick up a glass of champagne, and hide in the corner. The bubbles tickle my throat as it goes down.

I hold up the wall, studying my shoes. Their torn leather

peeks from the hem of my gown. I shift the fabric and pull my dress over them. Another server passes and I set the empty flute on the silver tray, replacing it with a full one.

I people-watch and sip the drink in my hand, imitating the strangers that walk about. Their faces don't move when they laugh. They dance ten feet away from each other, and whenever the song ends, they can't walk away fast enough. This party tired. I could be home in my fuzzy socks, painting my nails with Tasha. Or videoing B'onca.

Now that I think about it, I haven't talked to B or Mama in a minute. I'm sure they understand, though. College gets busy. Plus, I don't feel like hiding my true feelings about Wooddale or explaining that it looks better from the outside and how rotten it is on the inside.

A couple of kids head in my direction and I move out the doorway that I'm blocking. But they don't pass. They looking for me?

I lift my gaze from the floor and move it between theirs.

"Hey. You're Savannah?" the tallest one asks. "Benji's date, right?" I'm apparently popular round here. Her hair coils pulled up so tight, I'm afraid if I make her talk too much, she'll split in half.

"Hello," I say in a proper tone, mimicking her voice. "I'm Savannah, but Benji isn't my date. I mean, not like that."

"Were you in Jack and Jill?" the boy holding her arm asks. Only Jack and Jill I know is the nursery rhyme, and I know they aren't talking about that.

"What's Jack and Jill?"

The girl checks out her boyfriend and then me, her lips on the rim of her glass as she sips her champagne. "It's a social group for African American children. Only the crème de la crème are accepted. Benjamin and my best friend, Amanda, over there . . ." She points her skinny finger across the room to a tall girl with loose, curl-patterned hair. "They graduated from the program together."

"That's cool," I say.

Amanda glares at me across the room. Is this an ambush? Amanda probably who Benji meant to be here with anyway. She knows how to pronounce *bruschetta* without having to look it up on Google. She knows the social graces meant for the wealthy. She damn sure isn't from the projects.

"I have to go to the bathroom." I excuse myself, walking away before they can respond.

"No way he dumped Amanda for her," they whisper underneath their breath before I'm even five feet away. I trip on the hem of my dress as I run out the door. The wind almost blows me away as heated rain starts to pour down. I stand on the porch and hold my phone in the air. *No signal.* No signal means no Uber to rescue me.

And I want nothing more this very minute than to be rescued from this place. This place all wrong for me. All kinds of wrong.

"Leaving so soon, Savannah?" The voice behind me makes me jump. Lucas and his dark cloud.

"Why do you care?"

He comes over and stands beside me. "Want a puff?" He holds out a lit cigarette.

"This is a nonsmoking campus."

"Such a goody-goody," he says. "I'd say you never did anything to hurt others if I didn't see your blasphemous confessions."

"I don't know what you're talking about."

I knew this moment would come, but I didn't expect it to be this soon, and now. Darkness stretches across the campus. The wet grass sparkles as the rain lets up. The perfect time to make a run for it, but if Lucas thinks I'm running from him, then he'll forever come after me.

"Cut the shit." The sizzling of the tobacco is long. "You know, you wouldn't be here if it wasn't for me."

"Really? And here I thought it was because I *worked* hard. Unlike you, who had Daddy write a check for you."

"Working hard is a myth," he says. "You didn't work any harder than anyone else. You were just lucky. It's like God did everything right."

"Like you know anything about God."

"You know, I admit I wasn't the best student in high school." He lets out a short laugh. "In fact, I was a horrible student, but now I try. I'm student-body president and I actually make good grades. My parents are proud of me now. You won't ruin that for me."

For a moment I almost understand Lucas. The desire to

make your parents proud is one that can cause you to do things you aren't proud of, but the difference is Lucas proud of everything he's done. He has no shame in how he got here, and he wants to make sure I know that.

"I can't ruin something that's already on the brink of destruction."

"Don't you want to know how I helped you get into Wooddale?"

"Not really," I say.

"Jamison Presidential Scholarship," he says. "That sound familiar to you?"

The name of the scholarship that's paying for me to get harassed.

"Say what you have to say, Lucas."

"My mother's name is Janet Cunningham."

"All right, I'm leaving." I turn, heading back into the party. "Have fun talking in riddles to yourself."

"Janet Jamison Cunningham." His voice is full of pride.

My brain dances around what Lucas is telling me. The only reason I'm here is because of him. My success relies on him as well as his family. The scholarship that I worked so hard for is supplied by people who never had to work hard a day in their lives.

"When I was *accepted* into Wooddale, my grandfather donated a generous sum of money to start a scholarship for lower-income students." Lucas chuckles. "Who would have known that our generosity wouldn't be appreciated?"

He gets closer, his tobacco breath beside my ear. "You see, Savannah, if you tell anyone about that statue, and if anyone believes you, then it's goodbye to your scholarship—hell, your entire future. With a Wooddale degree, you can be anything you want to be, and without one"—he fiddles with the end of my hair—"you're a nobody."

Benji interrupts Lucas's idea of a threat. "There you are, Savannah. I've been looking for you."

Lucas gives my shoulder a tight squeeze. "Nice talking with you, Savannah," he says before going back inside.

"You okay?" Benji asks.

I nod and manage to give him some semblance of a smile, even though my heart rages in my chest.

I'm not backing down, whether Benji likes it or not.

SIXTEEN

If your daddy bought your way in how did you flunk in the first place? He can afford a library but not a tutor? #WooddaleConfessions

Y'all stay on my boy ass. Leave him alone. At this point nothing is going to happen and no lie his parties do be fye.

Your boy been shady to half the Black community on campus but a party is all that matters?

This is college. We got plenty of time to deal with this shit in the real world.

If we don't start now then we never will. We're adults now and this is happening in our own backyard. Whoever been making these posts is doing us a favor. Now I know to avoid him and his clique.

As for me. I'm going to play my role. Shoot, Lucas got mad connections. It's better to be with him than against him.

Good luck trying to integrate into a burning house.

SEVENTEEN

"Benji wants to talk to you." Tasha doesn't even let me respond before she welcomes him halfway in.

"I won't keep you long." Benji pouts a bit and I can't say no. Tasha makes a kissy mouth at me before I close the door behind us. The hallway is empty for the most part.

"What's up?"

"I know what I said at the scholarship dinner came off as . . ."

"Combative as fuck? Mean as hell? Aggressive?"

"Yeah." He rubs the back of his neck. "All of the above. I didn't mean for it to come off like that. I just don't want you to get hurt."

"I can take care of myself," I say.

I've been taking care of myself for a while, without him around. I'll continue to take care of myself when he isn't around anymore.

"I know you can. You're strong, smart, and resourceful." Benji props his foot against the wall. "But Lucas has people,

Savannah. He can ruin your whole life and you won't even see it coming."

"That's a risk I'm willing to take," I say. "If that means I have a chance at outing Lucas and the racism on this campus, I have to take it. What's that quote hanging above your desk?"

"If you stand for nothing, you'll fall for anything," Benji says. "But, Savannah, getting all in Lucas business, you'll still fall. And you're going to fall hard."

"Sometimes I think you're standing up for him." I eye the hallway. People walk by, being nosy as hell. "Lucas used to be your friend."

"*Used to,*" Benji says. "Yes, we used to be friends, because Lucas hasn't always been bad. There are layers to people, Savannah. You should know that."

I can't believe Benji just said that shit.

"Layers?" I yell a little louder than I intended. My foot taps the carpet. I couldn't stop it if I wanted to. "Fuck his layers. I don't care that he used to play Little League or y'all used to skip rocks. The only Lucas I've seen is the racist one."

Benji sighs. "You're impossible sometimes."

"Impossible? Well, if I'm so impossible, why are you around me, then? I'm sure Lucas would love for you to come crawling back to him."

"I'm going to let you cool off," Benji says. "I'll call you later."

I fling open the door. "Don't bother," I say before slamming it in his face.

I walk into the room and bang my head against the wall. Tasha is painting her toenails fire-engine red.

"I'm going through a crisis here," I say when she doesn't look up.

"What's your malfunction?"

"Benji and I just had a fight. He wants me to quit this Lucas thing so bad, and I can't help but think it's because he wants to protect Lucas and not me."

"Now, I truly doubt that," she says.

"Well, how come Benji keeps telling me to move on, every chance he gets?" I throw an oversized shirt over my head. "Hell, maybe he's a cheater himself. Two peas in a scamming pod."

"Benji ain't even like that." Tasha puts another separator between her toes. "Besides, have you met Benji? The brother is not a cheater."

"He's something. A jerk for one."

"You know I ain't totally on board with you doing this either."

"Tash—"

"But! I support you because I know that's what you want to do," she says. "That's what I like about you. When you put your mind to something, can't nobody stop you. Benji doesn't get that, though. All he sees is a girl he likes a lot walking into a line of fire."

"You think he still *likes* me likes me?" I sit on the edge of the bed, watching as Tasha strokes her toes back and forth with precise perfection. My own feet are sad. I need a pedicure . . . or five.

"Girl, yes. His feelings didn't automatically stop when you shot him down." She points the nail brush to me. Polish drips on the towel between her legs. "Now cut him some slack."

"I don't think I can," I say. "If he ain't with me, then how do I know I can fully trust him?"

"You don't know that about anybody," she says.

I lie across my bed and press a pillow over my face. "Why is college so difficult!" I toss it aside and study the popcorned ceiling. "It's supposed to be fun and exciting, but I ain't having much fun."

"Dang, and here I thought our weekly movie nights were popping," Tasha says. "Guess not."

I snort. She's so silly. "They have been. You've been the best part of my college experience so far."

"Girl, after this whole thing over with, if it's ever over with, I'll make sure your next three years are lit. Pinky promise."

I try to think of the next three years. Think of Lucas not receiving his diploma in the spring. Everyone knowing about what happens at Wooddale.

But I can't get there yet.

EIGHTEEN

I hold my phone up high so B'onca can see the courtyard with its tall trees and white folks playing Frisbee golf. She oohs and aahs at the vibrant green grass, towering brick buildings, and how many white folks are around at one time.

"This right here is the hangout spot," I say. "Everyone comes and does homework, and chitchats."

"You been giving me a tour for ten minutes and I ain't seen nare boy."

"It's a small campus. There are barely any boys and even fewer Black ones." I sit on the wooden bench across from the café. People-watching and soaking up some autumn sun has become my favorite pastime.

"I'm open-minded, you know? I wouldn't mind a Connor or Tate." B'onca is underneath the gym bleachers, our hideout when we didn't want to run drills. A bell screeches and footsteps scurry in the backdrop, but she remains.

"Don't you need to be in math class? Mrs. Curry don't play about being late."

If it wasn't for Mrs. Curry, I probably wouldn't have

graduated last year. She stayed on me like white on rice. One time I was late, and before an excuse was even out of my mouth, she was on the phone with Mama. I wasn't late again after that.

B'onca sucks her teeth. "Fuck Mrs. Curry. She be tripping. Won't let me retake this test I was two minutes late to class for. I *told* her I had to use the bathroom. Like, *damn.*"

"B, you literally only have a few months left of school. Just deal."

Funny that I'm motivating B when I can't even motivate myself to do my own work. At this point do I even need to worry about my grades? Lucas's family holds my scholarship within their hands. It can always be "defunded." Magically taken away one day, and there's nothing I can do about it.

"I guess. She talking 'bout extra-credit work to make it up." She rolls her eyes, patting a spot on her scalp. "We'll see."

"Girl, get it together and do the damn makeup work. Then you can come up here like we planned." At least with B'onca here, a piece of my college dream can come true.

"Now you know I'm not getting into that fancy-ass school. They gone take one look at my grades from this year and laugh their ass off."

"You never know until you try." *Mama's famous line.*

B'onca pokes her head out from behind the bleachers and the screen lights up with surrounding sunlight. Her cheeks are fuller than usual; her mahogany skin glows. "Looks like the coast is clear. I better get my ass to class."

Speaking of books, I need to get to it too. I start toward my dorm. "Do your makeup work, ma'am. I mean it. Did you at least take the SAT practice exam link I sent over? It'll help us gauge how much studying you'll need."

"I was gonna take it, but Scooter asked me to make a run with him, and that took all damn night."

Lord, Scooter. My feelings about Scooter ain't change even nine hundred miles away.

"Don't be trying to guilt-trip me with that look," she says. "I'ma do it. Matter fact I'm going over to the library this weekend. The quiet one downtown."

"You better. And I'll ask Mama to give you my old practice book. It has everything you need in it. B, you're smart; you can get in here."

Or at least she should *be able to get in here.*

My head hangs between my shoulders, the whole Lucas situation coming back to me, when my dorm comes into view.

"What you still looking down for?" she asks. "I'ma study." She rolls her eyes, smiling. "So dramatic, I swear. I'ma do it for real, for real. But trust you got an uphill climb helping me up my grades."

"Leave that doubt at the front door because it ain't got no place here. Get the grades, a strong test score, and you'll be here with me in no time, having white people all in your space."

"You living the dream, sound like." She laughs.

"Hey, they might get me a job one day."

145

"Aight, aight, point made." B'onca's middle finger is the last thing I see before I lose reception inside the building.

The air is cooler, and buzzing lights welcome me. I slip past the lounge area, full of students glued to screens with earbuds in their ears. I slide my backpack off my shoulder, an ache digging where its weight used to be, and make my way to the stairwell. A fourth-floor room means stairs but a damn nice view.

I grip the handle to pull the stairwell door open, but it swings toward me first.

My stomach sours as Lucas steps out, wiping red-stained hands with a paper towel. He flinches, staring dead at me. Then shoves his hands—towel and all—in his pockets.

His eyes burn into mine and we stand there a minute.

I shift on my feet. "Um, excuse me. Trying to get by."

He blocks the doorway and whispers, "You don't listen, Savannah. Everyone already knows what I did to get in here, and they don't care."

"They don't know the racist shit you've done to me or the others," I say. "Your daddy paying to get you in is just icing on the cake."

"Who's going to believe you? No one's going to speak up. No one is going to give you a platform. All you have are some anonymous cheerleaders on the internet."

"I have Daphne."

"Daphne." His words are thick. "Daphne Santos is a hack professor and a third-rate radio journalist."

"Well, you shouldn't be worried, then."

"Lay off, Vanna." He rams his shoulder into mine as he passes. He glances back. "Oh, and tell Meggie she'll be dealt with."

I throw a middle finger at his back as he walks away.

I hustle up the steps, damn near about to bust a lung. By the time I get to the fourth floor, the smells of Hot Pockets and ramen swell in my nostrils. A crowd blocks half the hall up ahead. Whispers grow louder and camera flashes bounce off the walls. *The hell they looking at?*

"Excuse me." I push my way through, trying to get a glimpse at what's so interesting. As I get closer, I realize the door they are gawking at is mine and Tasha's, covered with giant red letters.

GO HOME, NIGGA.

The painted words smeared across my dorm-room door, still dripping, streaks of red running down like tears. *What the fuck?* I just came from my last class of the day—art appreciation, how ironic. I wonder how Picasso would critique the graffiti-style "art" that attracts the audience. They snap more pictures and talk among themselves. Expressing their disbelief, their disgust. I stand, staring, trying not to puke. This my life. My home away from home. My path to a better future.

"I can't believe someone would do this," says one girl who lives a few doors down. She never says a word to me, and every time I come into the study room on our floor, I can't help but notice how she pulls her laptop a little closer to her body.

I push past the folks blocking my door, trying to hide the stinging in my eyes.

"Excuse me," I say. "Excuse me. . . . *Move*. . . . That's my room." I finally break through them and slam the door.

Tasha's magic-marker board with her schedule scribbled on it rattles against it before tumbling to the floor. My mind races a thousand miles a minute. I don't have to ask myself who did this. I saw the evidence with my own eyes. I'm not going to let him intimidate me. He can try and push me out. I'm not going to let him win. They've already taken too much from us. Add this to Lucas's docket. He not getting away with this.

I reopen my room door and a camera flashes in my face.

"Get the fuck away from my door!" I blink several times, the dots fading, and pull out my phone. I snap a picture of the hateful phrase and check the time. Four-thirty p.m. If I hurry, I can catch the dean of students.

My backpack bounces up and down as I jet across campus. The student services building is nestled on the far east side of campus. Far enough from the hustle and bustle of regular student life. I guess they think the isolated destination will encourage fewer complaints from students. I swing the heavy glass door open and ignore the cheerful hello from my Calculus I professor. I don't have time for friendliness. I run my index finger across the engraved wooden board of room numbers.

The dusty staircase smells of mothballs. The railing wobbles as I wrap my hand around it. I take shallow breaths and climb the steep stairs. I never met the dean, not personally anyway. He was at the Talk Back forum, sat in the last row and didn't say anything.

I tap on the door and let myself into the sparsely decorated office. Dimming sunlight sweeps in from the tall arched window, illuminating a small bald spot and a head of wispy white hair. There are no drawings of colorful deformed cats made by Dean William's children or pictures of him and his significant other in Switzerland or wherever privileged people go to vacation during the winter. Only a tiny potted red ficus sits on his desk, and a framed diploma from Harvard hangs on the wall above his head.

"Hello, do you have an appointment today?" the dean asks, looking up from a thick book.

Moby-Dick. How predictable.

"No, but this an emergency." I sit down in the worn quilted-brown-leather chair, not waiting for an invitation. He's going to hear what I got to say.

"How may I help you?" He presses a cat bookmark between pages and sets his book to the side.

I pull up the slideshow of photos on my phone. "This was spray-painted on my door today," I say, waving the bright screen in his face.

The dean rubs his stubbly chin, his hands dragging along the extra skin that hangs below. "Hmph." He leans back into his desk chair and takes the phone from my hands, not saying a word. I want to shake him by the shoulders, but I sit, patient. He clears his throat, setting the phone on his desk. "This is your door, correct?"

I pinch the palm of my hand. He may be a Harvard graduate but he isn't playing with a full deck. "Yes," I snarl through gritted teeth. "Lucas Cunningham, the president of Gamma Kappa Psi, did it."

He pauses for a minute, studying my face with this weird look on his. "Do you know for certain that he committed this crime?"

"Yes . . . well, no. I mean, I saw he had red paint on his hands. And we have beef, so I know it was him."

I wish I would have gotten a picture of his hands, but him writing a slur on my door wasn't the conclusion I jumped to when I saw them.

He furrows his brow. "You have what?"

I rearrange my language. "We've exchanged words in the past, so there's animosity between us."

"With the entire fraternity?"

"Probably. They stick together like a pack of rabid dogs."

"I'm very sorry that this happened to you." He slides the phone to me and reaches for *Moby-Dick*. "I'll be sure to look into this in a timely manner."

Tasha was right. That announcement the university sent out after Clive was only empty words. Our Black lives only mattered in that moment.

I shoot up straight. "That's it?"

"I'm sorry, Miss . . ."

"Howard."

"Miss Howard, you have no proof Mr. Cunningham did this. I can't go on a witch hunt without proof, but I will check into it and get to the bottom of this accident." He flips to his bookmarked page.

"It was no accident!" I try not to yell but I can't help it. I'm mad as hell.

"Savannah, you do not have to holler," he says.

"What do you expect I do in the meantime?" I mimic his proper tone. Maybe he'll take me seriously if I sound like him—like them.

"I will send the janitorial staff over to clean up the graffiti," he says. "Rest assured that your case will be moved to the top of my list."

It takes everything in me not to jump over the table and smack those thick-rimmed glasses off his bloated face. That would get his attention. I'm not coming about no stolen ramen noodles or insufficient funds on my ID card. This is a hate crime, and he isn't being supportive in the least.

"Is there anyone else I can talk to about this hate crime?" *Preferably someone Black,* I want to add. Maybe the president, but she seems harder to get to than the actual president. Each time Benji reaches out about something BSU-related, her assistant responds with how packed her schedule is.

His voice is stern. "Let's not throw around the term *hate crime*. This will be filed as a bias incident," he says. "Since no one was hurt."

I *am* hurt, but he ain't seem to notice nor care.

"Yeah, fucking right," I mumble under my breath.

"What was that?"

"Nothing." I gather my backpack and say a frigid goodbye as I slam the door behind me, hoping his ficus topples in the forceful quake.

I walk through campus with my head down. People stop and talk. A few come up to me to offer their condolences as if someone in my family just died. Pity moves across their faces. I don't want their pity. I want justice. For someone to speak up on my behalf. One of them had to see Lucas do this.

"Savannah, wait up," Benji calls out to me. Meggie bounces beside him.

I keep on moving.

"You . . . gone kill . . . me one day. Always making me run, and you know I got asthma," he says as he sucks on his inhaler.

"I didn't tell you to run. What's up?"

He puts away his pump and grabs his phone. "This is your room, right?" Benji shows me a status on Instagram posted by someone who lives on my floor. The caption underneath says, *Is it the '60s or the 2020s?*

Good point. There isn't much of a difference. "Yeah, I came back from art appreciation to that work of art on my door."

"Someone got me, too," Benji says. "*Half breed* instead of *nigga.*"

"Lucas," I say, and Benji nods.

"I'm sorry, guys." Meggie's apology is flat. "I never thought Lucas would do something like this. If I had known—"

I stop her right there. "*Did* you know about this?"

Her jaw drops like I just asked her the wildest thing she's ever heard. "I can't believe that's what you think of me. Of course I didn't know. If I did, I would have told you."

We have a stare-off until she looks away. "I swear on my life, Savannah."

The trust I have for Meggie is melting. I can feel it. Slowly dripping inside me. She's scared and I can tell. I'm scared too. Lucas is after me, and he's not going to stop. This is only the beginning.

"You still want me to dead it, Benji? Let him get away with this, too?" We haven't talked about Lucas since that day in the hallway. A sore subject that always puts us on opposite sides.

Benji shakes his head. "I just wanted to keep you safe, but this time, Lucas has gone too far. I'm sorry about what I said in the hallway. It was overboard, and you know I didn't mean it."

A sense of relief fills me. It's hard being mad at Benji. I just want to be friends again. Especially after this.

"It's in the past now." I remember our last conversation,

when he said I was impossible. "But I won't be too many of those *impossible*s before I cut you off for real."

He nods.

"You think Tasha seen this?" I ask.

I take out my phone and call her. She answers with sadness in her voice. "I guess that's why I got bombarded with pictures of skin-lightening cream today. I had to deactivate my social media, it got so bad." She lets out a sad, low laugh. But it's a mask, I know. A way to cope, because nothing 'bout this is funny. Tasha is darker than Benji and me. Her skin glows against the light. Radiates like she bathes in shea butter. Beautiful in my eyes, but my eyes don't matter at this moment.

"I went to the dean of students and he basically said get over it," I tell them.

"The dean thinks things have to be life-or-death for it to matter," Meggie says.

"He's not going to do anything?" Tasha asks.

"He said he's going to 'look into it.'"

"Which means we're going to have a funky forum, led by the administration no doubt, to discuss and to relate," Benji explains.

"You told him that Lucas did this, right?" Tasha asks.

"I did, but he said without proof he can't do much, and since this isn't a hate crime, technically—"

Tasha yells so loud the phone almost slips out my fingers. "What the fuck does he mean it's not a hate crime?"

"'Bias incident.'" I mock the dean's flat tone.

154

"Bias incident, my ass." Benji jiggles the change in his pocket. "I'm used to being called a half breed . . . an Oreo, but what he did to you two is unacceptable."

Tasha says she'll call us back. She's getting pepper spray in case Lucas tries anything physical.

"It's going to be all right, Savannah." Benji's fingers brush mine and I want to grab them, hold on to them, but I stop myself. "He won't get away with this."

I nod even though I'm not so sure.

NINETEEN

People call me "nigga" every day, just in a different way. Their racism isn't blatant, so it isn't racism in their eyes. Their racism is subtle. If you blink, you can miss it. Their racism passive. Sometimes I have a hard time deciphering it. Always wondering what the deeper meaning behind their actions is. When they cross the street while I walk by. Or refuse to acknowledge me at all, as if I'm invisible. And when they do acknowledge me, it's "hey girlfriend" in their sassy voices as their default greeting. #WooddaleConfessions

Damn that's deep.

I'm sorry you all have to go through this. They don't represent all white people on campus. We aren't all bad.

They represent enough for it to be a problem.

TWENTY

Every table in the coffee shop is occupied with students who look like they haven't slept in days. The young baristas are understaffed, and they try their best to keep up with the back-to-back complicated orders.

Instead of studying, I'm scrolling #WooddaleConfessions.

"Maybe I can DM some of the posts that said something about Lucas," I say to Tasha. She's sitting across from me, blowing on her twenty-degrees-too-hot hot chocolate. "If they come forward too, then the dean would have no choice but to listen."

She makes a low grunt.

"I gotta do something. Meggie been taking her sweet time getting back to me," I say. "We were supposed to have had some proof already."

I relayed Lucas's message to Meggie. Now I'm kicking myself for it. She's probably scared.

"How did my letter get in that drawer anyway? I never sent it to anyone but the dean."

Meggie. She started something she couldn't finish. That she might not finish. I can't think like that, though. I have to trust in her, because I'm not in the position to do this alone.

"You know how Meggie is," I say. "Her mind is everywhere, plus things like this take time."

"This school isn't exactly the best place to keep a secret. If Lucas already knows, that means eventually more people are going to know."

"Meggie says—"

"You putting a lot of trust in that Meggie girl," Tasha says. "Letting her know all your plans."

"Innocent until proven guilty." I swipe one last time before putting my phone away.

"That's only true for white folks and you know it."

We laugh. She ain't lying. "Either way, everything is going on hold until after finals. I'm drowning in all this coursework."

The dean for diversity and inclusion must have heard the news about our door and took pity on us. He gifted Tasha and me a free pastry or drink of our choice to help with studying. Literally the least he can do if you ask me.

Lord knows I ain't need the caramel macchiato that I'm sipping on. My hands tremble as I start my work. Technically, in order to keep my scholarship I have to maintain a 3.0 average. I *was* pulling A's and B's before the Lucas thing happened. Math got easier, but French upped its difficulty. I moved out of the D range, at least, and now I'm consistently getting C's. Maybe this was Lucas's plan all along. Stress me out bad enough that I'll lose my scholarship and get kicked out. He knows I can't afford this school out of pocket.

Ugh. Need to get my focus on the things that matter.

This Lucas thing matters too, though . . . don't it?

"I'm assuming the paint is off our door now." Tasha scoops some chili into her mouth. She booked a hotel over the weekend in the name of self-care. She asked me to come with her, but I wanted everyone to see my face each time I stepped out of my room. See what Lucas did to us.

"They didn't come until this morning . . . right before you got back."

"TWO DAYS?"

"Tasha, stop yelling—you know they already think we loud." I'm shocked, too, though, even knowing these folks. Forty-eight hours those words sat on my door. I tried to clean it myself, but I only spread the paint around. Forty-eight hours of pity, gawking, fakeness, trumped-up strife.

"They offered to move us, but I don't think it's fair for us to have to pack up our things."

"If anyone needs to move, it's Lucas."

We pore over the pile of materials in front of us. Tasha flies through math equations while I push aside my notes from chemistry, distracted with thoughts of Lucas again. Just can't shake it. The way he inflicts pain because he can . . . it baffles me. Black people ain't given no leeway. No benefit of the doubt. We're labeled instantly. The way Lucas floats in and out of these different communities with ease, and everyone on campus knows the type of person he is, pisses me off.

"Another person with a Lucas story," I say, scrolling through the long-winded message on my phone. It seems like everyone has one, but no one has spoken up about it.

Tasha bites her bottom lip and slaps her books closed. "Savannah, look, this is becoming too much. Just imagine what else he can do to get under our skin. A-and all this talk about him is getting on my nerves." Her voice cracks. "I can't even study no more. Ruining my morning. The way people attacked me online for no reason. Sent those pictures to me for no reason. Can't get that shit out of my head. I just—"

"He won't even have enough time to react when everything comes out in the open."

She doesn't respond.

I take my eyes off my phone and catch what looks like a tear dripping down her face and into her empty carton of chili.

"Tasha, what's the matter?" I scoot my chair next to hers and rub her shoulders.

She shrugs, tears flowing faster, and I dab her cheek with a napkin. "I don't know why I let that fuckboy get to me," she says.

"Lucas getting to you that bad? I'm sorry, Tash."

She sniffs. "Every time I become comfortable in my skin, someone knocks me down into a pit of insecurity. Can I be honest with you, Savannah?"

"Lay it out, sis."

She continues. "The main reason I came to this school is because I thought the kids here wouldn't treat me like the folks back home. I love my grandma and I'm glad she raised me, but you know how old people are. Being told not to swim too long or you'll get dark really messes with you."

"You thought the people here wouldn't talk about your skin?"

"Yes." She takes another napkin and blows her nose. "Nowhere to run, huh? Ignorant, right?"

"That's not ignorant, Tasha. I get where you're coming from." It don't matter how beautiful you are. It's always something or someone reminding you, consciously or not, of how much prettier you'd be if you were lighter. Bleaching kits are sold in abundance in Black neighborhoods. Companies only advertise Black women if they halfway Black with wavy hair.

Colorism in our community runs deep. Back to paper-bag tests done to make sure you come from the right folk. Elite clubs meant for light-skin folks. Blacks separating themselves from the dark. Basking in the fact they ancestors' gene pool was forcefully corrupted. Colorism goes deeper than the Mississippi River. Spans wider than the cotton fields of Virginia. It's embedded so deep inside us that sometimes we don't even realize we're perpetuating it.

Somewhere down the line . . . someone reminded Tasha. Planted a seed in her head that never stopped growing. That she's less than.

"I love my people, but sometimes I gotta take care of me." Her tears stop, but the pain in her eyes remains. "Should have known I wouldn't get validation from white people."

"We both learned our lesson about this place."

"Your hair?" she asks, and I nod.

Tasha did my hair up in scalp braids when I got tired of my Afro puffs. I grab at the ends, twisting them around my finger. "I wanted to straighten it to fit into this box that's too small for me to fit into anyway."

"Sometimes I regret choosing Wooddale," Tasha says.

"I could be at Hilbert right now. That's an HBU back at home. My life could be completely different. Might even be happy."

Mama thought she was setting me up for greatness. Wooddale may be one of the best schools, but it costs too much and I ain't just talking money.

"You think we gone survive here?" she asks.

The million-dollar question.

Prolly not.

TWENTY-ONE

Don't forget the forum is today! Show up and speak up. #WooddaleConfessions

This can get us out of class, right?

Because tbh I really don't feel like learning about Erik Erickson today.

Every time I scroll this hashtag it's full of fools. Show up and you just might learn something. Racism cannot be tolerated on this campus.

Who's going to stop it?

We are.

TWENTY-TWO

After word spread about the slur on our door, Wooddale made it "mandatory" for the campus to attend another forum about the "incident." A quick shower and I'm hustling my way through the courtyard around clusters of people studying. People not worried 'bout attending some "mandatory" diversity talk. Funny how it's only mandatory for certain folk.

I'm for damn sure going, though.

If I don't speak up as Memphis Savannah, will I ever be respected here?

The walk over goes by quick. Past the fountain and the old liberal-arts building filled with what I swear is mold, and behind the café sits Jasper Auditorium. Students talk among themselves as they crowd in. A good amount shows up, but not as many as what shows up for basketball games. Benji and Tasha wait at the top of the steps.

"Y'all see Lucas go in?" I ask.

"Nah, some of his homies went in but I haven't seen him,"

Tasha says. "You know he sends other people to do his dirty work."

"He probably won't show up, Savannah." Benji holds the door for us as we walk into the auditorium. The members of the BSU greet us. They seem like the only ones happy to be here.

People slump over, asleep or nose-deep in their devices, headphones plugged into their ears. Half caring about the goings-on of our lives. Lucas the main one who needs to hear what I got to say.

Elaina nowhere to be found, but one of her friends waves. "Hey, Vanna."

Vanna. Vanna won't be at this meeting.

Tasha, Benji, and I sit shoulder to shoulder in the front row.

"It saddens me that we are here," says a white professor with a printed headwrap. She white but wears headwraps and ethnic-printed attire 90 percent of the time. Whenever I pass her, she's bragging about her excursions in Africa or some other country where people of color reside. I got half a mind to snatch it off her, wearing my culture like a damn costume.

"Most of you are aware of the incident that occurred. We here at Wooddale pride ourselves on diversity, tolerance, and equality. Under no circumstances do we promote or condone the use of exclusionary language."

"*Shiee,*" Tasha says.

"As if it's her word to condone or promote," Benji whispers into my ear.

I hate that Professor Daphne couldn't be here to moderate. According to Headwrap, she had a family emergency.

"Savannah Howard, Natasha Carmichael, and Benjamin Harrington are here, correct?"

I wave my hand in the air. Benji sticks his up and puts it down just as quick. Tasha puts her phone into her purse. "Let's get this shit show over with."

"Will you three please come up?" Headwrap motions to the stage. We look at each other and hesitate. Benji takes the lead and walks onto the stage. I hesitate, but Tasha grabs my hand and gives me that *you got this* look. Bright lights block out the folks in the auditorium as we step onto the stage.

"These three students were victimized by someone we have not caught yet." Headwrap looks at us with fake compassion. "I want to offer my sincerest apologies."

I flash a plastic smile that fades as soon as she turns her attention to the audience. Benji muscles up a low grunt. We stand there, three in a row.

"I feel like we 'bout to be sold," I say to no one in particular.

"Today we are going to be open and honest about our feelings and learn together while promoting change," she says, as if it were the simplest thing in the world. "Have a seat, you three. . . . There is a mic being passed around."

"Nigga, are we really 'bout to explain to these folks why they can't say *nigga*?" Tasha sits down on one of the metal chairs lined up for us. The first student comes to a podium in the front. His shaggy blond bangs cover his eyes. He cracks his gum before he begins to talk. "I don't get the big deal about the N-word. It wasn't the *-er* ending. Everyone says it. Even *they* call each other that."

"They"?

The fuck?

These people, I can't—

I pinch the bridge of my nose. At the beginning of the semester, I became someone I didn't recognize. I don't know that person. But whoever she was, she is dead now.

Savannah earned a spot at Wooddale.

Savannah deserves to be here.

And since I'm here, I'm not doing this bite-my-tongue, let-them-touch-my-hair-and-don't-say-shit, try-not-to-be-*too*-Black, Vanna shit no more.

"The fact you called it 'the N-word' tells me you know you're not supposed to say it. You just want to be difficult." Old Savannah rises from the ashes and dusts herself off. I don't want to ever be that Vanna person again, whoever she was.

The mic passes again and jerks me out of my thoughts. "I agree with him," some girl in the crowd says. "Yes, it used to be considered a *bad* word, but it isn't anymore."

Before the mic passes, a whining creak echoes in the back

of the building. Everyone turns around as the door claps shut. Lucas slithers in with Elaina and Meggie right behind him.

Meggie. I blink my eyes three times because this must be a dream. A vision.

Tasha nudges me. "Ain't that your girl? Seems like she's sleeping with the enemy, *again.*"

Meggie and I make eye contact and it's like she wants to swallow herself. There has to be an explanation for this. Maybe she's acting as a plant. Getting more information from the inside. That has to be it.

"I knew she was a snake." Tasha laughs to herself. "Predictable as fuck."

They walk down the auditorium aisle like celebrities on the red carpet. People seated stop them to speak. Elaina even takes a selfie with one of her friends.

After forever and a day, they take their seats right in the middle of the room. Close enough for me to see into Lucas's eyes. Now that showtime over, students pass the mic again, but no one stands up to speak.

Silence hangs in the air awkwardly as the mic goes from hand to hand, but nobody has nothing to chime in. Until an unknown voice gathers the courage. "I'm not afraid to say it."

I squint into the crowd and tap Tasha on the shoulder. "Girl, who is that?"

"I don't know, but he's sitting with Lucas and 'em."

Not surprised.

"Nigga," the guy says, too bold for comfort. "There. Everyone says it, and look around—no one died."

No one died.

No one died.

Tell that to the thousands of Black men and women who die each day from that word. To the men and women who left the earth hearing that as their last word by the folks who killed 'em.

Headwrap intervenes, taking the mic from Tasha's hand. She didn't expect the forum to take a sharp left. "What's your name? You are going to be sent to—"

Before she finishes, a brash voice calls out. "Yo, my guy, what you just say? You not scared to say it, huh?"

The entire auditorium turns in unison, and my panic sets in at the tone of his voice. In Memphis, this would be when Mama would tell me to come inside. I'm not in Memphis anymore. Mama can't protect me from what comes next.

The guy who spoke out—he's tall and Black, might be a basketball player—towers over the boy, whose whiteness stands out in the dim room. Three other white boys start to surround the Black guy—one of them is Lucas. Two more Black students join in, their height unmissable—must be other basketball players. The sound of fists connecting with flesh bounces off the walls. Screams from the audience tell me what's happening before I can even see it. Who winning this losing battle yet to be determined.

Blows come back-to-back. From what little I can see, the men with the brown skin are getting the upper hand. The crowd gathers around, but no one stops them or helps. A few even pull out their phones. I can't stand my generation sometimes. Everything ain't meant to be recorded.

"Benji, you got to stop them," I say. If a white boy get hurt, they'll never give us a chance to speak again. A hurt white boy trumps three hurt Black kids.

Benji flies from the stage to help.

My hands shake around the mic. "Y'all stop. This is supposed to be a peaceful discussion. Stop it!" My teeth bear down together as someone charges our way. Hits connect with Benji's body and I freeze. A crowd of a few other boys pulls them apart.

"We have a zero-violence policy here at Wooddale that is punishable up to expulsion," Headwrap yells into the mic. "Break it up, now! Campus security will be here to escort you all out."

"That's not fair," I say. "That guy was provoked."

"That's not the way this works," she says. "Violence only promotes more violence."

"He's a racist and the guy was only defending himself and his people." Tasha walks to the edge of the stage for a better look. "This ain't right. Ain't right at all."

"I'm sorry, you guys." Headwrap dismisses everyone from the auditorium and watches the chattering crowd leave, a scowl painted on her lips.

"Man, let's just get out of here." Benji wraps his arms around the chiseled Black dude, helping him as he limps. Two others follow behind. *That's what's-his-name from my chemistry class.* He's face of the basketball team. You can't go to the school's home page without his pearly white smile flashing across the slideshow. Benji calms him down and we walk with them. His teammates take over and help him to the athlete dorms.

Folks who ain't go to the school stroll by, being nosy at an ambulance parked on the sidewalk near the building. Folks who do go to the school film the scene for their social-media pages. I wonder what caption they gone put under this one. We walk past Lucas being tended by a paramedic. He only got a busted nose that can be healed with a Band-Aid. Elaina boo-hooing like he's on his deathbed. Meggie nowhere to be found.

"Dude act like he got some broken ribs," I say. But he gone milk this for all it's worth, I guess. Even got crocodile tears on the brims of his eyes.

"Which is what he need, to be honest." Tasha kicks at a pine cone in her path.

The EMTs shine a small flashlight into his pupils.

"Jacob was hard to hold. I got more injuries than he does."

Benji shows us his hand. It's swelled up the size of two grape-fruits. Without thinking, I caress the tender spots and scrapes. He doesn't pull away.

"That was brave, what you did," I say.

"I didn't want him to hurt Lucas or his crew too bad. He'd be dealing with worse things."

We plop down on the damp wooden bench outside the café. Benji sits in the middle and puts his arms across both our backs.

"What you think gone happen to him?" Tasha asks.

Silence, nothing but rustling leaves blowing past. The folks from the forum retreat to their dorms. No doubt ranting to the others about the ruckus the Black folk caused.

"I don't know, but it ain't gone be good."

"What about Lucas?" Tasha sucks her teeth in annoyance.

"A slap on the wrist," Benji says. His arm curls around my neck. "Community service that he won't go to. Just like when we got in trouble as kids. He'd do most of the dirt but get in the least amount of trouble."

"I hate this damn place," I yell to the gray skies. "How have y'all lasted here this long?"

"I keep my head down," Tasha says. "Don't start none, won't be none."

"They done already started it," I say. "Someone needs to finish it."

But that's the problem—no one has. Lucas has been on

campus for four years and nothing has happened. If nothing changes now, then it never will.

Even after he graduates, another Lucas will just take his place. I can't be at Wooddale ignoring injustices every day.

Tasha won't speak up. Neither will Benji. Neither will the anonymous folks online.

That someone has to be me.

TWENTY-THREE

The next morning and the morning after that are dark.

The mood on campus matches the weather. I sit in front of the open windows listening to the rain splash against the pavement. Everyone is tucked away in their dorms, which gives me time to do homework without fear lurking behind me.

Lucas literally has eyes everywhere.

I spotted two frat dudes following me from class this morning. And another two were in the dorm, posted up on the wall, looking at me weird. That ain't no coincidence. No way.

My fingers clack on the keyboard as I read aloud to drown out my worrisome thoughts. Writing a five-page paper for my African American history class ain't on my radar when I'm trying to make my own.

Ugh. Forget this. I click the file closed without even hitting save and rake my fingers across my scalp.

The Cunninghams are staples in the Wooddale community.

Powerful.

I'm an outsider. No one is going to believe me. Believing me would mean everything they thought to be true was a lie.

I can ask Elaina to fess up to some of his seedy behavior. She hugged up with him all the time. She has to know something. Maybe slip a question in one day while she's high out of her mind. They might not believe us but they gotta believe Elaina.

Ruffling sounds at my back startle me and I snap around. "Girl, who—"

Tina, a redhead from French class, saunters toward me. Her room is a few doors down from Tasha's.

"Don't run up on people like that, girl—you scared me."

Her hair dangles over her eyes, matching the angry shade on her face I've only just noticed.

Uh-oh, what happened?

"Did you hear about Jacob?"

Jacob? The basketball player from the forum?

I hold my breath. "N-no, what happened?"

She tosses the morning's copy of the *Wooddale Gazette* in my lap. Sure enough, Jacob's face is plastered on the front, like a mug shot.

WOODDALE'S STAR
BASKETBALL PLAYER OFF THE TEAM

The air in my lungs burns. *Damn, son. This is bad.* Basketball season ended before it even began with this news. Jacob *is* the entire team. Tina crosses her hands, dabbing the corners of her eyes. I figure they have a thing going on. He's always hanging around her room and shit.

"I'm just so pissed. Jacob's freaking out because without the team, he doesn't have his full ride. He can't keep going here without it. H-he's leaving, Vanna."

"SUH-VAN-NUH," I clarify. "And I'm so sorry. This is so fucked up."

Ain't no story in here about Lucas and his partners. No, Lucas is untouchable. The thought of suspension never passed through his mind when he was swinging. Things like that don't happen to Cunninghams, not yet anyway.

"Why'd he even have to say anything at that forum? Everything was perfect. Now this!" Tina storms off, and I resist the urge to burst her bubble with a truth she is too egotistical to see: this ain't about her.

This 'bout Jacob. Me. Tasha. Benji. All us Black folks at Wooddale.

What's gone happen to him now?

Will it be the same thing for me when I blow the whistle on Lucas? Will I lose my shot at bettering myself because I spoke out against shit that's not right?

We get so little—but have the most to lose.

TWENTY-FOUR

Prayers up for Jacob. We see who the real animals are. #WooddaleConfessions

Didn't he start it . . .

No, he was clearly provoked.

He needs to learn how to control his anger.

Black people always being branded as angry. Maybe we're just fed up.

He can still play basketball though, right?

He's a human being not just an object for consumption.

Is that a no?

TWENTY-FIVE

"You write like a damn kindergartner," B'onca shouts over the FaceTime call as I time her on her practice SAT. It has been a few weeks since our last call, and this is our last go-around before she takes the real thing. She's advanced a lot. But I can't help wondering, will it be enough? People like B'onca and me, we don't get second chances. We don't get boosts or extra help.

We get one chance, and if we strike out, then that's it.

"You shouldn't be using my notes anyway," I say, propping up my phone on the bookshelf by my bed to give my arm a rest. "It's about what you know by heart." The timer in my hand beeps. "*Annnnd* time!"

"Man, this is some bull," she says. "Am I really only going to have sixty minutes to write an entire essay?"

"Yes, ma'am. Maybe even less."

"You better be glad I love and miss you," she says. "Or I'd be taking my ass right on down to the community college. You don't even need an SAT score to get in."

That's B'onca's favorite threat, but I know she's just talking to talk. She wants to attend community college as much as I want to wax my upper lip.

"How them grades looking?" I ask.

"You sound just like my mama."

I roll my neck like her. "And?"

She sucks her teeth. "Well, I'm expecting A's in everything except Mrs. Curry. She tripping, for real. Dropped me a grade because I was late again. Told her I was sick in the bathroom. She figure I was lying, I guess." She sighs. "Messing up my GPA."

Oh, how I wish things like that wouldn't matter for B'onca like they didn't matter for Lucas. A low GPA wasn't a downfall for Lucas. The difference between a 3.5 and a 4.0 GPA means everything to B'onca.

It's her way out of no way.

B'onca needs those points to make it. To Lucas they were only points. He already got his golden path laid out.

"Savannah, you think they'll accept me?"

Tears stall in my eyes. The desperation in B'onca's gaze makes it hard for them not to fall, but I blink away the tears.

Her eyes grow big on the phone screen like she's trying to look up close. "Girl, why are you crying?"

I let my head fall into my hands. "It's just that . . . I can't even lie to you. This shit is hard. This shit is hard *and rigged.*" It feels so good to just tell someone the truth. Someone who'll understand. Someone I won't have to prove it to with a damn court file worth of documents and four, five people on record.

Her face falls too, and I know she's worried. But B'onca

the strong one. Even if she never shows it. "So I need to get in on that minority token? I gotcha."

We laugh.

"You're silly, B. I don't want what I told you to discourage you. You keep working hard, aight? If not for anyone else, do it for yourself."

B'onca's door slams and rattles her laptop. "Here comes my mama. Let me go before she bust in here embarrassing me."

We say our goodbyes and hang up. The possibility of B'onca coming to Wooddale about as slim as a rich person getting into heaven. For folks like the Cunninghams, their heaven is already here on earth. I lie on the bed and watch day turn into night. Until the darkness isn't comforting to me anymore.

Restless, I grab my phone to text Meggie. Tasha says I'm naive for still trusting her, but I have to believe she's going to do the right thing.

> **Me:** You around? Any more information on Lucas?

I watch the three dots pop up on my phone almost immediately.

> **Meggie:** Savannah! Great timing. Christmas came early. I think. I'm actually on my way

to Professor Santos's before she leaves for
the night. Meet me at her office.

The dude in admissions. I cross my fingers. That, along
with quotes from the people I found, will put this over the
edge. Maybe B will have a shot after all. I knew Meggie wasn't
going to leave me hanging.

I toss on my sneakers and damn near run to the other side
of campus. Only a few lights illuminate the building. I knock
twice before stepping inside.

"You're quick," Professor Daphne says.

Meggie has two bags and a stack of files with her. She sets
her things down and holds up a manila folder, a wild look
in her eye.

"I'm scared . . . yet intrigued," I say.

"I'm the one who should be scared. I'm sure I broke about
a thousand laws to get this. Well, some nerd named Clarence
technically broke the laws. These are printouts of emails between Lucas and someone Clarence couldn't identify, about
his SAT scores. Let's hope it's your golden ticket."

The missing piece to our puzzle. The way to receive justice. *Justice.* The term holds no weight in these parts. Justice
cannot be given. It has to be taken.

Meggie sets her stuff on the desk and hands me a thin envelope. "Go on and open it. I'm dying to see what's inside. I
didn't want to open it without you. This is *your* baby, after all."

My hands grip the lightweight envelope. If everything I need is in this envelope, will it change things? If I send Lucas's tea spilling over, will anyone care? People like him invincible sometimes. Amazing what money can do. And will he find out it was me? Then it will be my world crashing down. I slide the paper out.

> **From:** LCJ2000@gmail.com
>
> Your last payment has been sent. Thank you for your services. Burn the fake ID and delete this thread.

Meggie jumps up in excitement. "*Ohmigod,* SHUT UP! We *got* him."

Now it's *we*? *She* must think I ain't notice how she always handing the onus over to me. I ain't miss it. But I ain't gone say nothing. She *is* helping.

Professor Daphne pushes her glasses up. "Let me see, please." Her face scrunches as she reads over the paper.

"This exposure is going to skyrocket your career, Savannah. Your name will be known years before you graduate," Meggie says.

Funny how white folks assume hard work equals results. That what they do, if it's done right, will matter.

That's they reality. Not mine.

"That's not all, either." Meggie scoots over and makes room for me next to her. She pulls out a thick stack of papers and my insides flutter.

"Damn, all that about Lucas?"

"No, most of it is about his parents, but there's something in there." She licks the tip of her finger and flicks through a thick stack.

Meggie's eyes light up. "Oh, that, yes. This is good. So, the summer before his freshman year, Lucas got into Wooddale off the wait list." She pulls out another sheet of paper and smooths its folds. "Right after . . . drumroll, please . . ."

I stomp my feet, trying to pretend to be excited and not slightly terrified.

"Meggie, get on with it." Professor Daphne cuts the suspense short.

"Lucas's parents gave a considerable donation to Wooddale."

Wow. "That's a huge coincidence," I say.

"It's not uncommon for Wooddale to accept donations," Professor Daphne says.

"I mean, it happens. His family name's on a building, for goodness' sake. But something isn't adding up. Lucas was also rejected from Wooddale's honor-society camp that they hold for incoming freshmen. Now, someone with his last name would be an automatic add, right?"

"Unless he bombed the SAT and then had someone else retake it for him. Even being a legacy can't fix bad grades and a bad test score," I say.

"Exactly. Lucas's application to the honor-society camp has his high school GPA on it. It isn't good, you guys."

Meggie pulls out the application for the honor-society camp submitted by Lucas, stamped **DENIED**. The 2.0 GPA reflects off the page like a glowing red flag.

Yeeessss. "It's still all so wild to me. You know how hard I had to work, and Lucas just squeezed himself in."

Mama floats through my mind, and her stern voice tells me I better do my best. This my best?

"It's not fair, and that's why I'm risking my entire academic career to get you this information, Savannah."

You? Shit, I'm the one that's gone catch heat.

"I think we all have something to lose here," Professor Daphne says. "If I don't report this, then it's my job on the line as well."

"Wouldn't that make you look bad, though, to be attached to a school blown out of the water?" I ask.

"I'll be a casualty, but I'll be fine—there are plenty more universities in the academic sea."

I pull out the rest of the contents and sift through them in minutes. Evidence, so much evidence. A copy of the check stub for "building improvements" donated by Lucas and Janet Cunningham.

Damn.

It's all right here.

"Just because I have proof doesn't mean anyone is going to listen to me. Lucas's last name holds weight on this campus and in this town," I say.

Meggie's shoulders slump. "Yeah . . . I mean, that's true, but that's why we have Professor Daphne on our side."

She is the only one on our side. The only one that can make this right.

"We have to get this out into the world. Even if not for the admission piece, Jacob got kicked off the team and lost his athletic scholarship while Lucas walked away untouched. There was a hate crime committed by him that the university is trying to sweep under the rug as if it never happened. But it did happen, and it happened to us. And no one's listening."

Professor Daphne flips through pages. Makes two stacks, one on each side of her desk. She folds her arms across her chest and leans back into her chair. "I'll take this to the president, and then we can go from there."

I almost throw my arms around her in gratitude but stop myself. "Thank you, thank you, thank you."

"When you're done with Lucas, he's going to wish that he just went into the family business," Meggie says.

There's that you *again. What's up with that . . . ?*

"You keep saying *you,*" I say. "I thought we were in this together."

"We are. It was just a slip of the tongue."

I can't help but think it's a Freudian slip, but I push that thought down. Meggie wouldn't get me all this information if she didn't plan on going all the way.

"Can we get her on your radio show as well? For an

interview. That'll really let Lucas know that we're serious," Meggie says.

"I can possibly make that happen, but I have to warn you, Savannah, there may be backlash. Are you truly ready for that?" Professor Daphne asks.

I chew a nail.

"Don't be nervous, Savannah. You're doing a great thing," Meggie says.

Easy for her to say—the risk on my head if I'm found out.

"Actually," I say, "can you wait until after Christmas break to bring it to the president? I want us to be able to focus on finals and not this."

"That'll work," Professor Daphne says. "It'll give me enough time to thoroughly check into the matter. I'm not questioning your source, Meggie, but I have to be sure."

"I understand. After Christmas break," Meggie replies.

"Are you still going to be up for it, Meggie?" I ask.

"Of course. I'm helping because I believe in you. At the end of the day, your voice and your story is what's going to bring attention to this."

My voice. My story. My Black ass on the line.

TWENTY-SIX

"Savannah, over here."

"Meggie?"

I peer around and there's her wispy hair and darting eyes peeking from behind the central courtyard great oak. "I need to talk to you."

I look over my shoulder before walking to her. "Why you hiding?" It's early morning and only a few students are out.

"I'm not hiding," she says. "There's just a lot of shade over here."

It's shady all right.

"I wanted to catch you before class. You might wanna lie low. Lucas is on a rampage."

Wooosah. "And how would you know this?"

"You know I always have my ear to the ground." She reaches for my hand and squeezes. "He's *pissed,* Savannah. About what happened at the forum and the hashtag."

Silence hangs between us and I finally break it.

"I'm walking around with a target on my back and it's like you're getting away squeaky clean."

"I'm not. Lucas knows how to mess with my anxiety. It may not seem like it, but I'm sure he's after me, too."

"You think I don't see you snickering with Elaina at lunch and things. You even came with them to the forum. You have to pick a side."

Meggie buries her face in her phone as a group of people saunter by, their stares like daggers. "I have to be in the thick of things. If not, how am I going to get information?"

"It seems like information isn't all you're getting. You want protection."

"Savannah, you're going to be fine," she says, fully facing me again now that the crowd has passed. "With Professor Daphne on your side? She's a powerful advocate." Meggie squeezes my hand again.

I guess that's supposed to make me feel secure, assured. It doesn't. Even if I do have Professor Daphne in my corner now.

"I gotta run. Remember to keep your head down. No posts for a few days," she says. "Even if people are upset. *Now* you have their attention." She stares past me. "You're being so brave, Savannah, *really* going the distance." She slips on her shades, covers her head with a scarf, and scurries off.

Going the distance. White folks don't ever get that we are the ones at risk. We got the most to lose. She the one planted the social-media idea in my head. Now she wants to run away. Meggie got this whole thing started and just disappeared.

Moving between social groups is easy for her. I ain't got that privilege.

The walk from the courtyard to my actual class feels like walking into death row. Whispers echo each of my steps. People don't even look away when I catch them staring.

I hide in the comfort of my hoodie, determined to keep these grades where they need to be. If they do kick me out of here for telling the truth, it won't be because I ain't proven myself academically.

That I have over Lucas, no matter what.

"A few more weeks until I can go home for Christmas break," I say to myself. Thanksgiving I couldn't afford to go home, and neither could Tasha. We spent those days playing cards, eating too many vending machine snacks, and finally relaxing. Campus isn't so bad when it's only a handful of people here.

I exhale before pushing the classroom doors open. As the semester progressed, French class got thinner. No one wants to learn a new language early in the morning. Tina's bright face greets me, all smiles. That's the last thing I expected.

"You look terrible, chica," she says. We bonded over how bad we were in French. Each time the professor explained something we didn't understand, we looked at each other with fear and disdain.

"Thanks, just what every girl wants to hear." I reject my usual spot in the front for a secluded table in the back with the other slackers.

Tina sits on the edge of the table. "Have you heard the campus gossip?"

"The story about the captain of the football team getting the cheer captain pregnant? A cliché of all clichés."

"No, *ha-ha*. About Lucas." She takes her phone out and sits it beside me. "Someone messed up his precious car."

I smirk at the work of art. The word *racist* smeared across his Hummer in three different artistic styles. "Damn," I say. "That's what his ass gets."

"You didn't do this, right?" She turns and looks over her shoulder and then to me. "I mean, I won't snitch if you did."

"Girl, I ain't ruining my life over no Lucas Cunningham." A half lie.

"Whoever did it better hope they don't get caught."

I agree and rest my head on the table, tuning out the professor's lecture on conjugated verbs, until an email alert flashes on my phone.

The dean of students would like to see you, immediately.

I pack my backpack and leave class. Administrators don't just call you out of class for no silly reason. I feel like a prisoner being led to the electric chair as I make my way to the student services building. My heart misses a beat when I reach my destination.

"Savannah, come in and have a seat," Dean William says, pulling out a chair for me.

"I don't mind standing."

"Suit yourself."

"What's so important?" I focus on a piece of lint on his wool jacket. "I was in class, you know."

"I specifically told you to let me handle things."

I drop my bag at my feet. "What are you talking about?"

"Lucas Cunningham's car was vandalized in the wee hours of the morning today."

"Okay, and . . . ?"

"Savannah, we believe that you did it."

"That's impossible. I have no idea what you're talking about right now." This might as well be a continuation of French class. I haven't touched Lucas's car, and if I had, I would have done more damage than spray paint.

"You have a motive. You think Lucas spray-painted derogatory language on your dorm-room door. Plus, we have video evidence."

Video?

What?

Unless I was sleepwalking, he a damn lie.

He swivels his computer screen for me to see. On the screen, a Black woman stands in a black hoodie with the hood up. Her eyes are lowered to the ground. It's a grainy imprint.

That ain't proof of anything.

"*Racist*, you wrote. That's a serious accusation to be throwing around, young lady."

"That could be anyone in that photo. All Black people don't look alike, you know." I roll my eyes. He wants me to admit to a crime I didn't commit. If I say anything, he'll scoop it up and use it against me. I'm not falling for the okey-doke. I've seen enough *Law & Order* to know I have the right to remain silent. I've seen enough dirty cops in my hood to know to keep my fucking mouth shut.

"Savannah, you have motive. It's no secret you dislike Lucas, and now this picture of a woman who looks awfully like you. Too much is leading back to you."

"Circumstantial evidence," I repeat like I heard on *Law & Order*.

"Be that as it may, you will have a judicial hearing with the board tomorrow to decide your punishment."

"I just *told you* that ain't me!" I clutch and unclutch my hand, working out the fire burning inside me.

"That is for the judicial board to decide."

I stomp my foot and curse underneath my breath. "Will Lucas also be meeting with this judicial board?"

"Why would he be?" he asks, as if that's the wildest thing he's ever heard.

"I can give you a lot of fucking reasons."

"Ms. Howard, I understand you're angry, but you will not curse at me." He walks behind his desk. "You have tangible proof stacked against you, and not just hearsay."

"You can't say you have proof when you only have a grainy photo that could be anyone."

He opens his desk drawer and pulls out a clear plastic ziplock bag. "How do you explain this, then?" He shakes the spray can that lies inside. "This was found in your dorm room."

"You mean Elaina's dorm room. I've been bunking with my friend Tasha. Remember the graffiti that I reported on our door?"

"According to our records, you never returned your key, which means you still have access to your original dorm," he replies. "This matches the paint found on Lucas's car. Ms. Howard, own up to your mistakes and the board may be lenient with you."

"There's nothing to own up to. If I did it, I would admit to it, but it wasn't me. You don't think it's a coincidence that that's the same color that was on Clive's statue and my door? Whoever did this had to be involved in those incidents."

Every word I say goes in one ear and out the other. The dean doesn't care to hear my explanation. I'm guilty in his eyes, and whatever I say not gone change the verdict.

"This ain't fair," I say. "HOW. IS. THIS. FAIR?" Tears sting my eyes, but I'm not gone cry in front of him. "You could be out finding the real person who did this, but instead you are harassing me."

He ignores my plea and writes something in his notepad. "Your meeting with the judicial board is in the chancellor's office tomorrow at eight a.m. Don't be late."

I leave his office and the tears stream down my face.

TWENTY-SEVEN

News floats around Wooddale faster than a racehorse. The path to the chancellor's office is lined with snickering faces and boisterous laughs from the bold ones. Before I was summoned today, the chancellor of the university was a hidden figure whose name only appeared in university emails. She's a woman, and that *almost* makes me feel a little better about the meeting, but she a white woman and that makes a world of difference.

"Have a seat. It's a pleasure to meet you." The chancellor holds her hand out. I look away. She clears her throat and flattens her hands to her side. The door pushes open and the room becomes chilly. I see Elaina through the crack of the door before it shuts.

Lucas strolls in looking like he rolled out of bed. I'm in the best clothes I have, even did my hair straight. It's not as big of a deal to him as it is to me. He doesn't feel any pressure to make a good impression. I want to snatch my sock bun out of my head. Wear my Afro in its natural, unmanipulated state. Speak in my Southern slang. Will the board listen to me if

I'm my authentic self? Would my boldness be mistaken for attitude? Would the chancellor believe my story less if I didn't conform?

Twice as hard to be half as good.

Someone from the *Wooddale Gazette* is going to write about what happens at the meeting. If anything happens at all. The chancellor is responsible for either making or breaking how this case or lack of case will be viewed by the majority on campus. The majority already got their mind made up: I'm a snitch and a liar. A freshman who just wants to ruin the campus and its reputation. There have been no scandals in the past fifty years—that have been reported, that is. To them and to the outside world, Wooddale is the epitome of wholesome. Nothing happens here. Especially nothing like this. Universities this prestigious have money to hide their scandals. To pay off people to be quiet.

I stand here.

In my cheap suit.

With shaking knees.

A scratchy voice.

And a story to be told.

"Lucas, have a seat," the chancellor says.

He sits in the back near the door and no one protests. I rock on the legs of the chair and steady myself when the chancellor begins to speak.

"We take the allegations against Mr. Cunningham seriously," she says. "And here at Wooddale, we pride ourselves on—"

I finish her statement. "Yes, we know. Equality and diversity."

"Yes." She clears her throat. "It's our duty to get to the bottom of this."

"It's been months," I say. "Months, and the only thing that's been done is a forum no one cared enough about to show up to. I had to get justice my own way."

"That sounds like a confession to me," Lucas says.

"No, I didn't mean it like that." I push the words I really want to say down. "I just mean no one has done anything for me."

"Yes, and I'm sorry," she says. "You're not the only case that we are looking into."

Are there other people like me in the background? Who don't have the chance to speak up? I never seen them before. Never heard of the others. Their stories will probably remain buried. Underneath the surface of ours. Like ours is buried underneath the surface of the ones before us.

"Is this school full of racists or something?" I ask. "How many secrets roam these halls?"

The dean and the chancellor frown in unison, adjusting themselves in their seats. They sit behind their marble desks with their designer clothes on, pretending that they care about what happens to Black folk.

"Let's stick to the case at hand. It's very important to us that we get the full story," the chancellor says, adjusting the collar of her blouse.

"Ask your dean." I glare at him. "He has the full story." I want him to go down the most, but if anything, he'd retire and live off the university for the rest of his miserable life.

"That is false." The dean turns to the chancellor, scratching at his double chin. "Ms. Howard here came into my office, without an appointment, barely intelligible—"

"You understood me just fine." My heels clack as I tap my foot.

"Please don't interrupt," the chancellor says, and her thin, cracked lips form into the fakest smile I've ever witnessed.

I mouth a sarcastic *sorry* and lean farther into the chair.

"As I was saying . . . Ms. Howard came into my office, flinging her phone around, going on about how Lucas wrote a slur on her door. I told her I would look into it, which I have been doing, and it is one of the reasons we are currently here."

"Allegedly," I say, "you were looking into it. I bet you continued to sit in your chair and read your book. The cleaning staff didn't even come until forty-eight hours later. Two days that word sat written on my door. Yet you were looking into it, right?"

"I was doing my very best," he repeats, refusing to look at me.

"Looking into it, my ass."

"She's obviously belligerent and can't even have a peaceful meeting," Lucas interjects, throwing his head back in frustration. "I don't understand why we even bother with them."

"Excuse me?" I say. "Who asked you anything?"

"You're excused." Lucas points to the door. His eyes are bloodshot red. "Can we get this over with, please?"

I know it's a sin to hate someone, but I'll gladly go to whatever hell was invented for people who do.

"We are a community, let us remember that," the chancellor says on some kumbaya shit.

"He's not a part of none of my community," I say.

"Likewise." Lucas folds his arms.

"What's the point of this?" I turn my attention to the chancellor. "Why am I here? Is it to be insulted? Because I can get that from the comfort of my dorm room."

Silence.

I stand and clear my throat.

The chancellor leans forward, studying me.

More silence.

"What are you going to do about slurs being written on Black people's doors?" I ask. "That's the real crime—"

She cuts in. "Ms. Howard, we did not find any evidence that Lucas was the one responsible for that. Whoever did it did a fine job of covering their tracks. We cannot punish Lucas for a crime that we're not sure he committed."

"This some bullshit. What about the paint on his hands?" I slap the table, and the buttoned-up suits in the room startle, like I'm about to pull a gun from my miniature pocketbook. I don't regret my anger. I don't conceal it either. At this moment, I'm proud to be the angry Black girl.

"Ms. Howard, I know you're upset. What was done to you

was a horrible act, and if I could catch the person myself, I would. However, as the late great Dr. Martin Luther King said, 'Hate cannot drive out hate; only love can do that.'"

White folks love quoting Martin Luther King. I imagine they google quotes of his as a pastime so they can use them at any moment. If white folks loved Martin so much, why did they have him shot down? Did love make them do that?

"I apologize that we did not send out a community email immediately when all this first occurred," says the chancellor. The dean folds his arms, still refusing to look my way. "I take full responsibility for that mix-up."

"And about the car vandalism," Dean William says. "If we give you a slap on the wrist, Savannah, who is to say someone else won't go vandalizing others' property?" His leathery face is smug.

"I DIDN'T VANDALIZE THAT CAR!"

"We have you on tape, Savannah," the chancellor says.

"No! You have some Black person on tape. We do not actually all look alike, you know? I can't believe this shit."

"You're not helping your case, Savannah," the dean warns.

My blood runs thick, but I hold my tongue, and sweat beads go unnoticed as they decide my punishment.

"Savannah, we really do believe that you add a great deal to Wooddale's campus," the dean says.

A.k.a. you help us meet our quota.

"Because we value you and since this is your first offense,

we won't be issuing a suspension. For now, you will be issued community service on campus," the chancellor says.

The breath stuck in my lungs makes its way up.

"However," the dean adds, "if anything like this happens again, we will have no choice but to void your scholarship and expel you."

"Listen, Savannah. No matter what you think, I find you quite charming," Lucas says. "I apologize for what happened to you and your friends. It truly was a tragedy. I will have my ear to the ground, and if I hear anything about the real perpetrator, I won't hesitate to report him or her."

"Go to hell, Lucas."

He leans his head back in his hands. "Ah, well, I tried."

"As for you, Lucas." The chancellor turns to him. "Although we do not have evidence to expel you, we will still have to launch an investigation into you and your fraternity house regarding this serious incident. Until we have concluded beyond a shadow of a doubt that you haven't committed any crime of vandalism, your house is shut down to all extracurricular activities, which includes parties."

Lucas jumps up from his seat. "*Come* on! That isn't fair. You're going to shut us down over their delusional story, without proof? The big end-of-semester party is coming up. You can't do that." He sounds like he's about to cry. *This* is what brings emotion out of him. How predictable.

"I can and I just did," she says, very matter-of-fact.

Defeat washes over him, and he turns around. He eyes us

as he walks back toward his chair. His mouth forms into a frown and I match his gesture.

"That's all," she says, dismissing us with her pseudo gavel.

Lucas slams the door on his way out.

———

If I am caught in any more mess, I will be expelled indefinitely. Scholarship gone down the drain. Shit, at this point, would that be so bad, to be expelled?

Mama would be mad, but maybe she'd get over it eventually. I think. I hope. This all is too much. I'm gone finish final exams, but after that . . . I don't know. I need the heat off me.

I whip out my laptop and send a message to Professor Daphne without even blinking.

> Professor Daphne,
>
> I'm sorry, but I prefer to not be named in this Lucas story. I also will not be moving forward with the interview. I apologize for wasting your time. Thank you for being so nice.
>
> Take care,
> Savannah

I dial Tasha and Benji on three-way and rehash the sordid story.

"You don't think Lucas set you up . . . do you?" Benji asks.

"I wouldn't put it past him." I fold my winter clothes and put them into my suitcase. I don't have to leave for break for another three days, but packing between studying is my procrastination technique. "The girl in the picture does look like me, but I never seen her before in my life."

"You're a persistent girl, I'll give you that," Tasha says. "I told you a long time ago, ain't no point in trying to go up against these folks."

I curl the side of my lip. "I just wanted to try and bring change to the campus."

"The only thing the people around here change are their checkbooks. Wooddale doesn't care about Black people," Tasha says. "You can tell the world that Lucas did x, y, and z, and they'll just say . . . what that white man tell you?"

Benji responds for me. " 'We're looking into it.' "

"Look what that did. Hell, did the president even say anything?" Tasha says. "She been mighty quiet this whole time in her li'l raggedy house, but I guess our lowly Black problems don't affect her."

"That doesn't matter. They don't matter. I care and that should be enough," I say.

I care. About the future Savannahs, Tashas, and Benjis that will have to walk this campus.

"I know you do, boo." Then her voice switches from soothing to stern. "But sometimes you have to accept defeat. We can't win against these white folks."

"I got half the mind not to come back after Christmas break," I say.

Mama will be pissed, but a pissed Mama is better than a pissed-off mob of white people.

"Dropping out is an option." Benji using his sarcastic voice. "Or you can stay in school and keep your head down."

No surprise that's what Benji recommends. Keeping my head down is what he wanted me to do all along.

"You already told Professor Daphne you ain't interviewing. So just let this shit go." Tasha adds to the pile-on. "Savannah, you're going to do it big one day. Make your hood proud and all. You can't do that if you're hiding from the Cunninghams in the backwoods of Tennessee somewhere."

The thought to not make a fuss preys on me all the time. I can hold my head down and pretend like everyone else. Pretend that everything is okay. That Wooddale values diversity. I can . . . but I can't.

I can't stay silent at Wooddale knowing what I know.

"Are you going to tell your mom?" Benji asks.

I damn near choke on my spit. "I'd rather die than do that. What she doesn't know won't hurt her, and she doesn't need to know this. At least not now."

"I heard that. For all she knows, you living the college dream," Tasha says.

I lean my head against the wall and look over at my empty side of the room. "More like a nightmare."

No one tells you how different college will be from high

school. They hype you up about the live parties and the friends you'll meet. The best four years of your life, they say, loud and wrong. It's headaches, heartaches, depression, anxiety, and stress all rolled into a shiny fifty-thousand-a-year package. Big Mama always told me stories about how I come from a long line of Black folk that been making sweet lemonade out of moldy lemons since the beginning of time. I don't get why my lemonade still tastes sour, then. Why that power ain't flow through me.

Professor Daphne emails back immediately, super disappointed but understanding. I can't bring myself to reply to her. I feel bad, but what can I do? I'm hanging on to my spot at Wooddale by a thread, and even though I ain't sure I want to return next semester—I don't want Lucas to take that option away from me.

He won.

That's it.

TWENTY-EIGHT

What happened to this hashtag? No one has posted lately. #WooddaleConfessions

I think it was that freshman who was posting at first. We see how that went.

Fucked up what they did to her door. Nobody deserves that.

Dude, did you guys see that Lucas got brought in for that? The fraternity house is shut down until further notice.

Damn. No more parties for real? We have to take them underground or something.

I'm feeling it. Like they did during Prohibition.

Somebody's door got vandalized with a racial slur and that's all y'all care about? Seek help.

Here for a good time. Not a long time. Am I right?

No.

TWENTY-NINE

"Hey, baby," a man with a bald fade and iced-out grill yells from the passenger side of a beat-up Nissan. I pretend I don't hear him as I read over the grocery list for the fifth time.

Right after my last final, I was on a plane back to Memphis. I dipped out as soon as I could. Now here I am at home and I can't tell anyone the truth about what's bothering me. That I ain't even sure I'm going back to that damn school.

The smell of stale cigarettes and BBQ fills the air. Mama put me to work as soon as I stepped off the plane. First it's groceries and then the laundromat. Tomorrow we'll sit around the table and pick greens for Christmas dinner.

I miss this avenue. Here I'm not Savannah, the angry Black girl. I'm not Savannah, Tasha's and Benji's freshman friend. I'm just Savannah, Freda's daughter. Although that isn't the best version of myself, it's the only version that I truly know, inside and out.

"Don't nobody want yo' uglass no way." The car speeds off, leaving marks in the middle of the street.

Well, *that* I ain't missed.

A Korean man greets me as I walk into the corner store. I wave to him behind the plastic barrier and peek down the narrow aisles. Light bread, Coke, and Budweiser scribbled down on the scrap piece of paper.

"Aye, where y'all light bread at?" I look over my left shoulder and yell to the clerk at the counter. He points to the back. I study the shelves and pick up the Wonder Bread. It'll be stale in two days.

A *ding* chimes on the door. My eyes move to the glass mirrors on the ceiling. Preparing myself for what happens next.

"Put your fuckin' hands up."

I drop the bread on the floor and the voice gets more intense. "Put your fucking hands up!"

"We have no money," the cashier blurts out, and I pray he has his hands in the air. My phone twitches in my hands, 911 staring back at me. I can't bring myself to hit the green button that will send the police speeding down the street. Calling for the police can end up with this guy dead over a petty theft. Lead to me laid in the street because they thought I was the culprit instead of the victim. I feel safer here on the floor.

"Don't lie to me. The entire hood come to dis store." I look around the shelf. A gun, or item that's the shape of a gun, hides in the robber's jacket pocket. I turn around and hold my hand over my mouth, my breathing so shallow I can't tell if I'm performing the natural function. The thief's face is a mystery. I don't even get a glimpse. The only thing I can make out is his Timberland boots.

The register opens and closes, and the clerk says, "No more."

"You better have more next time, muthafucka." The door chimes again.

I wait for the clerk to tell me that I can come out of hiding, and then I leave the squished bread on the tile floor and run as if the spirit of Flo-Jo possesses my out-of-shape body. My white tennis shoes click off the pavement. Oxygen ain't flowing right, but I keep running until the store a blur behind me. I stop a few streets ahead and pant against an abandoned phone booth with graffiti scribbled on the side.

My chest heaves as I rest.

"Savannah, is that you?" a voice calls out to me.

I turn my head and look up. "B'onca!"

Police sirens mixed with barking dogs ring in the background. I can't get my mouth open to answer her question. I could have died. A few hours at home, and I could have died.

"The corner store got robbed a few minutes ago." I gasp for the polluted air to fill my lungs.

B'onca acts like I said rainwater wet. "They get robbed every other day now. I don't know why they don't shut it down." That corner store is the only one that stands close enough to the projects for folks to walk to. I don't want it shut down. I don't know what I want. Feeling safe anywhere seems like a pipe dream.

"I was in there." I exhale. "I saw the whole thing." I wipe the sweat from my forehead.

"You gone be fine. Long as you don't snitch or nothing." She rests her hands on a swollen belly I didn't notice till now.

"You pregnant?" Disbelief drips off my tongue. She never mentioned a baby or that she even thought she might have been pregnant. That's what all those trips to the bathroom was about during class.

"Scooter trapped my ass." She sucks her teeth and adds, "You need a ride home?"

I nod.

"C'mon, sis, and calm down. It's only a robbery, and knowing the niggas around here, it was probably a fake gun." She rubs my back in small circles as we walk to her car across the street.

It sits low to the ground, and she grunts as she gets in. It takes me three tries to close the rusty door.

"Mama ain't tell me you were having a baby." I reach for the seat belt, but nothing there. This car not meant for grown-ups, let alone a baby, but I 'pose something better than nothing. B'onca looks different. I don't know if that's possible after three months, but she does. I don't know if it's because everything on her body spread out or it's something else.

"I didn't find out until a month ago. It was too late to do anything about it." She shrugs and puts the key into the ignition. It flutters at the first crank. The same with the second. The third time a success.

The car clanks as it rolls down Main Street. Nostalgia hits me as we pass all the spots of my childhood. There's the candy-lady house. She sold pickles for fifty cents and bags of hot chips for twenty. The tiny house now sits vacant with a FOR SALE sign out front. We stop at a red light beside the field we'd play hide-and-seek in. Now it got an orange fence up with a KEEP OUT sign attached to it.

I stare at B'onca's baby bump, which almost touches the steering wheel. "What about school?"

"What about it? I can't go to Wooddale with a baby on my hip. I'm sure that fancy school don't got day care. Rich teenagers don't keep their babies."

"Do you want to keep yours?" I ask.

"That don't matter now," B'onca says. "She'll be here soon."

I change the subject. "You got your test scores. How did you do?"

She looks over her shoulder. "It's in the yellow folder."

I reach in the back seat. Feeling past chip bags and old half-filled water bottles. "You need to clean out your car."

"Scooter was supposed to do it, but who knows when that'll be."

I hold my breath as I open the file. My exhale turns into a loud cheer. "You got a 1280. Damn, girl. You did it!"

"Yay . . . I did it."

"Wow, you'd think you got a 600 or something."

"None of it matters anymore. I put in my application like you said. Even if Mama did agree to take care of the baby while I went to school, it wouldn't be at Wooddale."

"That's not right. You know how many people on campus made less than you and still got in?"

Lucas's smug face appears in my mind's eye. He didn't even try as hard as B'onca. He didn't work for it, but he reaps all the rewards.

"They white," she says. "It's different for us. I'm not tripping about it, though. I got other things to worry about."

"You still should be proud of yourself," I say.

"Yeah, I'm proud," she says. "Now tell me, girl, how you liking it up there? Your mama brags about you whenever she comes to church. Let her tell it, you gone be the next Michelle Obama."

"Nah. I'd rather be here. Even with the robberies."

She pulls up to the projects we live in. Little kids play outside behind the black iron gates. I don't know if they're meant to keep us in or used as a reminder for the new folks to stay out. Mamas sit in front of their doors, watching to make sure their kids come back inside safe.

B'onca presses down on the horn as a car jumps in front of us. "I don't know why you acting brand-new. Things like this happen all the time around here. People get killed, that's life. You dodge it and live another day."

My face falls. "Damn, B. That's kind of cold."

Color returns to her fingers as she loosens her grip on the wheel. "That's why I click with you, Savannah. You see life with rose-colored glasses. That's good when you live in a place like this. And then you saw a world away from this place and went for it."

"Shit, I ain't no better than nobody."

She lowers the radio that's now playing an old Christmas song. "If I hear 'be more like Savannah' one more time, I might apply for a community college or something."

"If that's what you want to do, you should," I say. "There are a lot of programs to help young mothers who want to continue school." Our community center hands out flyers all the time about expectant mothers and staying in school. B'onca and I always dodged them. We never thought we'd need them.

"I was going to, but I had to pick up extra shifts at work. Babies don't feed themselves. I can barely feed myself with what I make working at the grocery store."

"You mama not helping? What about Scooter? You putting him on child support, right?" The faint sound of "Santa Claus Go Straight to the Ghetto" hums in the background. This the first Christmas song I ever remember listening to. The same year I got my first bike for Christmas.

"I'm glad my mama ain't kick me out. Shoot, with my sister and her kids, the apartment at full capacity." She grazes her hand over her belly. "Scooter ain't got no real job. Putting him on child support wouldn't do nothing. He said he got me, though."

I don't know what to say to bring comfort to her. "I'm sorry, girl."

She forces a smile. "It ain't nothing to be sorry about," she says. "I'm going to have a baby and you're going to have a life."

I place my hand on top of her swollen stomach. There's a little flutter and then a powerful kick. "You gone shape one."

"I wish I could teach her more," she says. "I don't know anything outside of Memphis. Don't know anything outside of what my mama told me I was gone be. Look at me proving her right. You proving the hood wrong, you know."

Last time the hood got proved wrong was when I was a little girl. Jeremy Porter got accepted to Juilliard on a music scholarship. The smoky smell of BBQ and cookout tunes went on that whole weekend. His mama moved out and I never heard anything about his after-Memphis life. I wonder, what happened to the folks who made it out before I did?

"Look at me, girl." I grip B'onca's shoulder. "You're going to be fine. You hear me?"

B'onca nods, and I almost think she believes me. I get out the car and help her up from the low seat. "Thank you. It feels like this baby in my ass."

I don't want to burden B'onca with all my problems. She got one big problem attached to her front side and I don't want to add any more stress to her.

I imagine what life would be like if I gave up my scholarship. If the men in my life were only Scooters. If I come home and end up with my belly poked out. Worn out. Dreams ripped away and no hope of them returning. Babies don't eat college credit. Minimum-wage jobs don't care about how smart you are.

B'onca gone graduate top of her class like me, but she wasn't dealt the same hand.

I wonder what happened in that robber's life to make him steal. Did he graduate top of his class too? Did life deal him a bad hand and he just trying to feed himself? Did he give up a scholarship to one of the most prestigious universities in the country?

I don't want him to go to jail.

I want answers about his life. Still looking for the answers to mine.

THIRTY

I've been scrolling Booker T. Washington's social media news-feed all day. Their homecoming looks live. I practice the steps to sorority moves in the mirror and grin at the way they holler to each other with vigor in their voices each time "BTU" is called out. The fashion . . . If I go there, my fashion will be on ten. Mostly out of pressure, but oh well.

I pull down my baggy tee and take a sip of my warm tea. The images on Booker T. social-media pages make my heart race. Soft brown faces lit up with white smiles.

I don't belong at Wooddale.

I belong somewhere like Booker T.

My mind is made up. I set my phone on the desk.

I'm not returning to Wooddale.

I just have to get Mama onboard. She asks me every day if things are okay at school. I don't have the courage to tell her what's been happening. To her, Wooddale is an oasis and not my personal hell.

The front door creaks open. I straighten my room up some more. Not wanting to hear a lecture from Mama. Her footsteps stop outside my door, and without even a knock, she comes inside.

"I'm going to miss you when you leave tomorrow," Mama says, wrapping her slim arms around me. She looks worn out, her stockings have a run in them, and her pocketbook slumps over her shoulder. "Girl, I swear you're nothing but skin and bones. You ain't eating up there?" she asks, spinning me around to get a better look. Pinching the meaty skin on my cheeks and arms.

"I do. It's just they don't have a lot of options in the café, and most of the time I'm only eating ramen or whatever else I can find."

"Well, we're giving you a big feast before you leave. Big Mama is going to be over in a minute and we're going to make your favorite dinner."

I have to ease into it with Mama. She never was one for the Band-Aid approach.

"Mama, have you ever thought of starting over? Doing things differently with your life?"

"When I could even think about starting fresh, I already had you and a load of bills. The only thing I could even afford to start fresh was a new grocery list."

"But you still had dreams, right?"

"Well, of course I had dreams." Mama sits on the bed, pulling me onto her lap. I used to hate when she did that— always screamed out how I was too big and I was going to

218

break her. She'd laugh and say, "I birthed you, so you already done broke me once. Twice ain't gone kill me."

I don't fight it this time. After this semester, the comfort of my mama's arms the only place I want to be.

"I was going to be a dancer," she says, stroking my hair. "I had the moves, the body, and the grace. I was going to be the second coming of Debbie Allen."

I lean into Mama. She smells of peppermint candies. I love when she tells me of her past but also feel guilty. If it wasn't for me her life could have gone a different way.

"The morning I found out I was pregnant with you, I was at an audition to be in a traveling dance group for the summer. Your grandma didn't want me to go, but she said if I got accepted, she'd think about it. But during that audition I fainted, and the next thing I know I'm at the hospital and the doctor saying I'm three months pregnant."

"I'm sorry, Mama."

"Don't be sorry. You're the best thing that ever happened to me. I may not be the second coming of Debbie Allen, but I get to be the mother of an intelligent young lady." Mama kisses my cheek.

Tell her.

"Mama, I'm not going back to Wooddale this semester," I blurt out. It's too late to transfer for the spring semester, but I sent in my application to Booker T. Washington for fall ahead of time.

"Where you going, then? 'Cause it sure ain't back here. Ain't nothing here but crime and poverty." The excitement in her voice leaves. She forces me off her lap and stands over me. Her eyes aren't glowing anymore.

"I don't fit in there, Mama. I don't want no uppity corporate job that bad."

"You foolish. You have to work hard to get where you want to be. You want to be working two jobs? Cleaning other people shit for nine dollars an hour?" she asks, fully expecting an answer.

"I just don't see what's wrong with me going to the school that I want to go to."

Mama snaps. "I told you I ain't paying for you to go to Hilbert, Dilbert, Bilbert, or nowhere else that ain't Wooddale."

"If I got this scholarship, I can get another. The school I'm thinking about is majority Black and only forty miles from Wooddale. I bet it's just as good as Wooddale."

"Girl, you don't know that for sure. You're being too sensitive, Savannah. You think you can run from white folk your whole life. No matter where you go, you gotta deal with 'em. I don't think a school with a Black woman president can be that bad. If it's good enough for her, it's good enough for you."

A Black president I ain't seen or heard from the entire time, except for wack-ass mass emails and well wishes.

"But, Mama—"

She cuts me off before I can explain.

"*But Mama* my ass. I tell you what, Savannah. Leave Wooddale if you want to. You won't get the little support I'm able to give you now."

"What you mean?"

She rattles off. "Exactly what I said. Drop out and you gone pay your own way. Getting a full scholarship is not as common as you think it is."

"Mama . . . you can't do that."

"Watch me."

I blink away the tears that cloud my vision.

Mama stands there silent for several minutes, tapping her foot, huffing and puffing.

"Savannah, what's really going on? Why you want to leave your chance at an Ivy League education so damn bad?"

I look around my room, at the sheets used for curtains. The wallpaper that needed to be redone years ago. The shoes Mama got on damn near a historic relic.

This on my shoulders.

I'm stuck.

"Nothing, Mama. You right. Everything's cool. I'll go to Wooddale . . . make everyone proud of me."

THIRTY-ONE

The whole café gets quiet as soon as Tasha and I step foot inside. Faint sounds of a lawn mower roaring, then popping, backfiring outside.

"Something on my face?" Tasha asks. We ignore the stares and make our way to the register. She scoots in front of me, surveying the food line. "I want more than chips."

"I'll take some of these." I hand the cashier the yellow bag of chips. She smiles at me, something in her eyes that I can't place. Like she wants to say something but chooses to mind her business. Change jiggles in my pocket as I dig out my ID from deep down in my too-tight jeans.

Eyes roll at us as I struggle with my jeans and the cashier lady folds her arms. Lips snarl up like they smell something foul. Even the Black folk who wear matching purple-and-green sorority jackets give us the cold shoulder. One girl stares extra hard, but eventually looks away too. I finally swipe my card and take my chips.

"Damn, it's cold in here," I say. I don't know what these

people's problem is, but damn near everyone whispers as we walk past. I peer for a glimpse of a friendly face, maybe Benji, but no luck. People push past me; their accidental bumps seem on purpose.

Tasha grabs a tray, but by the look on her face, she isn't no closer to finding something she wants. I bury my fingers in the chip bag and offer her one. "We could get out this fishbowl a lot faster if you just settled for a potato chip or some noodles."

"Hangry is a *real* illness that affects millions of people." She turns up her nose. "If we gone keep doing all this home-work, I gotta eat."

"Suit yourself." I take a salty nibble, eyeing the room, and spot Meggie. She quickly looks away and keeps walking. *What the?* I know she sees me. Tasha moves through the line and I catch up to Meggie's green backpack covered in comic pins.

"Um . . . hello?"

She spins around, looking like a deer caught in the head-lights. "O-oh hey, welcome back. . . . I didn't even see you there."

I roll my eyes at the blatant lie. If anyone knows why we are being shunned, Meggie does. She pops up at every social event, her nose on the periphery of every popular clique. Her trailer-trash secret still kept locked in my pocket. I ain't even told Tasha.

"Meggie, why everyone tripping?"

Tasha joins my side, a tray of mac and cheese with green stuff in it in her hands. "Yeah, what we do?"

Meggie lifts her collar over her mouth and whispers, "You're the plague around here."

"Plague? This the Book of Moses?" Tasha glares at Meggie.

"No, this is the Book of Wooddale, and Lucas Cunningham is their god." Meggie pulls a rolled newspaper from under her arm and hands it to Tasha and me. "I guess you haven't seen this."

There, big as day, is my mug, next to Tasha and Benji, with a big-ass headline:

GAMMA FRATERNITY TEMPORARILY SUSPENDED AFTER HATE-CRIME INVESTIGATION

"They pissed about our trauma?"

"They're mad about the outcome," Meggie says. "The fraternity house is shut down. Plus, that thing with the basketball player."

"Jacob is his name. And even still, what he did wasn't our fault," I say. "What do they expect us to do? Don't say anything when we targeted, like good little Negroes?" Truth be told, I can't believe Meggie ran this article. She the head editor, ain't she?

Meggie shrugs. "Personally, I'm on your side. These people have the brain size of a rabbit. Lie low. In time, this will all blow over."

"You think so?" Tasha asks, picking the green stuff out her mac and cheese.

Meggie shrugs again. "I hope so. I'll see you around, Savannah."

Damn, that's shady.

I nod. She throws up her pink hoodie and leaves.

"Ain't this 'bout a bitch." Tasha slumps over. "I don't like half these fools, but being shunned a whole 'nother ballpark. I'm not even the one who snitched on Lucas."

"First of all, I didn't snitch. I let the dean know there's a racist on campus. *They* decided to have that pointless mandatory forum and open the investigation."

"Still, why am I out in the cold?"

"You my friend, right?"

Tasha stops and pretends to think about it.

"Girl, forget you."

"I'm playing. Yes, I'm your friend." She grabs my free hand as we walk the maze of the cafeteria. I avoid eye contact and keep my gaze glued to the back of Tasha's curly hair.

"Some people don't know how to sit down and shut up," a low voice says. Chairs scrape the floor as people scoot far away from us as we settle at a table.

"Girl, these folks act like Lucas's parties were hosted by Drake or somebody." Tasha picks at a piece of "fried" chicken on her plate.

"You talking to us?" the sorority leader at the far end of the table asks.

Tasha shifts the bougie from her usual voice and speaks like she got some straight Memphis in her. "I ain't talking to myself. We don't want to sit at your funky table no way."

"Good, we didn't invite you." Sorority girl flips her hair over her shoulder and Tasha stands up fast, like she 'bout to go off, and I reach to stop her.

"Why are y'all even here?" the sorority girl asks. "No one wants you here. Especially you, Savannah. Since you've been on campus, all you've done is cause trouble."

"You don't have this energy for a literal racist that you have for me," I shoot back.

"Think about that," Tasha adds.

"You making it seem like we all angry, all the time, and I personally am *not*." Her sorors nod along in agreement.

"You *need* to get angry," I say.

"No, you *need* to get lost," she says. "Then we can go back to how things were."

"What? Ignoring the fact that Lucas don't like Black people unless they bow down to him?" Tasha says. "Remember, I was here last year. I know all you frat and sorority folks stick together, but it ain't worth it."

"You just need to get your freshman friend to fall in line."

"Don't worry about me," I say. "I never stay anywhere I'm not wanted. Matter fact, let's just leave." We both stand, giving the sorority girls one last look before exiting.

Tasha dumps her tray. "Rosa Parks didn't fight for us to be treated like this."

"This how they acting now. Wait till the truth comes out."

We leave the cafeteria and skirt past the courtyard and into Jester Hall, Benji's dorm.

"What are we doing over here?" Tasha asks.

"You heard them," I say. "They don't want me here and I'm not staying."

"Not staying where? The café? I mean, the food trash, so I agree. We can find somewhere else to eat from now on."

"No, I mean I'm leaving campus. The dorms at least. Tasha, I can't do this another semester. Now that basically everyone is against me, it's like what's the point of staying here? To be an outcast? Bullied? At least in class I have the professors as a buffer. In the dorms and everywhere else, I'm exposed. A target."

"You gone leave me here to deal with it?"

The sadness in Tasha's eyes makes my stomach drop, but I have to do this. For me. "Maybe you can come with me."

"Nah, I know wherever will be far and I can't be taking the bus on the regular."

"Tasha, you from Chicago, how you don't like public transportation?"

"Exactly. If I never gotta take a bus or train again, it'll be too soon. People don't wash they hands, you know. Where you planning on going anyway?" She points to the signs that cover the hall. "Every building on campus is full. Even the off-campus apartments have a waiting list."

Words stick in my throat, but I force them out. "I—I

know. That's why I'm here. Maybe Benji can find me a place to stay. He's from this town and he has connections."

"I'm glad y'all are friends again."

"He apologized *and* he letting me make my own decisions regarding Lucas," I say. "That's all I ever wanted from him."

On Benji's floor, we slip past the upperclassman rooms. A mix of country music and stale French fries hangs in the air.

"What about Meggie?" she asks. "She can't help you?"

"Judging by the shade she just threw me in the cafeteria . . . I'm not so sure anymore."

We stop at Benji's door; brass numbers 173 glint in the overhead lights. As I begin to knock, the door creaks open, light from his desk lamp illuminating his neatly made bed.

"Benji?" I push it open a little wider. "Benji, you in here?"

"He's such a man," Tasha says as we enter the room. "Never locks his door."

"He must still be in class. I'ma leave him a note and shoot a text." I pull a piece of paper from my pocket.

"I still say give him a chance at love. Especially if he comes through for you on this." Tasha folds her arms across her chest. "I'm the head stan of Savji." She studies the piece of paper I scribble on.

"Savji! Bennah is better." I shove her shoulder, laughing. "Give me a second." I search through his desk for a pen. BSU buttons are piled in one corner next to old tests and Fortune 500 business cards gifted to him from his parents. Below that, something shiny that's clipped on an envelope catches my eye.

A picture.

I lean in. Benji is standing on a large white boat, like the kind in those rap music videos, with his parents on one side. A familiar rich snob is hugged into his other side—Lucas.

Two older people with that same stink of uppity lean on Lucas's shoulders.

I turn the picture over.

January 2

Everything's fuzzy and I steady myself on his desk. This too much. This can't be what it looks like. Lucas's and Benji's parents are friends? They are still friends.

"Now, it don't take that long to find a pen. Stop all that snooping." Tasha's breath is hot on my ear as she looks over my shoulder. Her eyes settle on the photo of Benji and Lucas and her mouth falls open.

"I know damn well that is *not* . . ." She snatches up the picture, blinking, like maybe if she blinks enough it'll go away.

My hands shake as my mind dances around something I'm not trying to see. "This was taken two weeks ago."

Benji never told me much about his life pre-Wooddale. I don't really know him as well as I thought, I guess. I started to think maybe at the core Benji was like me and Tasha. That picture reminds me he isn't like us at all.

I take the picture from Tasha, her jaw still wide open.

"They seem *real* close," I say.

"There's got to be an explanation for this," Tasha says.

"I mean, sure, but he got *real* defensive when I told him that Lucas cheated his way in and I was going to expose it."

"Hold up, you don't actually think Benji would do something like that? Buy his way in?"

"Tasha, you haven't met his parents. They have the money and the means." A few beats pass in silence. "And friends that get down like that."

My mind races a mile a minute. I don't know what to think or believe.

"You tripping. I've been in a few classes with him. He's smart as hell."

"And anyone can pretend to be smart. Lucas is good at that."

"How about before you go jumping to conclusions you talk to him? We can stand here all day long saying what-ifs," Tasha reminds me.

If Benji's parents did buy his way in and Lucas is outed, that means Benji and his family could go down too. My head throbs. Justice worse than a headache. It's a migraine. "What I'm supposed to do? Professor Daphne already knows something's up."

I feel sick.

"Just ask him," Tasha says. "If he doesn't have anything to hide, he'll have no trouble telling you what's good." Tasha always comes through with the practical advice when I let my mind jump to conclusions.

She right. I'ma just ask. That's what I'll do.

"Now put the picture back and let's leave before he comes home and you gotta explain how you're a snoopy."

I tuck the picture just as I found it. Only a piece of Benji smiling toward Lucas is visible. Benji and Lucas only commonality is money, but Benji wouldn't do something like this. He just wouldn't.

THIRTY-TWO

Benji texted me back as soon as I left his room. I explained to him my situation before I found the picture. His smile still haunts me, but I need him. He's the only person I can think of that can come up with a solution for my housing problem.

My phone vibrates. A picture of Benji and me covers the screen. I hit the green talk button and hold my breath. I can't take any more bad news.

"Hey, I found someone to take you in," he says.

"Who you find that quick?" I hold the phone between my shoulder and ear and toss my clothes into a black gallon-sized trash bag. My two suitcases are at capacity.

"Mrs. Flowers. You met her at the gala, remember?"

I search my memories. "The short older lady?"

"That's her. She used to babysit me back in the day. Her kids are all grown and out of the house. My mom said she's been lonely, so this would be a good arrangement for her, too."

I guess my silence goes on for too long.

"Are you interested?"

"Yes, I can't be choosy, since my only other options are stay here with these people trying to force me out or be homeless."

"You know I wouldn't let you sleep in a homeless shelter. You're going to be all right, Savannah. I got you." He doesn't wait for a response before hanging up. I dial Tasha. She's at her LSAT tutoring session but answers first ring.

"Did you ask him about the picture?" Tasha asks me in a whisper.

"Not yet." I fold my sheets in a ball. "How do I even bring it up?"

" 'Did you buy your way into school like your white friend did?' sounds good to me," she says.

"I'll figure it out," I say. "I gotta have faith that he didn't do this. That Benji ain't like Lucas."

"Do you think this lady is going to let you stay for three years, or . . . ?"

"I don't know anything about this woman. How long she expects me to stay . . . All I know is she's rich with space. She did seem nice when I met her, though."

"If she is rich, I assume she doesn't expect you to chip in on anything. Send me some pictures of her house and the address just in case she is an ax murderer."

"Tasha!" That's the last thing I want to think about. Being chopped up into pieces by an elderly woman.

"What? You never know, shoot. Everyone is a suspect."

"All right, I'm through with you. You need to stop watching them serial-killer documentaries."

"They keep me entertained."

"You a fool. I'll see you soon." I hang up to kissy noises on the phone when my email dings. Another email from Professor Daphne. *Sigh.* I haven't responded since last semester when I opted out of doing the interview. I need to keep my head down. . . . Get this degree. Make Mama proud. Give us a better life. I swipe left and archive her email without reading it.

Sorry, Professor Daphne.

Lucas wins.

———

Benji shows up in the early evening in his white Range Rover with windows so tinted that I only see my reflection staring back at me. His dad bought it for him for his high school graduation, but Benji decked it out with his own money.

"Ready to meet your new roommate?" He gets into the car, flicking nonexistent dust off his steering wheel. He buckles his seat belt while staring at mine. He won't move the car an inch if I'm not buckled.

"Let's get out of here."

We ride along in silence for the most part. Benji plays the oldies station for me to relax my mind. He points out the expensive, fly cars that pass by. I comment on how I'll never be able to afford them.

You have to ask him.

Nina Simone's soulful voice plays. She sings about the things she doesn't have: a home, money, shoes, a god, culture.

"This song deep." Benji taps his hand on his knee to the rhythm.

"Ain't it? She recorded this song in 1968. I'll send you the YouTube video of her singing. It's hauntingly beautiful."

"Are you the old-school-music thesaurus?"

"The perks of being babysat by my big mama every weekend." Mama worked seven days a week most of the time before she got that nine-to-five job at the tax agency.

"It's blowing my mind that a Black woman sang this song in the 1960s."

"Nina deserves all the respect in the world. She wanted to be a classical pianist, but in the fifties that was unheard of for a Black woman."

"Damn," he replies. "What have I got?" Benji sings along, off-key. "Yeaaah . . . nobody can take away?"

"What you know about this song?"

"You not the only one who know old-school things, you know."

Nina Simone asks what she even have. I soak up her response. She got her: smile, head, nose, boobies, hair, life . . .

"Got my heart, got my soul, got my back . . ." The lyrics fill the car and I let my head settle on the headrest.

The lyrics make me want to take a stand and fill me with this lingering hope that maybe things ain't too bad. I may have lost myself at Wooddale in the beginning, but I've found myself again, deep inside.

Me.

Tucked away, but still whole. Still . . . *enough.*

I turn the volume louder, and Nina's singing voice blares over honking horns and screeching tires, singing 'bout all the things she *does* have. I sink into the leather seat and let the words wash over me. All this on my shoulders: the stress, the worries, the fear. But I got stuff to be grateful for too. Stuff nobody can take away, like Nina sings.

Life.

I got life.

I squeeze my eyes together and try to be grateful. I'm still here on earth, and that has to count for something. I can't get down with Nina's optimism though, and I switch the song to rap.

Benji doesn't care for the song and changes it to some music without words. "Don't you know not to touch a Black person's stereo?"

"I ain't never heard no Black person listen to this."

"Miss Savannah, Black folk created classical music."

I laugh and lean into the headrest. "Is that right?"

"Classical, jazz, rock and roll . . . all that."

"All right. I'll listen to this one song." I pretend to doze off. "If I don't fall aslee—"

He thumps me on the shoulder. "For real, though. How are you feeling about this whole thing?"

I sigh, long and low. "Like someone shot a hole in my chest."

Time passes and we talk about random things. It's like old times. He's being corny and I can't help but laugh. Right as I fix my mouth to ask Benji the hard question, I notice how the neighborhood changes. How far away we are from campus. At least forty-five minutes on the bus and that's on a good day, but I can't worry about that now. I'm just happy to be away.

As we get closer to our destination, the grass gets greener. The houses stand taller and wider. The neighborhood around Wooddale is rich, but this is a different ballpark. This area wealthy.

Women in athleisure run aside their fluffy dogs. Elderly couples walk hand in hand on their nightly after-dinner strolls. They look like they don't have any worries. All their problems end at five p.m., when they settle in for dinner with their families. Going on about their day at the firm, how Paula didn't show up for the PTA meeting, and how little Jimmy won the school science fair.

Why don't none of my problems end at five p.m.? They seem to work overtime.

"Don't be intimidated by the houses. Mrs. Flowers is loaded. But she's down-to-earth. She's from the South too—Texas, I believe—so you guys have that in common." Benji whips the Range into the circular driveway.

I let down my window to get a better view. The grass trimmed with rows of picture-perfect rosebushes. I take a deep breath. Wealthy folks' neighborhoods smell sweet, like apple pies baking in the summertime. Benji comes around to open my door and takes my hand like a chauffeur to help me out of the Range.

Mrs. Flowers still has her Christmas lights up. They reflect off the cream-colored brick. Benji sets my bags off to the side as he rings the doorbell. It's one of those newer video camera models. I wait on the doorstep as he gets more of my things out of the car. I ring again and quickly shove my hands into my pockets.

"Hold your horses. . . . I'm coming," a brash voice says behind the door before the wooden barrier swings open. "May I help you?" The familiar woman reveals herself. I have to look down to get a better glimpse of her. She looks different from the scholarship dinner. Her voluminous voice doesn't match her small stature. Her skin is brown and smooth, with few wrinkles. Her hair is a lustrous gray and sits in a low pony that hangs to her waist. She doesn't look a day over sixty-five.

As the old saying goes, Black don't crack, and brown don't frown.

"I met you at the gala." I extend my hand for a proper greeting. She ignores my gesture and closes her gray wool housecoat tighter around her slim figure. It seems that after years of living on the East Coast, her Southern hospitality is a little rusty.

"Is that supposed to mean something to me?"

Benji didn't tell her I was coming . . . *today*? Or maybe her old age makes her forgetful.

"I'm your new houseguest, Savannah. The one Mr. and Mrs. Harrington sent over. . . ." I rub my hands together. The heat flowing from the small gap entices me to come inside. "We met at the Wooddale scholarship dinner."

Her eyes widen like a light bulb went off in her head. "Oh yes! Forgive me, child." She steps to the side. "Come on in, baby. I'm not as sharp as I used to be. Mrs. Harrington did call and tell me all about you. Where's Benjamin?" She squints into the darkness.

"It's okay. I forget things all the time. Benji is here. He's getting the rest of my stuff." I step inside the decked-out mansion. The pictures on the wall range from old-fashioned portraits to modern-day Black art. The grand staircase reminds me of my favorite old problematic movie: *Gone with the Wind*.

"Your house is gorgeous. You can take five . . . no, ten of my apartments and fit it into your foyer alone." I graze the staircase banister with my fingertips, feeling like a Black Scarlett O'Hara.

"Thank you, dear. My husband—God rest his soul—and I owned a few cleaning businesses that did very well. We were one of the first Black families to integrate this neighborhood." Mrs. Flowers waves Benji inside. "Come on in here and give me a hug. I ain't seen you in a month of Sundays."

Benji drops my trash bags before he gives Mrs. Flowers a bear hug and lifts her off her feet.

"It has been a while, hasn't it? You're looking great. My mother says you started another charity organization."

"Yes, yes. Got to keep myself busy and out of this old house. Feels like I might get lost in here sometimes." She gazes over the room, studying the past fifty years of her life. "What's that there?" She shifts her attention to the trash bags.

"Those are my clothes and things."

"Oh." She frowns. The trash bags stand out against the elegant furnishings.

"I'll put these in the guest room," Benji says, lifting the bags.

"Do you remember where it is?"

"Yes, ma'am," he says as he starts up the wide stairs.

"Izola, Izola Flowers. Nice to see you again, dear." She finally reciprocates my handshake.

"Nice to see you again, ma'am."

"I hear you're from Tennessee."

I nod.

"I have many cousins there. They are probably all dead by now, though. I don't keep up with them that much."

"My condolences. And you're from Texas, right?" I'm distracted by all the paintings and statues.

"Yes, I moved here when I was twenty-five. I used to visit every year just to have some decent barbecue, before my knee started to give me problems."

I notice her tribal-decorated cane that sits next to the door.

"Benji is your boyfriend?" she asks.

As soon as she speaks his name, he resurfaces at the top of the stairs.

"No, we're just friends," I say.

Friends with a huge secret between them.

"Mm-hmm." She ain't believe me.

"You guys down here talking about me?" Benji asks, retrieving the last of my things.

"Boy, nobody talking about you," Mrs. Flowers snaps back. She sassy, so comfortable in her skin, just being who she is, and I love it. "Now take the rest of them here things."

He smiles as he walks up the staircase again.

"He's going to be something in life," Mrs. Flowers whispers to me. "And I can tell, you got his nose wide open."

"You think so?"

"I know so, dear. You don't become my age without having learned something about the matters of the heart."

"You have a great collection of books." I admire her bookcase that's filled from top to bottom. "I see you have *A Raisin in the Sun*. We had to read that in my African American literature class."

"Thank you. That copy is signed. One of my most prized possessions."

I run my fingers along the spine. This house is full of history, I can tell.

"I want you to make yourself at home here. I don't have

much company, but on Tuesdays I have a few friends over for spades. You're invited, if you like. My friends won't mind an extra person, especially a young person."

Benji returns. "That's everything."

"Excuse us a minute if you don't mind, Mrs. Flowers." I pull him outside, out of Mrs. Flowers's earshot. "Thank you again. You didn't have to do this, especially since we haven't been talking like that."

"I'm glad I could help, Savannah. I've been meaning—"

"I saw the picture of you and Lucas on a boat with his parents," I blurt out. The word vomit offers relief to the sickness that's been brewing inside me.

"What? How?" he stammers. "You been snooping in my room?"

"Tasha and I were looking for a pen . . . ," I say. "A-and that don't matter. You lied to me!"

"I didn't lie." He keeps looking everywhere but my eyes, like he's going over every possible scenario. Thinking what will happen if he confirms everything that I already know. That he and Lucas's family got more in common than he wants to admit.

"I appreciate you doing this, Benji, but we can't be friends. Not when you are lying to me." The words hurt to say. I truly do . . . did think of Benji as a friend. Mama said men's true characters come out eventually. Women just don't open their eyes long enough to see it.

242

"Let me explain the whole thing." Benji studies his feet. "We aren't friends, but we are *kinda* cousins."

For a second I forget how to swallow. Words are trapped in my throat, and it takes a minute to get them out. "Cousins! You're cousins?"

He nods. "I said kind of. Not blood related, but his dad and my dad have been friends since elementary school. It's not like I could tell my parents that I didn't want to go to their family events because Lucas racist. That I think someone I bathed with as a toddler is a racist."

"You could have said exactly that," I say.

"We already have enough awkwardness at Christmas without me making it worse."

"Lucas never said anything about you two being 'cousins.'"

You'd think he'd bring it up constantly. Just to get under my skin.

"He only acknowledges me when he wants to get something from me or to blackmail me, as you can see. We ain't been close in years. That isn't a lie. I swear on my life we haven't."

"I don't even know if I can believe you. Lucas is not only your ex-friend but technically a whole family member."

"You have to believe me. I'd never be hanging out with Lucas of my own volition. Especially after what he did to you."

I'm silent.

He is too. For several minutes we just look at each other.

"I need time," I say.

"I'll give you all the time you need."

"Try," I say. "I ain't making no promises. I gotta be able to trust you, and right now, I don't."

He nods, smiling sadly, and I resist the urge to cry right there. Benji says his goodbyes to Mrs. Flowers, and she and I watch from the porch as he gets in his car, beeps the horn, and drives away.

THIRTY-THREE

"Savannah, you have company," Mrs. Flowers says as Tasha enters my new room. It's Mrs. Flowers's daughter's old room. Everything just like she left it in the nineties. We went and got new queen-sized bedsheets, but other than that, it looks like it's straight out of an old hip-hop magazine or something.

"Savannah, I can't believe it," Tasha pants.

"You over there sounding like Benji," I say. "What's up?"

She leans on the computer chair and says between breaths, "I guess you ain't heard the news."

"I don't want to hear any more bad news."

That seems to be the only thing that comes my way these days. If I hear any more bad news I just might explode. That's why I like it here at Mrs. Flowers's house. It's a bubble away from campus and gossip. Which I hear less of now that I'm barely there. Here I'm out the way, and that's how I like it. I don't know how long I can stay this way, but this week has been wonderful.

"This good news." Her breathing returns to normal. "Great

news, actually. Lucas in a judicial meeting right now. He got caught cheating on his economics exam."

I sit up straight. Could this be it? "You lying."

She crosses her chest. "On God. Elaina was acting all dramatic on campus, trying to save face. Saying how Lucas doesn't need to cheat because he's so smart."

Smart enough not to get caught the first time. But not smart enough to not let it go to his head and get cocky.

"How long he been in the meeting?" I ask.

She checks the clock that hangs over the door. "He just went in when I left, and it took me forty-five minutes to get out here on the bus."

"Soon," we both say.

"You think we should call Meggie?" I ask. "I know she got some tea to spill."

"She was being shady as hell last time we saw her." Tasha plops down on the deflated beanbag chair.

"Right? I don't know anybody else to call, though. We might have to bite the bullet."

Meggie ain't on my side no more and that's clear as day. *However,* she doesn't know I think that, so she might give me the information I need.

Tasha points to the clear landline phone on the side table. "Use that. In case we have to slam the phone down on her."

"You're extra as hell." I dial the number on my cell phone. "It's ringing."

Meggie picks up. There is a collage of voices in the back and I can barely hear her. I press the receiver harder to my ear. "Meggie. Can you hear me? Hello?"

"Who's this?" The sound scrambles in and out.

"Savannah." I pick up the bass in my voice. "I heard about Lucas. I wanted to see what was happening."

"A party." Her voice fades in and out. "A party is happening."

I cover the receiver with my hand. "She says a party is happening."

"The fraternity house got reopened and they are throwing a day party to celebrate," Meggie says. The sound is clearer now. She must have stepped outside.

I shake my head. "That doesn't make any sense. What about the judicial meeting?"

She sighs into the phone. "They found him not guilty, basically."

"Not guilty!"

Tasha throws her hands in the air. "He has to commit murder in order to get got."

"The adjunct professor who accused him of cheating on his test recanted. Didn't even show up for the hearing," Meggie says.

"That can't be. He can't keep getting away with this shit."

"It's not too late, Savannah," Meggie says. "You can still do the interview. Professor Santos hasn't gone to the president yet, but soon. With your testimony there is no way that Lucas will be allowed on campus anymore."

I'm the key to this whole thing. Once again the pressure is all on me.

"Meggie, what are you even doing at the party?"

She takes a beat to answer. "It's for research."

I hang up, slamming the phone down.

"It gets worse," Tasha says. "Look at the picture I just texted you."

I grab my cell. A flyer clear as day with Lucas's face on it. The frat house has been reopened, and the frat is going to be rewarded with the Student Services of the Year Award.

"They can't be serious," I say.

Pillar of the community. The fact that the frat house even reopened in the first place is a crime in itself. No one cares about us. About the hatred Lucas stands for. They swept it under the rug. Lucas has to be called out. If not, then Wood-dale will keep producing more Lucases. Who in return will produce more hate. A never-ending cycle that deserves to have some light shined on it.

I tap the envelope icon on my cell and scroll through my old emails.

I need to put my big-girl panties on. If it's a mistake, then . . . oh well. I have to make mistakes to learn. But most importantly, I have to be true to what I think is right . . . not Mama, not Tasha, not Benji.

Me.

Dear Professor Daphne,

If you're still available, I would love to sit and talk with you about Lucas Cunningham. I'm available Mondays and Saturdays after 5 p.m. Looking forward to hearing back.

Best,
Savannah F. Howard

THIRTY-FOUR

Tasha and I came to the grand opening of a new pub near campus to relax, but that doesn't seem possible.

Lucas, Elaina, and Meggie walk in. All three giggling together like they have no care in the world.

I'm angry.

Angry that I trusted Meggie. Angry that I let her into my life. Angry that they get to have joy and I don't. That they get to be normal kids and I don't.

I'm tucked away in the corner booth. They don't see me, but I see them. Tasha walks over with a basket of buffalo wings and a light beer in hand. The light beer on account of her fake ID.

"Who peed in your cornflakes?" She sets the basket of food down, but I keep my eyes ahead.

"Look who walked in," I say. "Meggie. I can't believe she would do this to me."

I should have listened to Tasha from the beginning. The whole time Meggie probably was laughing at me with them for trusting her.

Tasha turns and follows my gaze. "Do you want to leave? We can go to the bar a few blocks up."

They sit down at their table and now's my chance.

"No, they are not about to run us out of here." I march over to them.

"Savannah, where are you going?" Tasha shouts, three steps behind me.

"Hey," I say with a smile. "I haven't seen you three in a while. Especially you, Meggie. You haven't returned any of my calls."

Meggie won't even look me in the eyes. "I've been around, just busy with friends and school."

"I can see that," I say. "I didn't know you considered *them* friends."

She takes a large gulp of her drink.

"Hey, Vanna. It's nice to see you. . . . I hope you're not mad at me anymore," Elaina says. I can't tell if her eyes are open or closed.

I wave my hand in front of Elaina's face. "How high are you right now?"

"What?" She tries to stand up, but gravity pulls her down. "I'm not high. I had one beer, that's all."

"This is how you control her with your drugs. . . . She doesn't even know where she's at right now."

Her head slumps forward and then back. "I'm A-OK, Savannah. I promise."

I can't do anything but shake my head.

Lucas drapes his arm around Elaina. "You're here to congratulate me on my community service award, I'm assuming. I do a lot of good work here at Wooddale. It feels nice to be recognized."

"You wish. I'll be on Professor Daphne's radio show soon. Exposing you for the trash that you are."

"Savannah, keep the cards close to your chest," Tasha whispers in my ear. I can't keep this secret anymore, though. I'm tired of keeping secrets. Tiptoeing around. Lucas intimidates everyone else, but he's not going to make me scared. Not this time.

Meggie almost chokes on her French fries. "I thought you canceled that. Professor Daphne didn't tell me anything about you rescheduling."

"That's because I told her not to," I say. "But it's happening, and, Lucas, you better get ready."

"What is she talking about?" Elaina asks.

"Savannah still seems to think I'm the one who vandalized her door," he says. "And that pathetic professor is giving her a platform."

"I thought we had moved past that," Elaina says.

"That isn't all I'm going to expose," I boast.

Meggie picks at her cuticles and looks at me with pleading eyes. Meggie isn't on my side. She probably never was. A coward if I ever saw one.

I direct the fire in my eyes to Meggie. "I can't believe you dissed me for these rich snobs. All we did together, and you just gave up and came crawling back."

She shakes her head. "It's not like that, Savannah, and remember, you gave up first."

She's right. I cowered and let them win, but not anymore. I can't be like Meggie, running away when things get hard. Staying quiet because it's the easy thing to do.

"Don't forget to tune in," I say. "You're going to be the star of the show, Lucas."

"I won't miss the chance to hear you make a fool of yourself," Lucas says.

The waitress comes by with their food. As she sets it down, I knock it over onto Lucas's lap. The buffalo sauce stains his white collared shirt and olive-green pants. People let out audible gasps, pulling out their phones to capture the moment.

He jumps up as the hot food makes contact. "What the fuck!"

Elaina's bloodshot eyes bug out. "Don't move, baby. I'll clean you up."

"If this was where I am from, your shirt wouldn't be stained with finger foods—that'd be your blood."

"Ma'am, I'm going to have to ask you to leave." The waitress goes to the kitchen when she notices I don't move.

"I think you've forgotten you're not in the hood anymore." Lucas grabs a handful of napkins from the dispenser.

"You don't scare me, Lucas," I say. "Not anymore."

"Get your ass out of here." He steps to me and I can feel his breath on my forehead. I look up at him, staring into his cold dead eyes.

The waitress appears with the manager and he threatens to call the police if I don't leave.

"Come on, Savannah . . . we don't need the trouble," Tasha says.

She hands me my pocketbook as we leave the scene of the crime. I apologize to the workers for making a mess.

"People were recording. You already know how that script is going to go," I say.

" 'Angry Black Girl Attacks Innocent Bystander—Community in Shock.' " Tasha answers like a news reporter. "When you get all this spunk?" She hooks her arm into mine as we walk the curvy brick path back to her dorm.

I press my shoulder into hers. "Seeing Meggie there all buddy-buddy with them. It triggered something inside me. The whole time she was playing both sides, getting me riled up just to let me down. I can't be afraid anymore—being afraid is what they want me to be, and I refuse. Refuse to let them control me."

"That's my girl." She continues our strut. "Sounds like you're ready for next week."

"As ready as I'm ever going to be."

THIRTY-FIVE

"Hiding out again?" The librarian chuckles, setting down a stack of books in front of me.

"Just for a little bit. I'm done with classes for the day. Might as well get some reading in," I say, grabbing the top book on mass communication. This semester I'm taking my first journalism class. I want to be prepared. The library has become my chill spot, the only place people don't stare or point at me in pity. We're about a month into the semester, and I'm doing my thing . . . best I can, anyway.

"Where's your friend?" she asks, pushing in the chairs around the square table. "The one who always got something brand-new on? You two might as well have been joined at the hip last semester."

"She's at a tutoring session now. We're on two different schedules, plus I've been living off campus this semester, so I don't see her as much."

That might be our new normal. I should be getting my acceptance (or sorry-to-inform-you) letter from Booker T. any day now.

"That's a shame, but I'm sure you two will meet up soon." She waves goodbye and pushes a cart full of books between two shelves.

I grip the pen in my hand, my mouse hovering over junk mail and advertisements for overpriced shoes until I find the email thread I'm looking for.

> Savannah, I'm thrilled to hear from you. This is a confirmation for our meeting on February 20 at 8:30 p.m. I am looking forward to hearing what you have to say.
>
> Best,
> Daphne Santos

I check my watch.

Six o'clock.

Today.

This very evening, the truth will come out.

I sit in the dim corner going over notes. Notes about Lucas have become my life. I know more about him than about myself at this point.

I have all this information, but not one solid source. Not one person from the hashtag wants to come forward.

Tasha made a different choice and that's fine for her. I want to do this. Do what's right for me. I'm at Wooddale to make a change . . . but change not just about me, my degree.

Giving up isn't an option anymore.

The lights dim in the library, and I pack my backpack with my heavy books that wear me down. The sun dips on the buildings over Wooddale. I need to change my clothes before the interview. Time for me to haul ass, get off this campus. I speed up my pace and cut through the alleyway, the flickering streetlight and honking horns my only guidance to the street. I skirt down the shortcut, past the econ building, through another alleyway.

Giant black trash bags piled on the side of the business building come into view. The smell almost repulses me enough to go the other way. But the shortcut is a solid fifteen minutes faster.

The alley T-bones into a thoroughfare. But except for a few cars, the street is practically bare. A burgundy sedan slow-rolls to a stop sign and lets me cross, my shadow blocking the reflection of its headlights as I move past. Up on the sidewalk, the car's headlights dim again behind me like someone is following me.

A man is on my trail as the car vrooms by.

I walk faster.

But the figure gets closer, his face clearer. Something isn't right. Where I'm from, you know when someone has beef with you. It's in the way they walk toward you. Never letting they eyes off yours. The way their mouths melt down at you like you the vilest person they ever seen.

The bus stop a few blocks ahead. Almost to the main street where the traffic is . . . crowds . . . people . . . safety. Sweat breaks on my brow and I move faster.

Whispers at my back make the hair on my neck stand up. "Savannah, you can't run from me."

Faster, Savannah. I quicken the pace to an almost-run.

"We either talk now or we talk later, but we're going to talk."

Lucas?

Shit!

I cut a quick glance and a guy in ripped jeans and a charcoal tee meets my eyes. He's too tall to be Lucas. "Savannah . . . what's up? Let's chat." The dude in a black coat to his right snickers.

I bust into an all-out run.

"Oh, come on, baby. Don't run."

Everything is a blur. My bag slams into me every time my heels hit the ground. I dash across an intersection and I can hear their feet pounding. I don't look. I can't. It might slow me down. *Just run.* One more block. The intersection is so close I can taste it, when three more guys round the corner, walking toward me, malice written on their faces.

FUCK! My hands fumble for my phone clumsily. This damn backpack has too many pockets. I spin around to face these dudes. My bookbag slides down my arms and hits the ground with a thud.

This is an ambush.

I'm surrounded and ain't no one coming to save me. I square up, fist raised to guard the face. Five against one with nowhere to run.

"Listen, just let me go, all right?" I wrap my ponytail a little tighter. This the wrong time to have these long-ass box braids. I keep my eyes peeled, ignoring the weak feeling in my knees. I study their faces, memorizing every mole and freckle, hair placement, and lip size.

Silence.

The dude in the coat slips it off and rolls his shoulders like he 'bout to start swinging. *Protect the face.* I replay the jacking rules I know in my head, keeping my fists high.

If this what it's come down to, I'm not going out weak.

My feet bump my backpack on the ground, and I stumble, my phone flying from a pocket and across the pavement. My fingers twitch.

They circle me, but no one strikes. It's like cornering me is the mission Lucas gave them, but after that they ain't know what to do. Like they legit scared to step to me. I lurch forward and the ringleader jumps.

Wow.

I scoop up my bag off the pavement. This amateur hour, apparently. "When y'all get the frogs out your throat, come find me." I'm not gone let a pack of blonds in Keds intimidate me.

"Savannah." The group parts and Lucas walks into the middle. "I'm not here to hurt you. I can't believe that's what you think of me."

I scan for a weapon. A rock. A stick. Anything to protect myself. A dark metal rod the length of a bat, like a piece of scrap metal, glints at the corner of my eye.

"Then why you got five big-ass men cornering me?" I ask.

"Seems this is the only way I can get your attention," he says. "I didn't think you were serious about going on Daphne's show. A little birdie told me that's where you're headed."

"Would that little birdie be Meggie?"

"I won't reveal my source." He snaps his fingers and his crew comes in closer. "I thought we had an understanding, that we were both just trying to make our parents proud. That you wanted to keep your scholarship and be somebody, but no. Seems all you want to do is drag my name through the mud."

"I can't dirty up a name that's already filthy."

"Think of everything you're giving up."

"I don't want it," I say. "The degree. The prestige. If keeping quiet is what it takes, then they can keep it. It's no good for me anyway."

He shrugs. "Suit yourself. I'm not into violence, but my friends here can be." The group parts again and Lucas begins to walk away. Until someone pushes him back.

"The fuck is your problem?" Lucas stops his boys from pouncing as Benji comes into the light.

"You straight, Savannah?" Benji asks.

"He was going to have them jump me."

I keep my eye on the metal pole just in case. It's still a gang of them versus us.

Benji drops his books to the ground. "You want to fight? Fight me."

"I'm not going to fight you, man. We're family."

"That didn't stop you from writing *half breed* on my door. You are reminding me more and more just how different we are."

"No. You remind yourself of that. Everything was cool before we came here together. News flash. You just became Black. That whole BSU thing was for appearances and you know it."

"I been Black my whole life. You and the other people in my neighborhood just chose to ignore it."

"You made it loud and clear now." Lucas pokes Benji in the shoulder. "We all know what you are now."

Benji steps closer. His chest with Lucas's. "Say it, I dare you."

They stay that way, looking into each other's eyes as if they are trying to find something. The past maybe. How life was before Wooddale. Friendship.

Lucas steps back first. "Let's get out of here. Savannah, it was nice talking with you."

They all follow the leader back into the alleyway.

Benji makes sure Lucas is out of sight before wrapping me in his arms. "You all right? He ain't touch you, did he?"

I breathe in his outside smell. "No. You showed up right on time."

"Let me drive you home."

We separate, grab hands, and walk to Benji's Range.

THIRTY-SIX

I wake up to Benji's no-word music. I must have nodded off.

In minutes, we're nearing Mrs. Flowers's neighborhood.

"Are you coming in?" I ask.

"Do you want me to?"

"Yes."

He pulls up to the front door. I don't notice how much my hands shake until I'm at Mrs. Flowers's steps.

"Fuck." I can barely get the key in. Benji takes it from me and opens it within seconds. The door clicks shut behind us and I press back against it.

"I can't believe them." My words come out cracked, weak. "They were really going to hurt me. Words are one thing, but physical violence?"

Benji helps me to the kitchen table. He sits next to me and takes my hand in his. There're no words to say. Not at this point. We've been on this roller coaster for so long, getting off seems like a foreign concept.

Mrs. Flowers's cane taps against the linoleum floor.

"Savannah, I didn't know you were having company tonight. Hello, Benjamin."

"Good evening, Mrs. Flowers. I'm sorry for showing up without letting you know."

"These men . . . boys tried to jump me," I say. "Benji showed up and drove me home."

"Tried to jump you?" She sucks her teeth and stands straighter with her cane. "That school is becoming too much." She walks into the kitchen and comes out with a glass of water.

"Lucas was there. He made them do it. Wants me to be silent by any means necessary."

"They sound like their ancestors. Just nasty," she says. "I'm sorry this happened to you, baby. You want to press charges?"

"The cops won't do anything." They'd "see what they could do." That's all anyone in this town does: the bare minimum.

"How did you get yourself into this mess? So tangled up with Lucas that he wants to mess you up in this way."

"It's a long story." One that I didn't want to drag Mrs. Flowers into at first. Older people shouldn't have to be worried about stuff like this.

"I have time. When you get to be my age, you begin to use the time you have and not the time you think you have tomorrow."

She refills my glass of water before settling into the chair with an exhale. "All right, I'm listening."

I explain my story—everything . . . talk the longest about Lucas. And she listens intently. For several seconds after I finish, she taps the arm of her chair like she's choosing her words carefully. "Do your mother and father know what you've been going through?"

"I don't talk to my dad. He hasn't been the most instrumental person in my life. Haven't seen him since I was eight," I say. "I haven't told my mama, though. She thinks everything is perfect. I'm the golden child. The first one in college. The first one not to have any babies young. It's a lot of pressure, being the first."

"Parents sometimes don't realize the weight they put on their children. At the end of the day, it's *your* journey, Savannah. And deep down, you know what is right. I won't tell you what to do, but I'll tell you this: your decision is something you'll have to live with for the rest of your life. Nobody else has to live with your conscience. Only you." She wraps her bony hand around mine and squeezes. "So make the choice that's true to who you are, the woman you are—the person you choose to be."

My fingers drum on my phone. Who am I? Who do I want to be? Will I look back on this when I'm her age and be okay with letting Lucas get away with this?

Nah.

This the last time. The last time Lucas Cunningham is ever going to hurt me.

THIRTY-SEVEN

Tune in tonight to Professor Daphne Santos's radio show. It's time for Wooddale to be the one blown out of the water. #WooddaleConfessions

I'm there!

Bet we can listen in the common area tonight.

I got the popcorn and sodas.

Damn, what happened now? It's been nonstop drama all year.

This sounds like it's going to be the season finale.

THIRTY-EIGHT

"Hi, Savannah. This is Daphne's assistant. Just calling to confirm that the interview is on for this evening. Professor Santos is looking forward to meeting with you. . . ."

The voice mail plays in the background as Mrs. Flowers pins my hair into place.

"Call us if you have any questions. See you soon."

"You remember what to say? Yes, ma'am; no, ma'am. Make sure you enunciating your words. People don't like what they can't understand."

Mrs. Flowers is trying to teach me things, but to be honest, I'm not going in there twisting my words. I've had to fake it for far too long.

"They gone dislike me no matter what I sound like."

Mrs. Flowers lets out a deep sigh. "At least wear the navy suit I set out for you."

"Yes, ma'am," I mumble. The suit in question is Mrs. Flowers's daughter's old debate suit. Dignified, but not too bright and welcoming. What I wear doesn't matter anyway. It's radio and not television. I look like I work in HR and not like an eighteen-year-old from South Memphis. But I guess that's the look she was going for.

After I'm all dressed, I hear a honking outside. Mrs. Flowers starts fussing about manners, which means it's Benji.

He wants to make things right—well, this is a start.

I race down the stairs and out the door, Mrs. Flowers hobbling behind me. Benji drives us to the station. Mrs. Flowers complains the whole way, even though he's going thirty-five mph in a fifty zone. I pull down the mirror overhead and dab on more red lipstick. Mrs. Flowers catches my eye. "Less is more, dear," she says.

I pause mid-dab and stick the tube pack into my clutch bag.

My phone chimes. It's Tina. Jacob's girlfriend.

Tina: Good luck. We're all rooting for you here.

She must know people I don't. Or she just trying to make me feel better about the situation. Everyone on campus already made it clear who they rooting for.

"The BSU still has eyes and ears to the ground. We're going to find the guys that did this to you."

Benji may be a lot sometimes, and although I don't need him to, he always fighting for me.

"They probably long gone by now."

"Nah, someone is going to slip up and say something. Bragging like what they did was cool."

"Let's just focus on the interview for now. Something I can kind of control."

"You're going to do fine," Benji says as we get closer to our destination. "You know what you need to say." The wealthy suburbs slowly turn into a regular neighborhood. Everyone's grass isn't neatly trimmed; some garbage cans overflow.

"Right now, I know what I need to say. What about when she actually starts recording? What if I clam up?"

"We'll be right outside the glass." He squeezes my knee for reassurance. "Just look out and I'll bring you back." It works for a minute, but the bouncing starts up again as we park in front of the radio station. WFIA is the oldest radio station in town, according to Benji. Professor Daphne has had her show for fifteen years and even though radio is dead she still has a strong listenership.

Benji helps Mrs. Flowers out and then comes around to me.

"You're doing the right thing." He takes me by the hand before closing the car door. "I know I said before you shouldn't do this, but I was wrong. I was scared, but this is not about me right now."

He puts a yellow folder in my hands. "Take this. . . . Call it me making it up to you."

"Wh-what is it?"

"Just take a look. I'm proud of you and I'll be waiting outside when you're done."

I open the folder. "Ain't nothing in here."

"Look in the pockets," he says.

Paper fills my hands as I rustle inside the pockets. I pull up a handful of check stubs: receipts all made from Lucas Cunningham Sr. to various Wooddale officials, their names not redacted—not like the other files Meggie found.

"Those aren't all of them, but those are the ones I could get my hands on."

Helicopter rides. Sushi dinners. Boats. Limousine rides. Vacations. Receipts for them all.

"Benji . . . how . . . why?" I stammer. The words don't come out right, but the gratitude shows on my face.

"I wanted . . . needed to prove that I'm on your side." He hugs me, his lips grazing my cheek. "This was all I could get on such short notice, but it's more than enough for Professor Daphne to take to the president."

"Where did you even get these?"

"Kind of pays off being the cousin of a monster sometimes. I went snooping at Uncle Lou's house. Thankfully, old people keep carefully organized receipts to everything," he says. "I should have done it sooner, but it takes a lot of guts to be brave. I don't know how you do it all the time."

I thank him as a white guy in a turtleneck, not much older than us, meets us outside the studio. He shakes our hands and introduces himself as Miles, the producer of the show. "Your story, what happened to you—I mean, right in our own community. We can't let things like this go on."

"You're darn right," Mrs. Flowers agrees. She waves goodbye as Miles leads me away. Her and Benji will have to wait in the car. A space issue.

My nerves on one hundred. Without Benji and Mrs. Flowers, I'm truly alone.

Miles goes on and on about the details of the interview and how long I will have to talk. Radio is different from regular news. You can be more open and real, but in shorter time slots. We stop outside a door with a faded gold star on it.

Daphne Santos

The woman who will have the weight on my shoulders in her hands. Miles knocks once and then lets himself in. Professor Daphne stands there in ripped jeans and an off-the-shoulder sweatshirt. I suddenly feel overdressed.

"It's nice to see you, Savannah. Are you ready for this?"

Words are stuck in my throat. I should say more. I am going to be talking to Professor Daphne for the next thirty minutes. I try to form words, but nothing but an *ugh* comes out.

Professor Daphne notices. "You're going to do fine. It'll be over before you know it, and I've been told I'm a fine conversationalist."

"My tongue already tied," I say.

We walk inside the booth and it isn't anything fancy. High-tech boards and mics decorate the area. Two simple plastic

271

chairs where Professor Daphne and I sit in front of three large mics that hang from the computer monitor.

"After you." Professor Daphne gestures to the sitting area.

I sit first in the chair across from her. She pulls her chair in a little closer to me. She doesn't look me directly in my eyes, which makes me more comfortable. Less like I'm getting interrogated. Professor Daphne passes me a pair of chunky earphones, and within seconds, we start.

"All right now. I hope that Gil Scott-Heron track got you in the mood for some activism. Today I'm here with Savannah Howard, a freshman at Wooddale University. Thank you, Savannah, for sitting down with me."

She winks and mouths, *You're gonna do great.*

She turns to the mic. "Now, you may have seen or heard about a statue defaced on campus last fall by a well-known member of the community. Allegations against Lucas Cunningham, who you all may know as son of financier Lucas Cunningham Sr., were brought up. Savannah is here to tell her version of the story."

She covers the mic with her hand and presses a red button. "Deep breath. You ready?"

I exhale and nod.

"Can you tell me more about what occurred, how it all got started?"

"Well, after Lucas got word I was digging into his past and present, he spray-painted a racial slur on my door and left hateful messages for my friends, too."

"How do you know it was Lucas?"

"I ran into him in the staircase and his hands were covered with red paint. The same color that was on my door."

She nods and gives me a thumbs-up, so I clear my throat and continue.

"I went to the dean of students to report it. He blew me off, and I was then accused of vandalizing Lucas's car. I was told that if I was caught up in anything else, I would lose my scholarship."

"Do you believe this was all connected?"

"Lucas didn't want me digging into him, and the chancellor didn't want anyone making her or the school look bad."

Professor Daphne adjusts herself in her seat. "And when you say the school would look bad, I assume you mean because of the racism that happens on campus?"

"Yes, ma'am. Well, that's part of it. But for me, that's where all this started. There are little things that are always erased before people even have a chance to notice that they happened."

"Little things such as what?"

"For example, last year someone had a Wi-Fi network named KuKluxFan that was linked to Lucas's fraternity house."

"How do you believe microaggressions such as these affect you and other people of color on campus?"

I pause and think it over.

"It's tiring. Sometimes I'm exhausted just being on campus. It's like a full-time job. I have to explain myself constantly.

Being a Black person at Wooddale, it's like you're forced to shed the real you."

"In a statement released earlier in the year by the chancellor, after the Clive incident, she sincerely apologized and even stated that they were actively promoting change on campus. Did that give you peace?"

"It didn't give me a sense of anything. No one really showed up for the Talk Back forum, not even the chancellor. I went back home over Christmas break to get over the situation, but it never happened. Even at home, I felt fear that something like this would happen again. If not to me, then to someone else."

"I understand. This must have been so hard."

"It was . . . is. And so many people swallow the racism day in and day out just to get their degree. A-and I almost did too. B-but, Lucas's hatred for me . . . I just . . . I—I couldn't anymore. I mean, we've always butted heads, but then I found out about his parents. . . ."

Professor Daphne shushes her producer, who's encouraging her to wrap it up. "Go on, Savannah."

I take a *huge* breath. "Rich white students at Wooddale are often unfairly admitted, leaving no room for Black students who worked hard to get in." My foot bounces up and down like the Energizer Bunny.

Professor Daphne nods along. "Well, it is true. There are more white students at Wooddale than any other race."

"N-no . . . not like coincidence. I'm saying there is a buy-in.

Lucas Cunningham cheated his way in, and that's why he's attacking me. I have proof."

"Bear with me a moment, listeners. I'm going to open what looks like an envelope of records Savannah has given me." Professor Daphne opens the file and thumbs through the pages. Names, check stubs, receipts, and copies of thank-you notes. They're all there.

"There is also an email proving that someone took Lucas's SAT for him."

"Now, people, right now I'm staring at evidence that makes a convincing case that students are buying their way into Wooddale," she says. "I will do my part in making sure this information gets into the right hands."

Professor Daphne points at the timer and gives me a thumbs-up. "Savannah, I want to thank you again for being here today. Is there anything you would like to end with?"

I adjust the mic in front of me.

What I have to say last is the most important part.

People need to hear it and hear it well.

"I know most of you hate me right now, but put yourselves in my shoes. What would you do if it was your brother or sister or mother or best friend being cast aside and treated unfairly? If those people you loved earned a spot at Wooddale but were being pushed aside because their checkbook is not as big as someone else's? And if you did have a loved one or two get in, how would you handle it if they were received with hateful language, treated differently, reminded every day the school doesn't want them there—basically saying go home?" I lean into the mic. "Imagine wearing my shoes and try to tell me you wouldn't speak up too. It's time for Wooddale to wake up and make a change."

Professor Daphne flicks something from her cheek. "You heard it here first, folks. Savan—"

Professor Daphne's producer walks in and whispers in her ear. Her eyes light up like city lights. "Folks, now, hang tight—we have a caller who's willing to corroborate Savannah's story."

She presses a button on her keyboard. "Are you there, caller? Can you state your name for us?"

The caller clears her throat.

"Yes, ma'am, thank you. My name is Natasha Carmichael, and the same thing happened to me."

THIRTY-NINE

Tasha and I walk down Mrs. Flowers's street. Cherry ice pops that we made from scratch drip in our hands. People mow their lawns and wash their cars, enjoying the unusually warm weather for March.

We aren't welcome at Wooddale anymore. People move away from us like we smell. Sometimes the professors don't even speak to us. Ignore our hands when we want to ask questions.

But I still wouldn't do anything differently.

"Gimme some good news. News that'll make me forget that we are the lowest of low at Wooddale," I say.

"I got the internship this summer. Your girl will be rubbing shoulders with Capitol Hill folks."

I let out a loud shriek. "Tasha! What? When did this happen?"

"The day we went on air," she says. "I keep waiting for the other shoe to drop. For somebody to tell me it was a mistake."

"It *isn't* a mistake," I say. "You *earned* that spot. Basically lived in the library all year, and your recommendations were lit."

"We both know qualifications don't matter at these types of places."

"I'm still proud of you for speaking up about last year," I say. "You didn't have to do it, but you did."

"They threatened you with physical violence," she says. "It wasn't about me anymore. They weren't going to get away with hurting my best friend."

We throw our ice-pop sticks in the trash, then stop at a park bench.

"I have good news too," I say. "Or at least I think it's good news. I got into Booker T."

"You're leaving?"

Plans for next year bounce around my head. Of me, Tasha, and Benji taking the campus by storm. Stirring things up. I don't know where my wants begin and end. I can't have my cake and eat it too. Choosing is the hardest thing. I want to go to Booker T., but the thought of making another transition makes me think of missing late-night food runs with Tasha and impromptu study sessions with Benji. Being the *other* again, but just in a new setting.

The alternative is to stay at Wooddale. Be an outcast. End up with other slurs on my door. Like Tasha said before, there's always going to be a Lucas Cunningham on this campus.

"I think Wooddale already made the decision for me," I say.

Two weeks pass and there is still no word from the admissions office saying that an investigation is happening. All I get are threatening calls about a libel lawsuit. Lucas still slithers around campus with his head up his ass.

After I put my everything on the line, it seems like no one cares.

I did all this for no one to care. Sometimes I wish I would have stayed with Tasha. She wants me to come back, says it's better to face them head-on, but I'm the opposite. Living here at Mrs. Flowers's gives me strength to continue to fight.

My phone vibrates on the end table next to me. I catch it before it falls off the edge.

Tasha: Look at this link! You big time now.

I tap the link that opens to a social-media page of someone with tons of followers.

A clip of Tasha's and my voice from the interview plays over a video of protest signs, Clive, and a picture of my door with the dripping red paint.

Me: 500,000 people have watched!

This has to get Wooddale talking. Instead of the silence that haunts me.

I pull my laptop open and get comfy. Midterms will be upon us soon and I'm finishing this semester strong. A notification from my phone diverts my attention away from my art-history notes.

Hello, my sister,

You don't know me, but I've been following your #WooddaleConfessions posts for a while (I was not sure it was you in the beginning, but it increasingly became clear to me).

I listened to your interview about the injustices being brought down upon you at Wooddale and I want you to know you're not alone.

Our university was built on the backs of Black people, yet Black people weren't allowed to attend until 1950 and that was only on paper. And trust me, they weren't greeted with sweet potato pie and a Black history parade. Wooddale has been locking out and redlining deserving folks since the beginning. When they aren't redlining, they're making sure the little color that makes it on campus is still not welcomed with sweet potato pie.

Because of this I've gathered a group of Black students on our campus and our neighbor school

Booker T. Washington. We would like to come and
stand with you in solidarity and protest Wooddale,
if you are so inclined.

Eli

The post makes my face light up.

The DM sits on my phone for a few minutes before I respond. I type and delete my response. I do this three more
times before I gather the courage to hit send.

Hi Eli,
I'm down whenever you are.

The next five minutes are the longest. I can't think of art history, only of the art that was left on my door four months ago.

My phone chimes and I knock over a vase trying to
pick it up.

Tomorrow, Lucas is due to get his Services of the
Year award. We can protest on the street outside
the building.

I'd forgotten about Lucas's fraternity award. They'll have
a plaque that hangs in their house, and future frat members
will think that they're the most charitable people around. That
they don't paint slurs and only help old ladies cross the street.

Not on my watch.

Savannah: That sounds like a plan.

Eli: I'll see you tomorrow. When one of us bleeds, we all bleed, my sister.

Our conversation ends and I run down the stairs two at a time. Excitement fills my voice. "Mrs. Flowers."

"What, child? I'm in the kitchen. You finally finish that art-history paper? It's been two days. You should have finished by now."

"No, ma'am, but I did something better. I got people talking," I say as I enter the kitchen.

"Child, speak in sense. Not that dramatic buildup you be doing . . . and help me with this here food since you down here."

"The radio interview. It's gone viral," I say as I begin to drain the chicken grease into a tin can on the stove.

"Viral?" she asks. Sometimes I forget Mrs. Flowers ain't from the plugged-in generation. *Viral* to her might mean a disease.

"It means that a lot of people have heard it. Exposure is good. It means those assholes—"

"Watch your mouth," she warns.

"Sorry. I mean those higher-ups at school have no choice but to face the accusations. It means there's no reason people shouldn't be looking into the admission process at Wood-dale."

"Lemme see that." Mrs. Flowers stops cutting the yellow squash. I hold the phone for her as she reads over the message.

"You sho' right. You done started something now." She picks up the knife and resumes making dinner. "You leading this thing, right?"

"Yeah, with them."

"Be careful. A Black woman speaking up for herself always has a target on her back."

"I'll be careful," I reassure her.

I smash the sweet potatoes in a white cooking bowl, adding a dash of cinnamon, Mrs. Flowers's secret ingredient to a delicious sweet potato pie. We sing along to the Stevie Wonder song playing from the Alexa that her son sent her for Christmas. She hadn't known how to set it up, so it was just sitting around collecting dust. I filled a playlist with every blues, jazz, and Motown song I could think of. I want her to have some things from her youth.

And I added some jams from Nina, definitely Nina.

I'm floating until I think of Mama.

Oh shoot.

If this keeps getting shared, Mama bound to see it. She always hooked to her phone playing *Candy Crush* or whatever game is the wave at the moment. She should hear this from me and not just the internet version of myself.

"I need to make a phone call," I say to Mrs. Flowers, who's

kneading dough. She makes everything from scratch. It takes forever, but the results are amazing.

The phone rings three times. No one says hello from the other end, but I hear breathing.

"Hey, Mama," I say.

"Who's this?" she asks, like she hasn't heard my voice for the last almost eighteen years.

"Mama, stop playing." I sit on the chaise in the hallway that never seems to be used and turn on the decorative light. I been meaning to ask Mrs. Flowers why she has so many unnecessary pieces of furniture. Must be a rich-folks thing.

"Mm-hmm. Haven't heard from you in so long, I almost forgot I had a daughter."

"I'm sorry, Mama. I just been busy. It's so much work to do here. When I think I'm done, more comes."

"Well, that's what college is. Hard work, but you got it. To what do I owe the pleasure of hearing from you, my prodigal daughter?"

"I have something to tell you. Don't be mad at me. I think I'm handling it really well."

Mama pauses for a long while. "What have you done?"

I can hear my uncle asking for something in the background.

"Don't you see I'm on the phone?" Mama shoos him away. "Go 'head, Savannah."

I spill my secrets. "I—I left my dorm, but I found someone to stay with."

Mama doesn't say anything, and I can hardly breathe. I

keep talking, filling the silence with my overdue confession. "She's a lovely older lady from Texas. She reminds me of Big Mama."

Maybe if Mama knows Mrs. Flowers is sorta kinfolk, she'll take the news better.

"Little girl, what you mean you left the dorm? You mean I'm sending you money for food and things and you don't even need it?"

"I mean, I still need to eat," I mumble. "And there's something else."

"What else?" She waits. "Open your mouth and talk."

"They accused me of vandalizing property," I say, clearer this time. "They have no proof it was me, though, Mama. It ain't fair."

Mama sucks her teeth. "When did this happen?"

"Last semester. . . ."

"*Last semester,* and you're just now telling me?" I pull the phone away from my ear. Mama's voice rings out clearly. "Savannah, I swear fo' God. If you wasn't so far away, I'd be kicking your ass up and down the street."

Thank God for the distance.

"I know, Mama. I'm sorry."

"Sorry my ass. What did these people do to you that made you so mad you left your dorm?"

"I found out one of the students bought his way into college instead of earning a spot like me. And he ain't the only one. People just walk in the door without working for it, and that ain't fair for you, Mama. You know how hard you worked to get me in through the front door and they just waltzed in the back one."

Silence.

"Then that's not all. That same student racist, Mama. He wrote 'go home, nigga' on my door and harassed my friends. Cheated his way in. Got the whole campus thinking I'm the problem when it's him."

I close the gap between my phone and ear.

"Mama?" I ask, making sure she didn't have a heart attack or an aneurysm or some other massive medical emergency from my pile of confessions.

"He did *what*?" Her tone is low, sharp.

"No one cared, Mama. Well, until now. That's why I called. I went on a local radio show, and the clip . . . it's going viral. I didn't want you to see it and learn about it that way. I—I wanted to be the one to tell you."

"I'm so angry right now I don't know what to do, Savannah Freda Howard . . . but . . ." She sighs. "I'm also very proud of you."

I turn up the volume on my phone. Maybe I heard her wrong. "What did you say?"

"That I'm proud of you. For standing up for yourself. Standing up for what's right."

"Thank you, Mama."

"Don't make this a habit, though, of crusading against the folks on campus. You have three years left at that school."

"Maybe."

"What you mean 'maybe'? They ain't expelled you, have they?"

"No, Mama, but I don't think I want to come back next year. For real this time."

"Savannah, you can't let this run you away from that school. What I tell you before you left?"

I sigh and repeat the mantra. "That I got in fair and square and that I belong here."

"That's right. Now you just have to prove that they are the ones who don't deserve to be there. The bastards."

"Mama, I don't think I want to continue to study at a racist institution, though."

She sighs and rebuts. "Baby, I been trying to tell you . . . the entire world is a racist institution."

Preach.

We say our goodbyes and hang up. To know she's proud of me, even if I'm not doing what she set out for me to, is a push I need to raise my voice a little higher. Come a little harder. I'm Freda Howard's daughter, a woman who raised me when she was still growing herself. I have that strength inside me, inherited from her and her mother and her mother's mother.

I'm going to use it to stand up.

I scroll the comments on the social-media post.

People are calling Wooddale.

Leaving Dean William voice mails.

287

Donors, some white, some Black, are standing up on *our* behalf.

The administration still hasn't made a statement.

But tomorrow we're marching against injustice. They will hear us.

FORTY

Today is protest day and I'm on edge. More than on edge—
I'm dangling.

If everything goes well, Lucas will be the one kicked out
and Wooddale will be forced to pay attention. I'll take a
whimper over silence.

My phone chimes. Meggie's name flashes on my screen.
"What does she want?"

> Meggie: I'm sorry, I can't be there today,
> Savannah. It just became too much for me.
> I can't lose my scholarship. Good luck at your
> protest. You got guts.

"She got some nerve," I say.

"Who are you talking to?"

I read the text message to Mrs. Flowers. "She hasn't been
around for months, and that's all she has to say. Can't even
apologize in person for being a coward."

Meggie got this ball rolling. She got me the information. Put my head into all this and then dipped. A very roundabout way to prove she was never down for me.

"A protest ain't exactly Disneyland, you know. Some people aren't built for them." Mrs. Flowers flips the bacon over in the pan. The grease causes her to jump as it splatters out and pops her on the hand.

"I never done anything like this before either, but I'm not backing down," I say, squeezing oranges into the crystal pitcher. Mrs. Flowers's hands aren't strong enough to do it anymore.

"Your other friends are going to be with you, aren't they?" she asks.

I roll my eyes. "Yeah, my real friends. Meggie shady. She the definition of throwing stones and hiding your hand."

"Don't worry about her. Worry about the people you have."

Tasha and Benji the only ones who I know for sure going to be there for me.

"You be careful out there. Those protests can turn bad in a New York minute," Mrs. Flowers says. "I marched with Dr. King, you know."

"No!" I almost spill the pitcher. "You never told me that." I sip the orange juice, checking its bitterness.

"I surely did. I was a young gal. Around your age, or maybe I was a few years older. . . ." She stares off. "Anyway, I was in Memphis, visiting family. While I was there, my cousin ran home talking about Dr. King here and he's marching with the sanitation workers for equal pay. My brother and I went with him downtown. I remember the barking dogs, and the police standing there with their sticks by their sides, ready to use them. My brother held me close to him, told me not to be scared. That this was something bigger than us. We marched and marched. A few days later, Dr. King was shot dead."

I stare at my hands and picture myself in her shoes.

Memphis, 1968.

I haven't thought about the ramifications of today. I've seen the news stories of men and women hit with tear gas and rubber bullets . . . and real bullets. Police storming folks' front yards with assault rifles. Even if they had nothing to do with the protest going on. Innocent bystanders harassed by folks meant to protect and serve.

"That's wild. You're a part of history."

"It's wild that you're making your own history. I was a part of someone else's, but you are creating something that people will talk about for years to come."

———

"Hello, my sister. I'm Eli."

He introduces the rest of his clique, who all have Afro-centric names. Their T-shirts host a variety of Black sayings across the chests.

"I've seen you around campus before, but you never joined

the Black Student Union. I figured you weren't into this sort of thing."

"We've been working in the background, spreading the word about Lucas, especially after you started reviving the hashtag," Eli says.

"I'm Tamia." A girl appears who smells of rosemary and has a dyed-blue Afro that reaches and blends in with the sky. She pulls me into a long embrace. "I'm sorry if you felt alone."

"I've had a few people by my side, but nothing like this." I admire her T-shirt, which says *Fuck it, I'll do it —A Black Woman.*

"Is this all who's coming?" I ask. There are maybe a hundred people lined up behind us on the outskirts of the university. After feeling alone all year, it may as well be a thousand.

Cars park past my view. The neighbors must be having a fit at all the beautiful Black people walking through this colorless neighborhood.

"No, lots more are coming," Eli says. "I made an event online and more than five hundred RSVPed."

"A few of my friends are coming as well." Tasha and Benji are on their way. They said that forty minutes ago, though.

I try not to panic.

The crowd that forms is intimidating. They are all here for us. I can hardly breathe. I have to tell myself to do it, remind myself of the mechanics behind this natural body function.

Ignore the images of men in bulletproof vests shooting rubber bullets into people.

Eli leads us to the abandoned field behind the school that's used for unofficial pickup games.

"This is the plan." Tamia begins to take over. "Eli and I will be in the front so it appears like we're leading the protest. We don't want to get you into any more hot water."

"Sounds good."

Eli makes a megaphone out of his hands. "The protest will start in thirty minutes, and if you haven't already, make your signs now. If the police come, we will stick together. No justice . . ."

"No peace," the crowd calls back in unison. This is what I've been missing. The unity. They march to the same rhythmic drum.

Hundreds of people are here, and this ain't even everyone.

The sorority leader who was salty about the frat house being shut down calls out to me: "You got this, girl." She stands with her crew holding purple banners that say CHANGE IS NOW on them.

I raise my chin in response. People I don't know came to stand for justice with me, even if we not best friends.

More students with Booker T. Washington hoodies join. They all come up to me to give encouraging words.

A girl holds her hand to her chest. "I'm sorry, sister."

I spot Tasha. The three active people in the BSU roll

behind her with makeshift signs in their hands. Tasha holding a **WE NOT Y'ALL NIGGA—WE MADE THIS HOME** sign in one hand and a **BLACK GIRLS ARE MAGIC** sign in the other.

Another sign, written in bright red paint, graffiti-style like the markings that brought us all here, catches my eye. **WE STAND WITH HER.**

"Thanks for coming," I say.

She hugs me. "Of course!"

My hands tremble holding the **BLACK GIRLS ARE MAGIC** sign Tasha hands me. All these folks came to stand with me? What gone happen if they find out I ain't brave like them? That I ain't strong like Tasha? That I ain't a fighter like Benji? What gone happen if they find out I ain't never want to be an activist?

We stand together, shoulder to shoulder, lining up like an army in formation, getting ready to march.

"I'm scared." I bite my nails.

"Nothing's going to happen," Tasha says. "They can't take all of us."

I turn around and spot Benji as he moves alongside random people in the back. I meet him halfway in the middle.

"You're here!" I spot an older couple behind him. "Even your parents here? Must be raining pigs somewhere."

"When my parents heard you on the radio, they decided it was time to speak up and tell what they knew about the Cunninghams. My parents are on your side, Savannah, and so am I. Even though I haven't acted like it."

All those feelings I said weren't realistic come rushing in.

"I hope you can forgive me," Benji says. "For not telling you about my family situation . . . for not being on your side from jump."

He reaches for me and I rest my head on his shoulder. His smell engulfs me. We stand, hugging for what seems like forever, his strong arms wrapped around my body. With him, I let the fears of where this protest could go leave my mind. I feel safe.

Eli interrupts. "Savannah, we should get started."

"I'm ready," I say, pulling away from Benji's embrace, our fingers still together.

"ATTENTION," Eli calls again into his fake megaphone. "We come together today for the oppressed people here, and for the ones who don't yet realize that they are. To speak on behalf of the unrepresented, and to shout to the open skies for the downtrodden. Let's show the people who reside behind these walls what we're capable of. If they won't tear down the walls of injustice, we will break them down."

The crowd locks arms in neat rows and stands in the middle of the street. Tasha and Benji on my left side, Eli and Tami are in front. We block traffic coming from each and every way as we march around and between cars. People film from inside their leather sanctuaries, with their windows up, of course.

"No justice, no peace!"
Clap.

"No justice, no peace!"

Clap, clap.

"Get out the streets, fools. Protesting doesn't do anything." We pay them no mind. Folks who don't know us from Adam throw water bottles, and whatever else clutters their front seats, at us. The occasional car honks in solidarity as they pull into their multimillion-dollar homes. Locking the doors behind them, I'm sure.

We sing the songs of our ancestors.

I glance at Tasha, who has tears falling from her eyes. The whooping sounds of police sirens ring out behind us. Our march comes to a halt across the street from Jasper Auditorium.

Lucas, Elaina, Meggie, and a handful of professors file out of the auditorium. They whisper to each other, staying close to the doors. I guess everyone else was too afraid to come outside.

"There's Lucas," I shout over the sirens.

The sounds of police threats fill the air.

"Disperse now or we will be forced to use force," they shout. "Disperse now."

"They just talking. We're being peaceful. Don't worry about it," says a boy wearing a black hoodie with raised brown hands drawn on it.

"Whatever happens, stick close to me," Benji says to me and Tasha. We nod and continue to chant, our voices blending in with what seems like a thousand people. There's no reason for the police to get violent, but it ain't like they need a reason. I pray to myself. If there's a God, I hope she listening.

Tasha gets out of line and marches across the street toward Lucas. Her sign lies against her side.

"Shit. We need to get Tasha," I say to Benji as I follow behind her. He's on my trail.

Tasha stands face to face with Lucas. "You are trash, Lucas Cunningham."

"No, you three are the trash. Why ruin my award day? Jealousy is very unbecoming."

"It'll be a cold day in hell before we're jealous of you," I say.

"Benjamin, I wonder what Uncle Ben and Aunt Billie have to say about your crusade?" Lucas smirks.

"You can ask them yourself." He points toward the crowd. "They are out here themselves. Seems that they care more about me than appearances. Too bad your parents can't say the same." Benji folds his arms. He a siddity boy, but he's got some fight in him.

"Savannah, more police are coming." Meggie tries to act concerned, but I ain't falling for that shit. Not anymore.

"Oh, now you care about what happens to me. At least Elaina and Lucas were up-front with me from the jump, but you played a good game and I fell for it."

"I told her you were a snake, and you know how you kill a snake?" Tasha steps to all three of them. "You cut its head off."

"Why are you all doing this?" Elaina says, looking skinnier than ever. "Lucas didn't do anything wrong and neither did his parents."

"You don't think buying him a spot is wrong?" Tasha asks.

"They had to do what they had to do," Elaina says. "Put yourself in their shoes."

"I'll never be in their shoes. I'll always have to work hard for anything that I do. That's why we're here, because people like Lucas always have things handed to them, but not anymore. It's a new day," I say.

"You're going to be sorry." She sniffles. She's tweaking, hard. "You don't even know what else he did—"

Lucas cuts her off before she can finish. "She doesn't know what she's talking about."

I step to him. "When we're finished with you, this part is going to seem like a picnic."

"No one is going to believe you," he says. "Even if they do, no one cares."

We walk back across the street.

"Lucas is scared. He knows his house of cards is falling down. Before he knows it, he's not going to have anything left. It's his karma," Benji says.

"Elaina already getting her karma. She coked out. Her eyes made of glass now," I say.

"They grew up with everything." Tasha sticks her sign up. "Tragedy don't always create ugly souls." I'm living proof of that.

Pop.

There's a ringing in my ears.

Pop, pop.

A stinging in my eyes. Everything happens so fast.

People run in every direction, taking cover from the bitter smell that fills the air.

"Don't . . . stop . . . running," Benji says.

Tasha's hand slips into mine. I follow the way her body pulls me.

"What's happening?" I cry out, but neither answers. I feel like we've run forever until we stop, settling in a wet grass pasture.

"Savannah . . . you okay, girl?" Tasha breathes heavy, coughing her lungs out. I can hear Benji taking hits of his asthma pump.

"I can't see." I panic, blinking my eyes, trying to get some form of a picture to show. Everything's a blur.

"Tasha, I can't run far. Go get help," Benji yells. "Hurry. Find my parents."

Her hand leaves mine.

"You'll be okay," he says. "It was pepper spray. They pepper-sprayed us. We weren't even doing anything, fucking pigs."

My eyes flutter some more. I can only make out pieces of Benji's face; with each blink more skin comes into focus. Students are still running from the toxic air. Others lie in the grass as their friends perform first aid on them.

"Are you okay?" I ask, rubbing my eyes. It makes the stinging worse.

He pats at his chest. "Yes, I'm fine. It didn't get to my eyes, just my throat."

"I feel bad, all these people choking 'cause of me," I say.

"You only had one shot to call them out," he says. "If you didn't do it now, you wouldn't have gotten the chance, and people do care. They knew the risk, but they still came."

Tasha returns with bottles of milk. "Some kids had these on them just in case. They must have known something we didn't. Benji, your parents said stay put. They are going to talk to the police, like that'll help."

Benji pours milk into my eyes. "They still want to trust authority figures."

"This is some bullshit, man. We were being peaceful," Tasha says.

"They don't care about that," I say. "They saw Black people and automatically assumed we were a threat." I grasp Benji's face. "Are you okay? Your asthma. We ran a lot."

"Now you care about making me run?"

I swat him in the chest. "Hush."

Eli comes over with Tamia, both out of breath. They smell like fresh-cut grass. "Are you guys okay?"

"The police are pushing everyone away from the school," Eli says.

"They still here?" Benji asks Eli, standing up. He wipes the grass on his hands on the back of his jeans.

"Yes, even more came. They suited up, too," Eli says. "I'm

sorry this didn't go as planned, sister." He directs his apology to me.

"Maybe this is the way it was supposed to go," Tamia says. "Peaceful protests rarely make history. Something needed to make it memorable."

I remember Mrs. Flowers's story. One of the reasons it held so much sentimental value was because a few days later, Dr. King was killed.

I perk up when I notice news trucks speeding to the scene. If the people at Wooddale don't care, then maybe people around the country will.

FORTY-ONE

Who up? That protest was wild. Savannah come collect your crown. You did that. #WooddaleConfessions

My eyes are still burning. Them cops gotta run me some coins after this.

Did you see how they swarmed us? Like we had guns or something.

Cause it was majority Black.

Yeap.

FORTY-TWO

The silence outside is haunting. Police sirens play in my ears over and over again. They not like the ones back home. Different somehow. Everything here been different. At home, I have the cicadas that most nights are drowned out by the winos who sit on the corner across from my building. Drinking Johnnie Walker to drown their sorrows. There's only quietness here. The type of quiet that makes your mind drift to places you don't want to be.

Tasha decided to stay over at Mrs. Flowers's tonight. She sleeps silently next to me, stirring every few minutes. The only one who can sleep at this slumber party. The quiet too much for me, too many thoughts in my head. I sneak to the door, careful not to close it too hard. Sneaking off to the unused chair at the end of the hallway. B'onca answers FaceTime just as I'm about to hang up.

Soft coos, and baby hands flail on the screen. "You're busy. I can call you in the morning." The shining grandfather clock strikes twelve in front of me.

"Nah, she all right." B'onca adjusts the screen, giving me

a full sight of swollen boob. "This child eat, and I eat, but neither of us gaining no weight."

"You gotta up the calories, B. Be strong for little mama."

"I know that. Everything for her now. Body, money, time. In a while ain't gone be left for me."

I want to tell her I understand feeling incomplete. Feeling like you giving all of you away. About the protest and the pepper spray. About running so far that after a while I couldn't feel the air in my lungs. About how everything changed today, and I have to change with it. Even if that means disappointing everyone around me. B'onca can't worry about that now, though. Her own sirens are going off.

"You getting enough sleep? You know I read this article that said a healthy sleep pattern is a healthy mind."

B'onca scrunches her face up. "Tell that to the fools who stay up all night outside."

"There's a program down at the center for new mothers."

"Mmmm, I'll see. She cry and I cry. She sleeps all day, and sometimes I do too. Folks say I'm too attached to her, that I'm feeling everything she feels. But this different." She looks down at the half-sleeping baby. "This real different."

"I'll be home in a few weeks for summer break. Hold on until then, I got you."

Auntie Savannah to save the day when she can't even save herself. That sounds about right. Doing everything for everybody but who gone save me?

"Thank you, boo." She waves the small limp hand. "Mia says thank you too. She got your present in the mail. I read it to her every night."

A picture book with a Black ballerina on the front.

"She gone be anything she want one day," B'onca says. "I'm gone make sure of that."

Another Savannah in the making. Taking on the walk of her mother. All those dreams poured into her from birth. Weighing her down unconsciously from patent-leather Mary Janes to prom heels.

"You mighty quiet. What's got you down over there?"

Choices.

I crisscross my legs, loosening the grip on my phone. "I'm still not sure if I'm supposed to be at Wooddale. But if I'm not here, where am I supposed to be?"

"The real question is where your mama gone allow you to go? You should see how much Wooddale gear she got now. The bumper tag and the door sticker. Even rocking the Wooddale sweatshirt. Gone have to have a good reason for her to trade that in."

"I applied to another school nearby. Met the folks and everything. Sometimes, like tonight, I want to pack my bags and go there, but then I think I shouldn't give up?"

"Girl, you all mixed up. School isn't out for a few weeks. Chill and see what happens."

"I don't think I've truly chilled since I've been at this school."

"You tell me all the time about them kids you met. You and Tasha went to the beach today, or you and Benji went on a *drive*. Folks like that don't come around too often. They Black, and they attend the same school as you do. You strong, girl, stronger than you know."

The sirens. The phantom smell of pepper spray silences all my thoughts. Pushes away everything I think I may know.

———

The email from Lora Price, the president of Wooddale, sits open on my laptop. I text Tasha in a panic.

> **Me:** She wants me to come to her house for a meeting.

She texts back within five seconds after I press send.

> **Tasha:** Naw girl that's a setup.
> Delete it, pretend you never saw it.

But I can't pretend forever, and this is what I wanted. For folks to pay attention. I button up my jacket and start toward the bus stop. Double-check the address again. The president lives right across from campus. She probably saw the whole protest from her bedroom window.

The bus driver opens the doors, looks at his newspaper and then back to me. "You're the girl from that protest yesterday."

I dig in my pocket for my change. "How you know that?"

He holds the paper against the clear barrier. "You all over the papers—the TV news, too."

Damn, what a surprise to wake up to.

The driver presses the paper harder to give me a better look. I drop in my fare, reading over the headline. PEACEFUL PROTEST AT WOODDALE UNIVERSITY TURNED VIOLENT BY POLICE. My face plastered across households in town. I want to vomit at the realization.

"Can I have that?" I ask.

"Sure." He slides the paper around the plastic.

I thank him and find a seat. The bus is empty, only an older woman who's fighting hard to keep her eyes open. The morning light hits the newspaper just right as I read over the events of yesterday. There's me on the front, and beside me are Tasha, Benji, Eli, and Tamia. The news describes the protest as peaceful, but in the paragraph underneath, the police chief says, "Acts of violence won't be tolerated in this community." His police force is the only force of violence around.

Protesting yesterday made me feel whole but not complete. Like I was a part of something bigger than myself, but I don't have a sense of what that bigger picture is. I roll the newspaper up and stick it in my bookbag. My phone chimes, a text of a link from Benji.

Benji: We're superstars . . . or something.

Or something, all right.

The link automatically plays. In the clip I stand next to Benji and say with the Southern accent that I've tried all year to keep at bay, "I didn't want any trouble. I just wanted justice."

In the clip, my eyes are swollen and a deep shade of red.

Justice. Not pepper spray, or to be treated like criminals. To be treated like we did something wrong when the only thing we ever wanted was to be heard.

I scroll through the comments. Two catch my eye. The first one says we made it to the national news. The second is a picture of Lucas with *#LucasCunningham* watermarked on it. They didn't say his name on the news. They won't even show his face. Lucas Sr. got clout everywhere. Social media musta caught wind of what they're trying to pull. That shit don't even matter, though. Lucas will bounce back from this scandal. In a few years, people will forget the Cunninghams. In a few years, Lucas will run his family business. In a few years, he'll still be on top. This week of news segments won't stop his privilege. No matter how many hashtags are created, people gone just move on to the next.

But right now, I'm glad people are listening.

The bus moves through town, only stopping once to pick up another elderly passenger. Soon we're at the Wooddale stop.

"See you on television," the bus driver smirks.

I give a quick smile before getting off. The area doesn't look like it's lived in by millionaires no more. Debris left over from last night. Empty water bottles are strewn about on lawns. Signs with powerful sayings lie lonesome in the middle of the street with tire marks over them.

The president's butler greets me and escorts me to her front room. I've never seen a butler who wasn't on television. I never even knew they still exist these days. I stand off to the side, making sure not to touch anything or look at anything for too long.

"Have a seat, Savannah. It's a pleasure to meet you," President Price says as she enters the room.

She looks regal in a long silk kimono that has bluebirds rolling on the sides. I admire her blown-out hair that still has volume and texture. I bet she's never caught slipping with a bad weave or a fingernail unpolished. Different bougie treats sit on the coffee table between us. She offers me a sweet potato tart and I accept. I bite it and my knees go weak. It's so good. Buttery and crisp—still warm, too. *Sooo* good.

I take a cup of cappuccino, too. The foam got a leaf decoration on top. I've never had one before, but when in Rome.

"You have been a very busy young lady, haven't you?" she asks.

I put down the tiny glass on the white cloth napkin.

Steadying my hand so I don't mess up her carpet that's so white, it's amazing that someone lives here. I can tell this room used for special occasions. I picture her sitting on her chaise beaming with joy each time her kids come home. They tell her that they're getting married to some senator's son, they're traveling to Africa to explore their roots, or starting their own Black-owned hair line. Whatever rich Black folk do in their spare time.

"It wasn't planned or anything. Sorry I had to protest against your school and all that."

"We all have to stand up for what we believe in every now and again. When I was your age, I was raising awareness about apartheid."

She doesn't look like the type to protest or run a university. Her face is soft, and she talks matronly, like the best secret recipe for chocolate chip cookies resides in her kitchen. If I was five, I'd want to snuggle up underneath her arm. I'm too old for it, but I kinda want to do the same.

I ask her, trying to sound as non-accusatory as possible, "Why you showing up now, after all this time?"

"Professor Santos and I have been in communication, and all along I've had things in motion. I didn't want to inform you about them." She takes a short sip of her tea and clears her throat. "As of today, a formal investigation has been opened against Mr. Cunningham—Lucas's father—and the director of admissions."

Ding-dong, the witch is dead.

"What about Lucas?" I set aside my tart, crossing my legs at the ankles like I've seen Tasha do.

"You'll be happy to know Lucas has officially been removed from campus for breaking code of conduct. It'll be coming out soon, but I thought you should hear that from me."

"And Elaina?" I say. "What about her?"

"Elaina provided us with information about Lucas. While we are grateful that Elaina told the truth, she will not be allowed to finish the semester nor return in the fall," the president says.

"Then there is the dean, who treated me like trash, and Jacob, who lost his scholarship for no reason."

"All of that will be taken care of, trust me."

Trust her? As if she has given me any reason to.

"I wanted to do something for you, which I hope will make you feel better."

I lift my head. "What is that?" I halfway expect her to say money. That's being too hopeful, though. I lower my expectations. Just 'cause she got money to blow don't mean she spending it on me.

"We will have a day honoring you. I know it doesn't change what you have been through, and for that I'm sorry. But, Savannah, I want you to know that you—of anyone—*deserve* to be here. On campus. In our dorms. Walking our halls when you please. You exemplify what our campus *should* stand for."

That's nice. Real nice. I shift in my seat.

But it isn't enough.

"I don't want to seem ungrateful or nothing . . . but I don't think I'll even be back next school year."

"Don't you have a full scholarship?"

"Yes, I do, but . . ."

"But nothing, Savannah." She drops the proper act and, within seconds, gets real serious and real Black. "Listen, I didn't make it where I am today by squandering my opportunities. It's rare that you get even one shot in life. You better make it count, girl."

"Yes, ma'am, but I can't walk around here knowing what I know. I'm tired of being one of the only Black faces. I'm tired of having to go the extra mile to prove myself. Of having to protect myself in general. Most of all I'm tired of attempting to fit in. I'm tired."

"Who said you have to fit in? Savannah, it's clear you don't fit in, and that's okay. You have a powerful voice. You're smart, motivated, and damn talented. If Wooddale isn't giving you what you need, you have to make it."

"That's a lot of pressure to fall on me."

She shrugs. "What's life without a little heat?"

"I'll think about it, but I can't make any promises now. No offense, but this is something that I have to decide for myself and not be coerced into by a woman that I met five minutes ago."

"I agree, and I won't fight you on it. However, I will leave you with this." She stands and walks toward the mantelpiece that holds her many awards. "No matter where you go in life, there will always be someone trying to keep you down. I'm one of the highest-ranking people in my field, period. Yet in interviews, I still get asked about my home decor, because I'm a woman. On the other hand, I get questions about why I'm not more assertive, and that's because I'm Black. A quiet Black woman is a unicorn in society's eyes. You think I'm going to give up my job, though, what I worked so hard for, because of a few ignorant people? At the end of the day, I'm still a winner, and so are you, Savannah."

This lady doing the most. None of these words make up for the fact she left us to defend ourselves, but I don't have time to debate her. Every time she sees my face on TV, she'll remember how she messed up.

"Thank you again." I stand up to give a handshake and she pulls me into a hug instead.

She calls in her butler and he brings me a goody bag of assorted pastries. I wave goodbye as I cross the street.

———

Mama's voice beats in my ear as soon as I press accept.

"I told you not to be out there acting a fool, girl. Who you think you is, Assata Shakur? What if something happened to you, Savannah?"

"Mama, I'm okay. It was only pepper spray," I say.

"It was only pepper spray this time. Who knows what they'll do to you next time? What am I saying? There better not be a next time, you hear me?"

I groan. "Yes, Mama. This entire office can hear you, you're so loud."

"Don't get ornery, li'l girl. Where you at, anyway?"

"I'm at my professor's office. I got an appointment today."

"I can't wait for you to come home for the summer, so I don't gotta worr—"

"Mama, I have to go." I interrupt her rant. "She's ready to see me now." I notice Professor Daphne has stepped outside her door.

"Okay, baby. Call me when you're done and let me know how it went. At least you're trying to finish your freshman year strong."

"I will, Mama, bye." I hang up the phone with no intention of calling her later.

"Sorry I'm popping up like this. Things have been wild," I explain, walking past Professor Daphne.

"I bet. I heard about your visit with the president today." She sits down in her chair and crosses her legs. "And I saw you on television last night."

"Seems like everyone and their mama saw me. My phone won't stop blowing up with good wishes . . . and then there is my own mama"—I tap the screen of my phone—"who I was talking to outside. She this close to buying a plane ticket to get here."

"She's worried about you. In her eyes, you are still her little girl."

"Sometimes I wish I was still a little girl. You know, before life got real difficult." I squeeze the ice cream stress ball that sits on the table. "Take me back to before puberty and I'd be fine. The only worry I had was what I wanted from the ice cream man. Or how late I could stay out playing basketball with the kids next door. Before I became hyperaware of my body image and unaware of everything else."

"But then you wouldn't be here leading protests. You wouldn't have met Tasha or Benji. Need I go on?" Her sandy-brown hair falls into her face. She pushes it behind her ear.

"You're right," I say, "but it's like everything hit me all at once. College. Being Black, being too Black. Being a woman, being an outspoken Black woman. I don't know how to juggle these things at once. It seems like yesterday, I was Savannah from up the street, Freda Howard's daughter, who hid behind her mama's legs when strangers got too close. Now I'm Savannah, wannabe activist, and to be honest, I never set out to be that. But now it's like I'm forced to, you know?"

"You think that's what people expect of you now? To always be the person they saw on television? Or heard on my radio show?"

"Exactly, and it's eating me up inside."

"Contrary to popular belief, Savannah, it isn't your job to save the world. Sometimes our talents come to us in different ways. Not saying that you must lead this life, but if this is the route you choose to take, you create the pace you want to run at. I want you to do a quick exercise." Professor Daphne hands me a sheet of scrap paper from her desk. "My mother made me do it before I enrolled in grad school."

I lay the paper on the coffee table between us. "What's the exercise?"

"You list every dream about your future that you remember having, from when you were young until now. No matter how big or small."

"What's this supposed to accomplish?"

"We never realize how our dreams evolve and change over the years. Sometimes it helps to write them down and see them in tangible ways. See how those dreams connect and what's the common points between them."

"What dreams were on your paper?"

She thinks back. "I wanted to be a scuba diver once upon a time."

"Girl," I say, like she my homey, "a scuba diver?"

"Yes, that's before I became sensitive about my hair." She fluffs at her natural.

I write my dreams down. Scratching out the ones that are too silly to have any meaning.

"Once I wanted to be a ballerina." I pinch at the fat on my thighs. "Then this happened."

"You grew legs?"

I laugh again.

"We live in a world where we are inundated with other people's lives. You go two steps up and then you see someone on social media who's gone twenty steps further," Professor Daphne says.

"I felt that way my entire life. Everyone is biking the Tour de France while I'm still learning how to pedal," I say.

"It's a nasty, lengthy cycle to break, but when you're finally free, it's like you see the world in a different light."

"I don't have many career dreams." I go over the lines on my paper. "I did have a dream. That got snatched away from me."

"What?"

"To attend a historically Black college. I got accepted to Booker T. Washington the other day, but I don't think I'm going to attend."

"Why aren't you going to accept the offer? If that's what you've been dreaming about, you should go for it."

"The scholarship. I can't support myself if I don't have money, and Black universities aren't exactly rolling in cash."

"Money is an obstacle that you can overcome. There are scholarships, grants, and, of course, working. If it's what you want to do, don't let anything stop you. You'll regret it in the future."

"What I thought I wanted in the beginning may not be what I want now."

"And that's okay," Professor Daphne says.

"Yeah, that's okay. College is about growing, right? I'm not supposed to be the same person, thinking the same way and feeling the same things. I'm supposed to keep steadily growing until I'm the person that I want to be."

"Savannah, if you remember nothing else from our time together, remember this . . ."

I perk up and Professor Daphne leans in.

"You have the power to choose what's most important to you."

FORTY-THREE

After piles of pros-and-cons lists, my mind finally made up. That's the easy part: telling myself that I'm leaving. Telling other folks, now, that's gone be the hard part. I need to do this for me, though. A decision that needed to be made without the input of anybody else. Not even Benji or Tasha.

I sit outside, across from the community garden. I haven't been here in a while. Not since frost covered the deep brown soil. The garden club already started planting for the summer. Tiny pictures with different vegetables and fruits mark spots in the ground. Around this time next spring they'll be blooming, but I won't be here to see them.

I swallow my fear and dial the familiar number.

"I've told you fifty thousand times don't be calling me at work. Someone dead?"

She never answers the phone with a regular hello. "No, Mama. I . . . I need to talk to you."

"You're talking now."

A long pause follows as I inhale the gardenia scent that

floats through the air. My mouth feels like I've been eating peanut butter sandwiches with no milk.

"Savannah, I'm gonna hang up."

"No, wait." I clear my throat. "Mama, I've decided I'm not coming back to Wooddale next year. Indefinitely."

"Indefinitely," she mocks. "We've had this conversation once before and I spoke my piece."

"Now I'm going to speak mine," I say. "Mama, I don't want to argue or anything like that."

"Okay," she replies. "Speak your piece."

I scramble to put my words together.

"You got two minutes and you just wasted thirty seconds of it."

"I got accepted to the historically Black college here on a partial scholarship. I'm going to apply for grants and get a small loan. Mrs. Flowers will board me as long as I continue to do my fair share of chores around the house. That'll save at least ten thousand dollars."

I pause and wait for her rampage. It never comes.

"You there, Mama?"

"Mm-hmm, I'm still here. You got a minute and thirty seconds."

"My friend Eli can hook me up with a part-time job. He's involved in politics and what have you."

"Is that the li'l boy I seen you on television with? The high-yellow one?"

"No, that's my friend Benjamin."

"He looks like more than a friend to me," she says. "Remember you there to get a degree."

Mama always tries to flip the subject and turn things around.

"Can we focus on school right now . . . please?"

She sighs, and I hear a buzzing sound. Mama's voice turns proper in an instant as she directs someone to a meeting.

"I'm tired of fighting you on this, Savannah. If you want to throw your life away and go into debt, that's your business. I've washed my hands of the situation."

I bite my jaw to stop myself from smiling like the Kool-Aid man.

"Mama, I promise I won't let you down. You'll see. I can make it on my own."

"Is Wooddale really that bad?"

"It isn't all bad. . . ."

It kills me to admit, but I'll miss Wooddale a tiny bit. I'll miss walking to the café after a lecture with Tasha and Benji. I'll miss knowing exactly where my classes are. Professor Jacobson made learning about the Harlem Renaissance new and fresh in his own weird white-person way. The food became manageable. I learned never to go into the cafeteria on "culture" day. I won't miss the teasing, though. Or the constant reminder that I don't belong. The butchering of my name. I learned not to speak loudly as well. I learned to never walk past the fraternity members alone. I learned that speaking up would be met with criticism instead of listening ears.

Wooddale isn't all bad, but it damn sure isn't good for me.

There's something about Booker T. Washington. What they represent. How there aren't any "all-Black tables"—just tables. How my hair isn't a political statement—it's just my hair. There I can move in and out of the world as my whole self, not even think of being anyone different.

Don't have to be an activist just because I'm Black.

The voice just because I'm Black.

I can just be Black, whatever that means to *me* and no one else.

ACKNOWLEDGMENTS

If you've made it here, that means you've finished *Required Reading for the Disenfranchised Freshman* and I have a real book out. I know I will forget people—as the old people say, charge it to my head and not my heart. To everyone who has ever had a hand in rearing me, supporting me, and reading early drafts of *Required Reading,* thank you. Without you I would not be here.

Thank you, God, for giving me a vision and the freedom to carry that vision to this point. I'm forever grateful.

Molly, the best agent and listening ear. Thank you for guiding me through this debut season. You've made it bearable and a lot of fun. We deserve more dancing shrimp after this.

Phoebe! Not only is *Required Reading* better because of you; so is my writing as a whole. You've given me tools that will last a lifetime. Thank you for believing in me, my dream, and Savannah.

Jess, girl, I could write a book about you. You chose my words once upon a time, and who knew I would end up here?

Thank you for being my fairy godmother, my friend, and the best mentor on earth. I want to be like you when I grow up.

To Nic. Thank you for the guidance you gave me at the beginning of my journey. It is my goal to pay it forward.

Mercedes! Thank you for being my critique partner, editor, decipherer, and publicist all in one. It'll be your time soon, and I will be right by your side cheering you on.

To my closest friends, Marcus and Alex, thank you for being there when *Required Reading* was only a thought in the group chat. You both inspire me daily.

Laila and Akure, for listening to all my bookish rants and pulling me back in when I got too ahead of my thoughts.

Jasmine, Bee, and Kayla, for always reminding me not to take life too seriously.

Mama and Daddy, thank you for being supportive parents.

To Grandma and Grandaddy, for always keeping books about people who look like me in the house. You set the blueprint for me to write stories such as this one.

To all my Memphis folks. We on the map, mane!

ABOUT THE AUTHOR

KRISTEN R. LEE is a native of Memphis, Tennessee. After graduating from college, she began to write about her experiences attending a predominantly white institution, which led to the first draft of *Required Reading for the Disenfranchised Freshman*. She's worked as a mentor for foster youth and has interned in a school setting, where she counseled middle schoolers. Writing stories that reflect often-unheard voices is what she strives to do. Discover more about Kristen online at kristenleebooks.com.